THE TREASURE OF PARAGON BOOK 3

USA TODAY BESTSELLING AUTHOR

GENEVIEVE JACK

Manhattan Dragon: The Treasure of Paragon, Book 3

Published by Carpe Luna, Ltd, PO Box 5932, Bloomington, IL 61702

This book is a work of fiction. Names, characters, places, and incidents are either products of the author's imagination or used fictitiously. Any resemblance to actual events, locales, or persons, living or dead, is entirely coincidental.

First Edition: October 2019

eISBN: 978-1-940675-54-1

Paperback: 978-1-940675-51-0

v 4.0

ABOUT THE BOOK

Deadly secrets. Hidden enemies. Colliding histories.

She's supposed to be dead.

For Rowan Valor, faking her own death is a regular necessity. How else would an immortal dragon manage to live in a place like Manhattan for close to three hundred years? But changing her identity leaves the community center she founded vulnerable, and for the sake of the children, she must find a way to undo the damage.

He's leading a new life.

Human detective Nick Grandstaff entered law enforcement to escape his violent roots. But closing the door on his past has resulted in an unnatural obsession with his work. Perhaps it's for the best that his longest relationship has been with his dog. What woman would choose to be with someone with such a dark and tangled history?

To have a future together, both must face their past.

When Nick investigates a case that leads him to Rowan's door, their passionate connection promises to heal old wounds and grant them both the once-in-a-lifetime love they deserve. But fighting a common enemy entangles them in the dangerous supernatural underworld of Manhattan where power is shifting, and unbeknownst to Rowan, a former ally has become a deadly enemy.

AUTHOR'S NOTE

Dear Reader,

Love is the truest magic and the most fulfilling fantasy. Thank you for coming along on this journey as I share the tale of the Treasure of Paragon, nine exiled royal dragon shifters destined to find love and their way home.

There are three things you can expect from a Genevieve Jack novel: magic will play a key role, unexpected twists are the norm, and love will conquer all.

The Treasure of Paragon Reading Order

The Dragon of New Orleans, Book 1
Windy City Dragon, Book 2,
Manhattan Dragon, Book 3
The Dragon of Sedona, Book 4
The Dragon of Cecil Court, Book 5
Highland Dragon, Book 6
Hidden Dragon, Book 7
The Dragons of Paragon, Book 8
The Last Dragon, Book 9

Keep in touch to stay in the know about new releases, sales, and giveaways.

Join my VIP reader group
Sign up for my newsletter

Now, let's spread our wings (or at least our pages) and escape together!

Genevieve Jack

CHAPTER ONE

She was supposed to be dead.

Rowan felt remarkably spry for a corpse. But then she'd died multiple times since coming to America over three hundred years ago. New identities were necessary for an immortal. Every so often Rowan would shed her proverbial skin and start over with a new last name, a new address, a new life. It was easier to do in New York. The city that never slept rarely slowed down to notice one mysterious woman with unfinished business or the fate of one of her identities.

She wasn't a thief, but Rowan had come to steal.

A dragon was born with a certain set of instincts. Keen observation was one of them. A natural affinity for anything rare and valuable was another. For example, Rowan had spotted the teardrop-shaped blue diamond around Camilla Stevenson's neck from across a crowded gallery—an example of her keen observation skills. Understanding that the stone was, in fact, the six-carat Raindrop of Heaven, sold at auction recently for $1.2 million? That was her talent for recognizing the rare and valuable.

She didn't need the money.

Rowan was rich. Very rich. It wasn't cash luring her up the path to the white brick mansion in the Hamptons, an enchanted lockpick weighing down her pocket. It had more to do with her history as an exiled princess of Paragon than any financial motive. She'd witnessed her brother's murder at the hands of her uncle before she was cast into this world, and Rowan had no patience for corruption. What the wealthy Gerald Stevenson and his wife Camilla had done made them the exact type of elitist scum that drove Rowan to distraction. She'd steal the diamond not for its value but for revenge.

For a human, playing Robin Hood in the Hamptons would be a ticket to the slammer. The place was crawling with security, and there was only one gated drive in and out of the property. Humans, though, couldn't make themselves invisible. Nor could they fly.

Besides, there was no better alibi than being dead.

The night hummed a familiar tune. Crickets chirped, insectile lovers calling to each other from the grasses; the waves brushed the beach in a soft caress behind her; and a warm spring breeze off the Atlantic rustled the branches of the hawthorn trees that grew along the main drive.

"Thank you, Harriet," she murmured as she slid the enchanted lockpick into the lock of the french doors at the back of the Stevensons' home. It was a sophisticated lock. Stevenson was a real estate developer and was no dummy when it came to home security. But security systems had their limitations. For example, most weren't able to record an invisible intruder or detect a lockpick charmed with ancient English Traveller magic.

The door parted like the lips of an eager lover, and she slipped into the dark interior. No alarm. No dog. That was fortunate. A few lights were on, but she knew no one was home. Gerald and Camilla were hosting one of the biggest political fund-raising events in the city that evening. How could they effectively rezone and gentrify every part of Manhattan if they didn't consistently line the pockets of their political allies?

Fucking assholes.

The gem practically sang to her from the master bedroom on the second floor. It was time to save the jewel from the Stevensons' filthy hands. She trailed down the hall, allowing her invisibility to fade to conserve energy. Invisibility and flight took their toll; she'd need that energy for the journey home.

The hardwood creaked beneath her feet. Rowan paused outside the bedroom. A delicious scent she'd never smelled before met her nose, sandalwood and dark spice. She breathed deeply and felt her eyes roll back in her head at the intoxicating fragrance. What the hell was that?

A fine shiver traveled through her body, straight to her core. Whatever it was, she wanted to roll in it. She made a mental note to find out where Gerald Stevenson bought his cologne. It couldn't be Camilla's. It was too masculine. Too heady. It took effort to pull herself together, but she managed to slip into the master bedroom and refocus on the task at hand. The Raindrop of Heaven wasn't going to steal itself.

The room was a white-walled wonder with decor that belonged in the Museum of Modern Art. At its center, a bed the size of a barge was flanked by two twisted wire sculptures worth more than most people's yearly salary. No doubt they were paid for in cash. People like the Stevensons loved to use art as a way to launder their wealth and evade the taxman. All the more reason they were overdue for some bad luck.

And she planned to deliver it.

Once she oriented herself, she found the door Harriet had described in her vision and had to smile at the Traveller's accuracy. The best decision she'd ever made was to save her dear friend from tuberculosis in 1904 with the gift of her tooth. She'd never regretted using dragon magic to bind herself to the powerful Traveller whose psychic gifts and practical magic rivaled any witch's. Harriet's friendship had proved priceless over the years, and her magical abilities had come in useful on more than one occasion.

The Stevensons' giant walk-in closet was built of cedar and had a convenient keypad on the jewelry drawer that served as a safe. Rowan held the lockpick against the keypad and watched the keys glow purple, one at a time. The magic revealed which numbers to push and in what order, and she enthusiastically followed its suggestions. The drawer popped open with a hiss.

The Raindrop of Heaven winked up at her from a bed of blue velvet. She caressed the cool facets of the diamond before plucking it from its cushion along with two matching earrings. She shoved the lot in the zippered pouch around her waist, pure satisfaction curling the corners of her lips.

Take that, you corrupt piece of shit.

Rowan's nostrils flared. The delicious smell from the hall was back, even stronger than before. Cloves and sandalwood. Her inner dragon stirred and licked its lips. She whirled to find a man standing in the bedroom behind her, staring at her through the open door to the walk-in closet. A bear of a man, big, rough, and all male. He scratched the stubble on his jaw, amaretto-colored like his hair, and scanned her with eyes the gray of stormy seas. His arms crossed over the chest of his sport coat, and his head cocked to the side.

She cursed under her breath. She'd been so distracted by the smell, she'd forgotten to make herself invisible again. Too late now. He'd seen her. The real her.

Thankfully, he was alone. She could handle one man. It wouldn't be pretty, but she could handle him. Their eyes met.

In a voice edged in grit, he asked, "Who the fuck are you?"

DETECTIVE NICK GRANDSTAFF STARED AT THE WOMAN in the Stevensons' closet and tried to decide if she was real or a lovely hallucination. He was leaning toward hallucination. After all, he'd been awake for going on twenty-four hours now, and she was too perfect to be real. Only a figment of his imagination could strike all his personal erotic notes. Long, dark waves cascaded down her back. Silky. Shiny. Touchable. He imagined his fingers buried in that hair. He'd startled her, and when she turned toward him, her amber eyes overwhelmed him as if he'd stared into the sun. And oh God, her curves. Curves for days. Curves that made his palms itch to touch her.

"I'm a friend of Camilla's," Fantasy Woman said, moving toward him. She folded her hands innocently in front of her hips. "She said I could borrow a pair of shoes."

He snorted. After years working as a homicide detective, Nick was a human lie detector. He could hear the lie in her voice as clearly as if the words came out of her mouth colored red. Whoever this woman was, she was up to no good.

"I wasn't aware Camilla had any friends."

Fantasy Woman laughed through her nose as if she couldn't help herself. He thought he might die from the thrill the sound sent through his body.

"What's your name?"

"Nick." He frowned. She was supposed to be giving *him* information, not the other way around.

She inhaled deeply. Those amber eyes narrowed on him. Bedroom eyes. Soul-stealing eyes. Goddamn, she was sexy. He felt her presence warm his bones like a tropical breeze.

"What are you?"

"Detective," he mumbled. What the hell was with the oversharing? He mentally shook himself.

"*Detective* Nick." Her gaze flicked down to the gun holstered under his shoulder. "If you know what kind of people Camilla and Gerald are, why are you here?" Again, she inhaled, leaning toward him. Did he stink? It had been a long night. He resisted the urge to sniff himself.

"Look, sweetheart, I'm on duty here. Security. You need to tell me your full name. Nobody cleared you to be here. I'm going to have to call this in and get a verbal confirmation from Camilla."

One of her hands reached out to dance her blood-red nails across the tops of Camilla's shoes. Goddamn, he could imagine how those nails would feel on his skin. Gently trailing down his chest. Digging into his back. He shifted, wishing he had something to hold in front of his pants. He needed a cold shower and to get his brain out of fantasyland.

Ignoring his request for a name, she hooked her long, elegant fingers into a pair of black Louboutins. The overhead light glinted off her ring as she removed the shoes from the shelf. That thing was a monster. Anyone who could afford a ruby of that size didn't need to be borrowing anyone else's shoes. Close now, she looked at him through her lashes and waved the shoes as if they were all the explanation he should need to let her go. He blocked the door with his body.

"Easy enough to clear this up," he said. "I'll give Camilla a shout." He raised his phone to his ear.

In the blink of an eye, her hand wrapped around his wrist and squeezed. He paused, his finger hovering over the Call button. Her touch sent a delicious rush through him that made his cock twitch. He lowered the phone.

"Did you know the Stevensons' actions are shutting down a community center that serves at-risk kids?" She glared at him. "How can you defend people like that?"

"Huh?" All he could see was her lips. All that existed was her perfume, a smoky citrus-and-cinnamon scent that drove him wild. His breath hitched.

"Camilla and Gerald bought the land out from under them. They're shutting it down. Over a hundred needy kids use that facility. It's a lifeline for some of them. You know how guys like Stevenson work. He'll probably turn it into a Baby Gap."

Nick swallowed. He'd been an at-risk kid himself at one time and had spent many afternoons inside his local community center. While he wasn't aware of the specific scenario, he'd be the last one to approve of such a thing. Still, it didn't matter. Although he sympathized, she didn't belong here, and it hadn't escaped his notice that she still hadn't told him her damn name.

"I don't know anything about that." He planted his hand on the doorframe, boxing her in. "Tell me who you are now and I'll clear this mess up with Camilla." He suspected she wasn't there for shoes, but he wished she was, wished there was a reason he could let her go and maybe get her number while he was at it.

He blinked and she was gone, ducked under his arm. She strolled through the bedroom toward the doors to the balcony. Damn, she moved fast. And as he looked back into the closet, he could see why. A jewelry drawer was open and whatever had been inside was gone, three empty impressions in the blue velvet.

He whirled and drew his gun, leveling it on the woman. "Stop!"

"Are you going to shoot me, Detective? For borrowing shoes?" Her red lips spread into a smile.

"Drop the shoes and put your hands up," he said firmly. "Don't make this harder than it needs to be."

She set the shoes down on the bed and opened the doors to the balcony. The ocean breeze coasted in around her, delivering another dose of her scent to his nostrils. He loosened his grip on his gun. He wasn't worried. She was unarmed, and there was nowhere for her to go.

"You can't get out that way, ma'am," he said, his voice thick. "You're too high up to jump without injuring yourself. Step back into the room and let's talk about this. Tell me who you are."

She backed onto the balcony and flashed him a wicked grin. "I'm a ghost."

Nick almost discharged his weapon. In the blink of an eye, his fantasy woman completely disappeared.

CHAPTER TWO

Nick Grandstaff found himself in Gerald Stevenson's world-class kitchen with a vague memory that there was something he'd forgotten, something important. His mind felt cloudy, and the faintest scent of oranges lingered in his nostrils. He rubbed his temples and concentrated. Nothing but brain fog. What the hell was he doing in here?

Jesus Christ, was that an espresso machine or a space ship? His stomach growled. Maybe he'd been hungry. That didn't make sense—he never ate on the job, especially not his client's food.

He turned on his heel and returned to the family room. Rounds, he was doing rounds. Shaking his head, he gave his neck a hard rub. He had a splitting headache. Fuck, this thing was a migraine. He could hardly think.

Methodically, he walked through each room in the mansion. When he reached the master bedroom, his temple throbbed and his gut twisted. He'd seriously have to hit the ibuprofen when he got back to the security desk. Everything was in order. Balcony doors closed and locked, weird art still overlooking the bed in a creepy way that made him question the Stevensons' sanity, nothing amiss on the balcony or in the massive bathroom or walk-in closet that was as big as his apartment. His eyes fell on the bedspread.

It was rumpled like someone had sat down or tossed something on top. It wasn't like that before. During his first walk-through, he'd thought the beds were so tightly made you could bounce a quarter off the top. He frowned. Nothing else was out of place.

At a jog, he surveyed the interior of the house, then locked up tight before inspecting the grounds on his way back to the security office in the guardhouse at the property entrance. He didn't find anything peculiar. Head pounding, he slipped into the guardhouse and pulled up the video surveillance. The Stevensons didn't have a camera in the bedroom, but they had one in the hall. Maybe he could see something.

He selected the file and navigated back to the time he'd started his last tour of the property, 1:00 a.m. At 12:59, the hall camera picked up a tightly made bed, as he'd remembered. He kept watching. He should appear at any moment. The picture froze, then blipped. The bedspread rumpled. He looked down at the time. One o'clock. He backed up. Unrumpled. Rumpled.

He checked the other security files. Every room empty but the ones he'd been in. No one had come in or out. Another stab of pain pierced his frontal cortex. *Fuck*, this was ridiculous. He pulled open a drawer and dispensed a dose of Excedrin into his palm, washing the pills down with coffee he'd left on the desk before he'd walked rounds. It was cold and stale.

While he waited for the fuckers to kick in, he leaned

back in his chair and advanced the digital recording slowly back and forth again. Exactly as before. Not rumpled. Rumpled. What the fuck? Did the Stevensons have a cat? A ridiculously powerful air-conditioning unit?

It didn't matter, did it, as long as the thing he was hired to protect remained. He wouldn't be able to rest unless he knew for sure that rumple wasn't a sign of something more.

Nick hustled back to the house, up to the master bedroom, and slipped into the closet, cursing his decision to take this gig. His partner, Soren, had begged him to fill in for him tonight. The guy was celebrating his anniversary and said he couldn't find anyone else. Nick had wanted to say no but, in the end, caved under the social pressure. Now he held his breath and entered the code for the safe Soren had given him. If the jewels were missing...

A diamond as big as his thumb sparkled from its place on the blue velvet, flanked by a set of matching earrings. All pieces accounted for. He closed the drawer again and rubbed the back of his neck.

That was it. He was officially losing his mind.

Checking that everything was exactly as he'd left it, he smoothed the rumple in the bedspread and returned to the guardhouse. Maybe he was overthinking this. Soren had said this job would be easy money. He was overqualified. All the experience in the field was making him paranoid. Aside from his dog, Nick's entire life was his career, and he loved the work with everything in him. He'd been overextending himself, burning the candle at both ends. It happened, and based on the hours he'd been putting in, he was overdue. That was it.

With a laugh, he started a fresh pot of coffee and swore he'd give Soren hell the next time he saw the bastard.

It took Rowan over an hour to undo the mistake she'd made with the detective. Every part of her ached, but then what did she expect given the significant amount of magic she'd had to use to bamboozle his brain? Nick Grandstaff—that was his last name according to the identification she'd found on him—was one distracting man. Once she'd dosed him with Harriet's elixir, she hadn't been strong enough to deny her curiosity about him.

She'd been stupid to let her guard down. Stupid to shed her invisibility in the first place. Beyond stupid to then *talk* to the man.

The only explanation was that he'd simply set her off-balance. She'd never reacted to a human the way she'd reacted to Nick. It was as if she'd been confronted with a triple chocolate cake after going a day without eating. She'd been *enthralled*. Maybe she'd gone too long without the pleasures of a man. Or maybe the stress of faking her death had made her careless. She shook her head. Who was she kidding? It was precisely carelessness that had resulted in her need to scrap that identity in the first place.

The glass doors to Zelda's Folly, the art gallery in Chelsea she owned and operated with Harriet, was a welcome sight. She turned her key in the lock and was relieved to find Harriet waiting for her in the office, although the gallery had been closed for hours.

"Look what the cat dragged in," her friend said. She smoothed her expertly coiffed gray hair and leaned back in her seat. Harriet had been working all night but still looked fresh in a rose-colored suit with chunky pearl jewelry. "You must let me know if you are delayed, Rowan. I was worried we'd have to hold another funeral."

"Sorry. I should have called." Rowan pulled the lock-pick from her pocket and tossed it on the desk. The enchanted object was no longer the shiny silver file Harriet had given her but a crooked, rusty antique with a flat section and a kink, as if it had been placed on railroad tracks like an old penny.

"Ye gods!" Her thin lips drew back. "What happened?" Harriet came out of her chair and rounded the desk to pull her into a hug. Her neck smelled of Chanel No. 5. "Are you okay?"

"I had to use the nuclear method."

"Oh, Rowan. Caught again? My word, you are a terrible thief."

She arched an eyebrow. "At least this time I didn't get arrested. I dropped my invisibility to save energy and a security guard walked in on me. I had to put the full whammy on his brain."

"How did he even know you were there?"

"I have no idea. Maybe he's an overachiever who walks the house and grounds regularly or something."

Harriet frowned. "Did you get the Raindrop?"

Rowan reached into her zipped pouch and scooped the necklace and earrings out. She laid them on the desk. "I left the replica behind. Had to."

"If the replicas are ever assessed by a professional, they'll never pass as the real thing. It's a weak enchantment, layered on top of a set of plastic Barbie earrings and a cupcake pendant. Even an amateur witch could unveil the truth with a snap of her fingers."

Rowan laughed at the thought of Camilla sporting a cupcake around her overly Botoxed neck. "By the time they learn the truth, it will be too late to do anything about it. I wiped the detective's mind. He'll be lucky to remember his name."

"Detective? I thought you were stopped by security... a rent-a-cop?"

"He told me he was a detective, and judging by the NYPD badge in his pocket, he wasn't lying. I don't think this was his regular gig. I'm guessing he was filling in for someone."

Harriet's eyes widened in alarm. "He told you? You had a conversation with him?" Her voice strained in her throat. "My goodness, did you two have tea and cookies before you wiped his brain?"

"I admit it wasn't my brightest moment. Honestly, I can't explain what came over me. Harriet, he walked into the room and all logical thought flew out the window."

"What did you say his name was?"

"Nick Grandstaff."

Harriet stilled, then disappeared behind her desk. Rowan watched her bony hands dig in the recycle bin beside her chair.

"What are you doing?"

"Checking something. I've heard that name before." If she had, Harriet would remember. As old as she was, her mind was like a steel trap. Sure enough, when she sat back in her chair, there was a folded paper in her hand. "Here it is. Detective Nick Grandstaff, NYPD, recent recipient of the Governor's Medal of Valor for pulling a teen girl from a burning vehicle."

"No shit?"

"Not even a little. This guy is the real deal. A hero. I hope you didn't bamboozle him too badly. This city needs him."

Harriet passed the paper over to Rowan, and she scanned the article, her eyes lingering on his picture.

"Nice to look at as well, isn't he?" Harriet stared at her with piercing blue eyes that narrowed perceptively.

Rowan shrugged.

Sighing, Harriet added, "Since you are ambivalent to the detective's attractiveness, you should be aware that a man with a strong mind like his might fight the serum. I don't recommend letting him see you again or having additional long-winded discussions. It could jar the memory loose. Which identity did he see?"

"This one." It mattered. She had several identities, but this was the one that was public-facing. Unlike the Rowan version she'd recently buried, the detective had seen the face of the owner of Zelda's Folly and the director of the youth center, Sunrise House. She *needed* this identity.

"Oh, Rowan." The frown of disappointment Harriet sent her cut right to her heart.

"I made a mistake. It is what it is." Rowan removed a small empty vial from her belt. "By the way, I'll need more forget-me juice."

"It will take time to brew. My stores are low and some of the ingredients have to be shipped in from Europe. As far as this goes"—Harriet rotated the rusty pick between her fingers—"it is irreparable. I'll have to start from scratch. I hope you're not planning any more heists in the near future."

She scoffed. "Not anytime soon. Now that I've had my revenge on Gerald Stevenson, I'm retiring my cat burglar suit."

"Good. It's not like you don't have enough jewels."

Sweeping the Raindrop into her hand, Rowan rubbed her thumb across the large, tear-shaped diamond. "True, but it's in my nature to collect things. There would be something poetic about liquidating Stevenson's prized possession and using the money to buy the land under my building back. What are politicians going for these days? One million? Maybe two?"

Harriet waved a hand dismissively. "I'm sure you'll find out. Just be careful. News of your other identity's death is spreading. Your brothers came by the old apartment this afternoon looking for you."

She froze. "Here, in New York? Did you say brothers, as in plural? The only one of my brothers who knows where to find me now is Alexander, and it couldn't have been him."

"No. Although Alexander did send another painting." She gestured toward the back room where they processed shipped artwork.

"Who was it then?"

"Tobias and Gabriel."

"Oh, that's right. Tobias must have remembered the old place from his visit... goddess, that was forty years ago."

"I gave them the box. They were with a woman named Raven."

Rowan had to sit down as realization dawned. She chose a chair in front of the desk and folded into it. "Tobias and Gabriel were together?" That didn't make any sense. All of her siblings had gone to great lengths to stay separated for their safety. When they'd come to this realm, their mother had warned them to keep their distance, and aside from a few limited visits, they'd adhered to that edict.

"He did not introduce Gabriel as his brother, but I recognized both of them from your drawings. Of course, neither knew who I was. I passed myself off as Mrs. Fernhall, the landlord. However, I was worried the witch might be on to me—"

"Witch?"

"The woman who was with them, the one they called Raven, was definitely a witch. I could smell her from across the room. I don't think she suspected me. Probably never ran into a Traveller before."

Rowan frowned. This couldn't be good. If her brothers shirked her mother's command, there had to be an extreme reason. "They wouldn't have come together to find me if it wasn't important."

"What are you going to do?"

"I'm not sure. Last I knew, Tobias was working as a doctor in Chicago. I think I still have his number. I'll call him."

Harriet nodded. "There's no shortage of drama in that family of yours, is there?" Her eyes roved toward the back room and Alexander's painting again.

"We're dragons." She shrugged. "We run hot and are fond of a little fire."

Harriet laughed.

Rowan stood. "I've got to get some rest. I'm tapped."

Harriet rounded the desk to give her another hug. "Don't worry about tonight. There's nothing we can't fix. Besides, the universe has a way of smoothing these things out."

"Thanks, Hattie."

The old woman pecked her cheek. "Do you want to take a peek at Alexander's painting before I go?"

"More of the same?"

Harriet nodded. "Worse."

"He's in a dark place."

"Artists go through peaks and valleys."

"Yes but Alexander has spent centuries in the valley of the shadow of death..." Rowan tilted her head. "I don't have the energy. I'll look at it in the morning."

"Tomorrow then. Rest well, dragon."

Rowan waited until her friend had exited through the front door, locked it behind her, and pulled down the security gate. Once Harriet was safely inside Rowan's hired car and in the hands of her driver Djorji, she headed for the back of the gallery. Down the stairwell, she descended into the basement. The vault door there was military-grade, and she carefully tapped in the code to unlock it. There was a hiss and then the grind of metal sliding against metal.

Overhead lights automatically blinked on as the door swung open, and Rowan released a held breath. The sight of treasure inside filled her with warmth and set her soul at ease. This was her treasure room, her sanctuary, the very best place for her to rest and heal. Every manner of gemstone winked at her under the fluorescents, along with gold coins, silver plates, and jeweled goblets that would be considered antiques today, as well as the occasional pearl necklace. She closed and sealed the vault door behind her, then fished her prize out of her pouch and tossed it on the heap. The Raindrop of Heaven and the earrings blended into the hodgepodge of valuables.

Rowan undressed. She paused to knead the muscles in her back and shoulders, sore from the long flight. Once she was entirely naked, she took a deep breath and spread her wings. Red scales arced and stretched in her peripheral vision, each wing possessing a claw at its crest. A long, deep sleep in her dragon form was just what the doctor ordered. She'd be as good as new in the morning.

She killed the overhead lights, then folded in half, resting her hands on the floor and welcoming her dragon form like the friend it was. Her body expanded, bones bending, flesh reordering itself as she grew and stretched to fill the subterranean space. She yawned, and her dragon teeth clacked together at the conclusion. In the fluid way that only dragons can, she dove into her pile of treasure, burrowed to the bottom, and allowed sleep to wash away the night's worries.

CHAPTER THREE

Chicago, Illinois

Tobias woke to darkness with the feel of his mate's firm breasts pressed into his back. Sabrina was practically wrapped around him, drawn to his above-average temperature in her sleep. Their subterranean apartment stayed a comfortable seventy-two degrees all year round, but her vampire nature meant she ran cold at night, and they'd discovered she unconsciously sought him out under the covers. He didn't mind one bit.

A repeated buzz came from Sabrina's side of the bed. He cast an annoyed glance in the direction of the sound and watched her phone light up. That was weird. Tobias looked at the clock. Not even sunset. Who was texting her at this hour? The comfort of her nearness evaporated as she sat up, read her messages, and frowned. Without saying a thing, she set the phone back down, rolled over, and snuggled against his chest. His hand trailed down to cup her ass and tug her against him. Obligingly, she hooked her leg over his hip.

"Hmmm. I love twilight," Tobias rumbled. "Best part of the day."

She sighed and planted her forehead against his chest. "We need to get up. My father is on his way here."

"Huh? How? It's still light out." Tobias jerked fully awake. Sabrina's father was a badass vampire mob boss who scared the crap out of him. Although his mate was the master of the Chicago vampire coven, Tobias hadn't gotten over her father's intimidating presence. Calvin Bishop was ancient and deadly. So deadly even his inner dragon got the willies in his company.

"His human security detail is transporting him in his coffin," Sabrina said. "It must be serious. My father does not travel during the day without cause."

It had only been a little over a week since Sabrina's father had left to establish the Racine coven, leaving Sabrina behind as master of the Chicago vampires and Tobias as her consort. As far as Tobias was concerned, the transition had gone off without a hitch. Had they done something wrong in such a short amount of time? Tobias hadn't heard any complaints from Sabrina's fellow vampires or the humans they dealt with managing the city on a day-to-day basis.

He flipped on the Christopher Spitzmiller lamp beside the bed, and a warm glow permeated the room. The Chicago vampire coven lived forty feet below the surface in a series of tunnels that branched all over the city. It was the perfect place for a vampire to sleep, safe from UV light as well as interference from humans during the hours they were most vulnerable. Even though Sabrina, as the only human/vampire hybrid, could tolerate sunlight, as master of the coven, she chose to keep the same hours as her people. And Tobias, as a bonded dragon, kept the same hours as his mate.

"I'm getting dressed and hitting the coffee. You cannot expect me to face Calvin or whatever major drama is coming our way without being fully caffeinated." Tobias bounded out of bed and started pulling on his pants.

"I'll text Chef and say we need a full human breakfast, pronto." Sabrina tapped furiously on her phone. Chef Angie was new to their world. Sabrina's father, being a full-blooded vamp had only fed on humans when he was master. But although Sabrina could feed on blood and often fed on the energy of her mate, she enjoyed regular meals as well. Thank goodness their longtime security detail, Paul, had a wife who had studied the culinary arts. She was more than happy to come into the fold.

In a matter of minutes, they were both showered, dressed and presentable and had just sat down in front of a meal fit for a vampire master when Paul opened the door to their luxury underground flat and announced, "Calvin Bishop to see you."

Two men carried in her father's coffin and set it down beside the table. They cleared out of the room fast enough to make Tobias's spine tingle. This was not good. Not good at all. Paul locked the door behind him.

Tobias took a slow drink of his coffee, studying the long black box that contained his mate's sleeping father. His gaze darted to Sabrina's. He drank more coffee, ate another bite of toast, pushed his eggs on his plate, drank more coffee.

"Okay, I give. Are we supposed to open this thing or wait until he wakes up?" he asked.

"The sun is setting now. It shouldn't be long." Sabrina

had no need of either window or watch to know that. Her vampire instincts distinguished the exact moment of sunrise and sunset without any external help. She'd told him she could feel the night in her blood. When the sun set, she described it as a shot of tequila coursing through her veins.

"He should be..." Sabrina raised an eyebrow in his direction and carefully lifted the lid.

Calvin sat up with a creepy factor worthy of Bela Lugosi, stiff backed and in a manner that seemed to require no effort at all, as if gravity did not restrain him as much as it did everyone else. Tobias dropped his toast.

"Sabrina, my darling." Her father swung his legs over the side and, in one swift move, leaped to his feet and pulled her into a hug. He turned to shake Tobias's offered hand and greet him as well. "I see Barnard and Max were able to reach you with my message in time. Thank you both for meeting me here at this hour."

"We live here, Dad, and it's nightfall. Where else would we be?" Sabrina asked.

He shook his head. "Obviously I feared that when you got the message from the Forebears, you and Tobias might do something foolish, like run."

"What message? What's so important that you risked traveling in daylight?"

Calvin frowned. "Haven't you been checking the coven's messages?"

She held up her phone. "Only like every five minutes. Ask Tobias."

"I think her phone is permanently attached to her left hand," he confirmed.

"Not those messages. The old system. The official system?"

"The tubes? No. We haven't gotten anything that way in ages."

At the look on her father's face, Sabrina stood and rushed toward the room that used to be his office. Tobias followed after her. They'd been renovating the apartment, and Calvin's old desk had been removed, but they were still waiting on furniture. The room felt empty and cold in its current state. Tobias hadn't spent any time in there since he'd moved in with Sabrina.

"What are the tubes?" Tobias asked.

Approaching the one bookshelf that was still crammed with books, Sabrina lifted one leather-bound volume and patted the wall behind it. Tobias's eyebrows lifted when he saw her open a small metal door, perfectly hidden. He would have never guessed it was there. Chewing her lip, Sabrina pulled a canister from a pneumatic tube inside.

"Just like the bank," Tobias said, trying to lighten the mood.

Her expression turned grim. Tobias knew that look. Sabrina only made that face when she was deeply worried about something.

"Only one group of vampires still uses this system of communication—the Forebears."

Tobias swallowed. The Forebears were the vampire rulers, the most ancient and dangerous of their kind. He waited while she twisted the top and read what was on the roll of parchment inside.

To all coven masters in all world territories,

It has come to our attention that a reliable dragon sighting has occurred in the Midwestern United States. Dragons are extremely dangerous and pose a significant threat to the future of our race. By royal decree, any vampire who delivers the dragon(s) to the Forebears, either dead or alive, will be rewarded.

She lowered the parchment and looked at her father. "It's signed Turgun. I didn't even know he was awake."

"I have a feeling Aldrich woke him up after your coronation. He must have seen more than we thought he did," Calvin said.

"But if he saw, wouldn't he—"

"Contact us about the incident? He did. Yesterday. He called me. The paperwork to transition you as master of Chicago hasn't been processed yet by Forebear administration, so I am still acting master according to their records. Despite Aldrich having attended your coronation, he followed protocol. You know how they do things there."

"I take it the Forebears are old-school?" Tobias asked.

"The oldest school there is," Sabrina said. "What did you tell him?"

Calvin cleared his throat. "I told him I thought the dragon was a complex work of magic created by a local witch who was loyal to the coven. Unfortunately, he was quick to point out the body count. A simple illusion couldn't take anyone's head off, he suggested. I was able to convince him that if the dragon existed, it must have been injured during the altercation with the wolves and disappeared, because it hasn't been seen since. It is the truth, yes?"

It was true in the sense that Tobias had been injured in his dragon form defending the coven. And he did leave to go home and shower and sleep and hadn't transformed into his dragon since. But there was a huge lie of omission there too. Tobias was the dragon, and he had become Sabrina's consort and was helping her lead the coven. That ceremony had not included Aldrich or any of the Forebears. But that didn't change that Sabrina's coven had seen him shift and knew exactly what he was.

"Oh, Dad, the entire coven knows about Tobias. What do we do?"

The older vampire scowled in a way that showed his canines, as if his teeth were too large for his mouth. He turned his full attention on Tobias.

"You and your brethren need to disappear. This will blow over. Turgun will become bored and go to sleep again, but only if there is no trace of anything draconic when they come here. Under the right circumstances, we might be able to convince them there was never any dragon at all. That it was all a magical hoax. But only if there is no trace of you or your siblings."

"Father, no!" Sabrina shook her head desperately.

Tobias didn't like the idea either. They were newlyweds. They couldn't be apart, and she couldn't leave the coven.

But her father pressed on. "You, Sabrina, must order your coven to remain silent. Insist they forget they ever saw a dragon. As master, you have that power. Compel them one at a time if you have to."

"That could take days," she said.

"I will help you."

Tobias held up a hand. "Can we go back to the part where I need to not exist? I live here. Where exactly am I supposed to go?"

Calvin gave him a stern look. "Wherever our people won't find you."

Once he saw Sabrina's reaction, he knew what she was thinking. There was a place. His brother and his mate had a safe house in New Orleans and they owed him a favor, but it would mean he'd have to live apart from Sabrina. It would also mean crawling to his brother for help. The notion filled him with dread.

He groaned. "Please tell me there's another option."

"I'm sorry, Tobias," Sabrina said. "It's the only way."

CHAPTER FOUR

Rowan woke in her treasure room, feeling refreshed, and shifted back into her human form. After a quick shower in the bathroom she'd had built outside the vault, she dressed quickly in a skirt and blouse she kept on hand for such occasions. Keeping her treasure room at the gallery made sense; no one would question a giant vault in the basement of a business that specialized in priceless works of art. However, it would be risky to keep such a thing in any of her many residences. Due to its sheer size, a residential vault would be distinctive and a tempting piece of gossip for the workers who installed it. Not to mention, it might elicit questions when she had intimate guests. Not that she had guests often. Her love life had been embarrassingly anemic the past several years.

Still, while it made sense for her treasure room to be at the gallery, it wasn't exactly convenient. Her preferred residence was on the Upper West Side and she needed to stop there before her 3:00 p.m. appointment at Sunrise House. She had a meeting with her lawyer to discuss what they could do concerning the building situation, and she needed to remember to call the hospital in Chicago to try to connect with her brother Tobias.

"Do you want to see Alexander's painting before you go?" Harriet asked when she reached the main floor of the gallery. The older woman was already behind her desk, exquisitely manicured and dressed in a lightweight, robin's-egg-blue cashmere suit that popped divinely next to her gray hair and classic pearls.

"Of course." Rowan couldn't hide the sad tone of her voice. Her brother Alexander was a talented artist, but his work always depressed her. The gallery bought it, of course. Rowan's money was what had kept a roof over his head all these years. It wasn't a horrible investment. His work sold on occasion for respectable sums, although not what she sent to him. She overpaid on purpose. It was her way of caring for Alexander when she couldn't physically tend to him.

Harriet led the way into the back room where they processed incoming shipments of art and supplies. The painting was six by eight feet and wrapped in brown paper, although one corner was pulled back. Clearly Harriet had taken a peek.

Rowan peeled back the wrappings. "That damned bird again."

"Every painting this last year. And the native woman." Harriet held her elbows.

"She was his mate. It was her death that broke him. He never fully recovered."

"Hundreds of years and he still pines for her."

"Over three hundred now."

"To be loved like that." Harriet laughed, her eyes flicking toward the ceiling as if the idea was enviable.

"Don't say that. When dragons mate, they mate for life.

Their immortal life. Not the other person's. When Alexander's mate died, he lost half of himself. His mind couldn't handle it. His mate, Maiara, has been dead and buried for hundreds of years and he's still obsessed. It's a fate worse than death. I plan to avoid it like the plague."

Harriet raised a sculpted eyebrow. "With your love life, you have nothing to worry about."

Rowan feigned offense. "Says the woman who hasn't been laid since Eisenhower was President."

Harriet pursed her lips to suppress a smile. "You don't know everything about me."

Studying the painting, Rowan said, "Is it just me or are the colors getting darker?"

"It's not just you. I compared this to pictures of the ones we've sold. Not only are the colors darker, he's aging the native woman. It's subtle, but I can see it. She's fading."

"What do you think it means?"

Harriet rubbed her knuckle along her jaw. "It means your brother has lost his marbles."

Rowan snorted. "Yes. A long time ago." Tears burned along her eyelids. He was getting worse, and there was absolutely nothing Rowan could do about it. She taped the paper back into place, covering the painting.

"I better go."

"Should I call Djorji?"

"Yeah, but tell him to pick me up at Friedman's. I'm starving. Going to have a late breakfast."

Harriet kissed her on both cheeks, then picked up her phone to call her driver. Rowan's stomach growled. She strode out the door and walked the few blocks to Friedman's, relieved to see there was a spot open at the counter. She ordered a coffee and blueberry pancakes before calling the last phone number she had for Tobias.

We're sorry, the number you have reached has been disconnected.

She'd expected as much. No one used a landline anymore. She hung up and called his work number. "Can I speak with Dr. Tobias Winthrop please?" she asked the woman who answered. "He's in pediatric cardiology."

There was a moment of instrumental music and then a voice response unit answered. "You've reached the office of Dr. Elizabeth Allen. Press One for the appointment desk."

She tapped the button. Another woman answered. "I'm looking for Tobias Winthrop," Rowan said.

"Dr. Winthrop closed his practice a few weeks ago. Dr. Allen is taking his patients. Can I make an appointment for you?"

"I really need to reach Dr. Winthrop. Did he leave a forwarding number or address?"

There was a long pause. "I'm sorry, ma'am. No, he did not. As far as I know, he isn't practicing anymore."

"Thank you." Rowan hung up and tapped the phone against her forehead. Tobias would never find her. The box Harriet had given him was meant to let him know she was okay, but there was nothing in it that would give away her location. And it appeared he'd gone underground as well, likely recycling his identity just like she had. She sighed. Whatever reason he and Gabriel had for trying to reach her would have to stay a mystery.

She pulled up the latest book she was reading on her phone while she waited for breakfast. It was a romance about a vampire who falls in love with a human. Silly stuff. Immortals and humans didn't mix. It never ended well. But she couldn't put the thing down.

"Excuse me, miss?"

Rowan turned her head to find an NYPD badge in

front of her face and a man staring at her from a considerable height. Her stomach did a strange little flip. Detective Nick Grandstaff's steely gaze burned into her with the intensity of a thousand blazing suns. She white-knuckled the edge of the counter. It wasn't the badge that sent a wave of shock with an anxiety chaser through her chest. It was Harriet's warning. What if his strong mind resisted the serum?

Admit nothing. "Can I help you?" she asked through a tight throat.

"Did you notice a man in here earlier, about five foot six inches tall, white-blond hair, slight build?"

"No." It was hard to speak. Her tongue had swollen in her mouth and grown uncomfortably dry. The light from the window shone directly on his face, turning his eyes the color of sterling silver. Pale, heavenly eyes that stole her breath. And his scent, it hit her as it had the night before, in through her nose and straight to her crotch. She uncrossed and crossed her legs against the building tension between her thighs and forced herself to blink. She ended up fluttering her eyelashes. *Fuck*, she had, hadn't she? She'd fluttered her eyelashes at the detective like a draconic Betty Boop.

"Okay. Thanks." He continued to watch her, his eyes narrowing. "Have we met before? You seem familiar."

"No," she answered quickly. Too quickly. She shook her head. By the Mountain, she sounded guilty. She reined it in and smiled. Too many teeth. She stopped smiling.

"You've never been by the twenty-fourth precinct for anything, have you?"

"No." She inhaled sharply. She'd been to the nineteenth precinct when she was arrested, but that was another identity, another name, another face. "No, I don't think we've ever met before." She forced herself to drink some ice water. "I'd remember you," she added under her breath.

"Oh." Nick nodded.

There was a clunk and scrape as the server slid Rowan's pancakes in front of her and focused on Nick. "Can I get you something, Detective?"

"Coffee. Black. To go." Nick's eyes never left Rowan's face.

"So, uh, what did this blond guy you're looking for do?"

He shook his head, a crooked grin revealing a chipped molar she found positively endearing. "Just need to ask him some questions."

She wondered what had caused that chip and how he'd gotten the scar that cut through his left eyebrow. There was one along his jaw too that caused an insanely sexy break in his stubble, hardly visible. She hadn't noticed either the night before.

"In other words, it's none of my business," she said, resting her chin on her fist.

That crooked grin flashed again, and Rowan almost fell off her stool. She took another sip of ice water.

"What are you reading there?"

She tucked her hair behind her ear, her cheeks heating. "Nothing that would likely appeal to you. It's a vampire romance. *Love's Last Breath.*"

"Never heard of it. But I like vampires. Dracula. My favorite book of all time is Mary Shelley's *Frankenstein.*"

Her mouth fell open. "Truly?"

"Yes. Someone important to me had a copy in their hands the last time I saw them. I like the story well enough, but it's the memory of it, you know?" His voice was soft. Between that and his furrowed brow, she got the feeling he was sharing something deeply intimate with her.

"It's an incredible tale about the importance of family and personal connections, don't you agree? It's not Frankenstein's nature that turns him evil but his abandonment and isolation." She loved the book. Had loved it since its release.

"Are you sure we haven't met?" He scratched the side of his neck.

Rowan gulped and had to look down at her pancakes to break the power of the twin tractor beams pulling her toward him. The man emitted his own gravity. How could he be human? He had to be human, didn't he?

"Do you make it a habit to approach women in diners and ask them if you've met before? It seems like a line better suited for a bar."

"Excuse me?"

"I've told you we haven't met, twice now."

He rubbed the back of his neck. "What's your name?"

"Rowan," she said softly.

"Nick." He leaned a hand against the counter beside her plate, and she wanted to sit on her hands to keep from touching him. Instead, she played with her knife beside his fingers, never touching but close enough to set her heart racing.

The server returned with a to-go cup and dropped it in front of Nick, who pulled out his wallet and paid the man.

"Now that we've met, maybe we should get to know each other better. Have dinner or coffee."

"You already have coffee."

"Dinner then."

She looked down at her ring, the ruby a blood-red reminder of why she needed to stop flirting with this man and eat her breakfast. She was a dragon, and she'd wiped his memories last night. Spending time with him could only lead to disaster.

"I don't think it's a good idea," she said, meeting his gaze again.

He lifted his cup and gave her a little nod. "Okay then. Enjoy your pancakes."

She watched him leave, holding her breath until his scent faded from the air.

CHAPTER FIVE

There was no blond guy. Nick wasn't proud to admit he'd invented a reason to talk to the dark-haired beauty he'd seen in the window of Friedman's, but the truth was, he'd been walking back to his car after questioning a neighbor about a case when he'd seen her at the counter and hadn't been able to resist speaking with her. Yes, he was attracted to her, but Nick was a disciplined man and simple attraction wouldn't be enough to draw him inside or cause him to lie. What he found irresistible was the familiarity. She was the memory of a song he could almost hear and couldn't quite remember.

He was sure he'd met her before. The way she brushed her hair back from her face, the angle of her wrists when she rested them on the counter, the crease in her brow as she stared at her phone, the way her full lips pressed against the rim of her coffee mug. Her perfume. Oh God, her scent. Orange peels and smoke with a dash of spicy cinnamon. It was distinctive and he'd smelled it before, he was sure, but he couldn't remember.

Part of him expected that he'd known her as a child,

maybe gone to elementary school with her. He'd grown up in an abusive household, and some of those years had been lost to him. He'd met a lot of people during that time, faces that were a blur because nothing stood out in his mind but hunger and the damned belt his guardian used to beat him with. But she'd denied recognizing him at all. Goddamn, his brain hurt thinking about it, and the weirdness last night wasn't helping the feeling that all was not right in his head.

He'd lost time. He'd been upstairs at the Stevensons', then in the blink of an eye he was in the kitchen. Maybe he needed another psych eval. He rubbed his temples. He'd long ago dealt with his abusive upbringing in therapy and so far hadn't suffered any long-term psychological issues. Could a person have delayed onset PTSD? Maybe. But he wasn't having flashbacks or anxiety attacks.

The entire ride back to the precinct, he stewed over his actions and was so deep in thought he didn't notice his partner, Soren, standing in the door to his office until the man said something.

"How'd it go last night?"

Nick snapped out of his reverie. "All right, I guess."

"Thanks for covering for me. Rhonda woulda divorced me if I missed our anniversary again for my side hustle." He reached into his back pocket and pulled out a folded check. "Here's what we agreed on."

"Thanks." He rubbed his eyes. "Hey, can I ask you something about that job?"

"Sure." Soren shrugged.

"You ever have anything weird happen when you're there?"

"Weird like what?"

"Like things move and shit. Like does the air-conditioning blow real hard or something?"

"I don't know what the hell you're talking about right now, Nick, but you're kinda worrying me. What the fuck happened?"

"Come in and sit down for a minute."

Soren took the chair across the desk, and Nick gave him a play-by-play of finding himself in the kitchen and the rumpled comforter.

"But you checked the video and there was nothing there?"

"Yeah. One second it's flat, the next rumpled. The diamonds were still in the safe. Nothing missing."

"Did you bookmark the recording?"

"Yeah, of course I did."

"I'll take a look. I need to run out there this afternoon anyway to review Mr. Stevenson's security plan for some big gala he's planning."

"Thanks." He cracked his neck. "I just can't shake that something about that night was wrong."

Soren frowned. "Coming from you, that gives me the willies. Your gut feelings have a habit of saving lives."

"I promise you, my instincts are not infallible."

"But they're pretty damned sharp."

"I'm not sure about that. I saw a woman this morning I could have sworn I'd met before. She wouldn't give me the time of day."

"So she's definitely met you before."

"Okay smart-ass."

Soren's smile faded. "Seriously, my friend. I think you just need some rest."

"You're probably right."

"And as for the girl, if she turned you down, she ain't worth it." Soren smacked him on the shoulder.

Nick grinned. "Or maybe she knows what's good for

her. I suck at relationships. Can't get beyond the dating stage. As soon as it gets serious, I head for the hills."

Soren frowned. "Weren't you serious with that one who..."

"The one who died. Katy."

"Sorry."

"That was seventeen years ago. I was barely twenty-one, and the fact is, it was casual. I mourned her, but it wasn't like I was married to her." Almost everyone in Manhattan had known someone who'd lost their life on 9/11. Katy had been a good friend, a fun date, and an undeniable hero, but he hadn't loved her in the way Soren loved Rhonda.

"And no one special since?"

He shook his head. "Not my bag. Too busy saving the world."

Soren laughed. "Northern Manhattan anyway. You take on almost twice the cases of any other detective in the borough. And that last one. Ugh."

The last case he'd cracked had been difficult. Domestic abuse. Husband murdered his wife. Nick had solved the murder just in time to pull the bound teenage daughter from a car her father had set on fire. He'd been awarded the Governor's Medal of Valor for that one. The honor didn't help him sleep at night, but knowing the murderer was behind bars did.

"I like to know I've made a difference. And it's not like I have a Rhonda at home waiting for me."

Soren stood and gave him a wink. "Well, don't work too hard. You know what they say about all work and no play." He gave a two-fingered salute before slipping out the door and returning to work.

Nick frowned. "Yeah, it keeps you from getting your heart broken."

"Miss Rowan, do you like my picture?"

Rowan stopped behind Elijah as she navigated the rows of children painting at their desks. For three decades, she'd been running Sunrise House, teaching art to children in the way Alexander had taught her when she was a whelp. Art had come naturally to her brother, but not to her. Only through his patience and perseverance had she learned that bringing a paintbrush to canvas could be an escape. She'd desperately needed an escape back then, from the Obsidian Palace, her mother's expectations, and from the wants and needs of her native realm of Paragon. Her goal was to provide that same escape to these children.

She loved these kids. She provided a safe place for them from the time school let out until the early evening when, under the best of circumstances, a parent or relative could be home to meet them. Under the worst circumstances, she was the only real adult influence in their life, and she took that responsibility seriously.

All the children came from disadvantaged backgrounds. Some were simply poor. That was the best scenario. A poor child who was both healthy and loved was very lucky indeed. It was the neglected kids she tried to focus on. The ones she knew left an empty house and went home to the same. She fed them, provided clothing, paid for their transportation. She had children who came all the way from the Bronx. Everyone was welcome, and she enrolled as many as the large building she owned could hold. Sunrise House was in an ideal location, in close proximity to the train and those in need. She was free now and she was rich, and she applied both those blessings liberally to helping the children of Sunrise House overcome their circumstances.

"Oh, this is very good, Elijah. I love your use of color and perspective in this piece." Rowan made sure to put on her most serious face as she assessed Elijah's painting over his shoulder. The nine-year-old didn't want a flippant compliment but her undivided attention. He'd painted Sunrise House as many of the children here did. In many ways, this place was home to them. "Tell me about your painting."

"I wanted it to look happy since everyone here is always happy." Elijah turned to look at her, and she could see dusky circles under his dark brown eyes. "This is the sun, and I made just one cloud in the sky because it's a sunny day. This is Sunrise House, and this is you and me holding hands."

"What's this?" Rowan pointed to the corner of the painting where there was a figure sitting in a dark box.

"That's me at home. The lights in our house don't work anymore, so it's always dark."

"Your family doesn't have electricity? Is your water working?"

"Yeah, the water still works."

Rowan forced her face to remain impassive for Elijah's sake. She'd look up his address later and have her lawyer, Adrienne, pay off the family's bills and get the lights back on. It was something she did regularly.

"Did you have dinner yet? The chicken is here." Today was Wednesday. Roasted chicken, white rice, broccoli, salad, fresh fruit, bread. She was firm with the catering company. Healthy, well-balanced meals. "You can go get some if you're hungry."

He jumped out of his chair and raced toward the cafeteria. A few children followed; others stayed with their art. There were two hundred kids in the program with employees and volunteers from the community providing academic help, athletic training, instruction in the arts, and even college preparatory studies for the older teens. This place was her heart and soul. She gave these children what she never had herself from the adults in her life—someone who cared about them and their individual dreams.

"Miss Valor?"

Rowan turned to find Adrienne, her lawyer, behind her, clutching his briefcase.

"Not here." She notified the head art instructor that she was leaving the floor and then motioned to Adrienne. "Come with me."

He nodded and followed her into her private office. Adrienne Sarcosi was a balding man with a fringe of white hair trimmed neatly around the sides of his head. Perceptive blue eyes peered at her from over a nose that roughly resembled a plum tomato and a set of thin lips that seemed to blend into his pale, spotted face. Adrienne was a good friend and an even better lawyer, and what he lacked in traditional good looks, he made up in loyalty and smarts. Rowan had admired him for decades.

"Did you get it?" she asked once they were safely inside her office.

"A temporary injunction, yes. Gerald Stevenson can't evict you until the land lease expires, per your contract."

She breathed a sigh of relief.

"Don't get too excited, Rowan. You know how this works. The Stevensons have a lot of money. In my professional opinion, people like that get what they want eventually, and he wants you out sooner rather than later."

She cursed. "We should have seen this coming. I should have never bought a building on a land lease."

"How could you have known that Gerald and Camilla

would buy the land out from under you from the church who'd owned it for almost a century, or that the blank check you offered them wouldn't be enough to buy it back? You must know this is about gentrification and corporate greed. They don't want a community center here. I'm sure they plan to bribe the rezoning board and turn this space into a strip mall. The deal was as crooked as they come, and there's not a single thing we can do about it."

"Can't you find something on Stevenson? Keep him wrapped up in court cases until he lets us stay just to get the bee out of his bonnet?"

"Suing them would open your corporation up to a level of scrutiny you do not want." He lowered his chin and gave her a steady glare. She was a dragon who had lived many lives hiding behind Firebrand, Inc. Officially, the company bought and sold art and antiquities. Unofficially, it allowed her to own property that was not attached to her personally, giving her the freedom to change her identity or become invisible on a whim. Adrienne was right; piss Stevenson off and he'd dig into her past. It wouldn't take long for him to realize she didn't have one.

"Did you offer them cash? I have almost unlimited funds, Adrienne. If we can't bribe Stevenson, can we bribe the companies that plan to move in here?"

He groaned. "I tried. After some serious digging, I have reason to believe that this is about more than money. Turns out the Stevensons have no intention of managing the property themselves. They're working on behalf of a corporation called NAVAK, Inc. I can't find any information on NAVAK. Their records are as tightly sealed as yours are, Rowan. If I didn't know better, I'd wonder if there was another dragon behind the corporate curtain." He pushed a piece of paper across the table with a logo and an address in the Cayman Islands.

She lifted the page and took a closer look. The logo was a diamond shape with NAVAK in gothic lettering inside it. She'd never seen anything like it before. "It's not a dragon. We're very territorial. I wouldn't rule out another supernatural entity, but it's not one I'm aware of, and I've been running in these circles for a long time. Maybe it's a foreign entity buying up American real estate."

"Possible."

"Anyway, keep trying. And just in case, start shopping for an alternative space of similar size. These kids need stability. I can't have them with no place to go. Not even for one day."

"Of course. But you need to be aware that a space like this is almost unheard of in Manhattan anymore. You bought this building decades ago. I'll be lucky to find something half the size for twenty times as much as you paid for this."

"Money is no object."

"I'll get started right away."

"Thank you, Adrienne."

She sat down at her desk and examined the logo again. If it was a supernatural corporation, there was one person who might know. She shook her head. No way would she go there. Not unless she was absolutely desperate.

CHAPTER SIX

The next morning, Nick awoke to a cold, wet nose assaulting his cheek. "Good morning, Rosco."

His German shepherd gave him a lick up the side of the face and chuffed in his general direction.

"Yeah, yeah. Okay." He rolled out of bed and pulled on a pair of running shorts and an NYPD T-shirt, then grabbed the leash off the hook by the door of his rent-controlled, one-bedroom apartment. The park was beautiful this time of year, but he had another motivation for the exercise that morning. The woman, Rowan, was on his mind again, had haunted his dreams until he woke up in the middle of the night with his dick in his hand and her face emblazoned on his mind.

It wasn't like him to obsess about a woman. Rowan had made it clear she wasn't interested. What was he, some kind of stalker? He knew nothing about her. Probably would never see her again.

He pounded the pavement faster, Rosco finding his stride beside him. So he had a little crush. He needed to treat this like one. She was Beyoncé or Gisele. Out of his league and out of his reach. He needed to leave it at that.

"Hey you, Mistah Nick!"

He jogged to a halt and waved to Regine under the bike overpass. The homeless woman was a regular fixture on his morning jogs. He'd discovered early on that she liked where she was, liked the freedom of being transient, and wouldn't entertain any talk of shelters. Occasionally he could convince her to accept small comforts, a coat in the winter, clean blankets, a cup of coffee. Most of all, he liked her. Loved her spirit and her refreshing authenticity. Regine was who she was.

"Miss Regine, how are you this sunny morning?"

"Good, good, Mistah Nick. You know, that udda woman who come here, Alice, she brought me this magazine yesterday." She held up a *Cosmo* and gave him a wide smile. "Quiz in here about how to know if you're in love or lust. I say who care? I take either."

Nick chuckled. "I wouldn't have taken you for a *Cosmo* girl."

She laughed until her shoulders shook. "I read to remember all the crazies out there." She pointed toward the city outside the park.

"I'll let you in on a little secret, Regine. We're all a little crazy."

"Ahhh. You a good man, Nick. When you gonna get yourself a woman?"

He shrugged. Visions of Rowan stretched out across his sofa sprang up in his noggin like she was taking up residence there. He rubbed his head.

"Ohhh, Mistah Nick. What that look? I think you in love."

He pointed at the scar running through his eyebrow. "Who'd love this ugly mug?"

"You all right." She waved her hand dismissively. "Womens only care 'bout you treating 'em right. You treat your woman right?"

"If I had one, I could tell you." Rosco bumped his knuckles with his nose and Nick checked the time. "Sorry, Regine. I gotta run. Rosco needs to do his business, and I'm going to be late for work." He pulled a few bills from his pocket and handed them to her. "Here. You need coffee with that *Cosmo*."

She clucked her tongue. "You a good man, Mistah Nick. I think you be very nice to your woman."

"Thanks. I'll know where to come if I need a reference." He took off running again, her laugh filling the air.

No sooner was Nick showered and dressed and in his vehicle than his portable squawked at him. Death scene, not too far from him. Soren was already there with the first responders, and the coroner was on his way. Nick hurried to the address the dispatcher gave him.

"Nick," Soren said. "Called you the second I got confirmation. Female, early twenties, found naked by the morning garbage crew, no ID."

Nick assessed the scene. The body had been dumped like a used tissue. That's the first thing Nick thought when he saw the woman. She was already gray and her position was such that it was pretty clear she'd been disposed of after death. No one alive would remain in the oddly splayed position and, although her wounds were ghastly, there was no blood at the scene.

"What do you make of this?" Soren asked him.

"She wasn't killed here. No blood. What do you think made those marks?"

"Her wounds? Neck, back, arms, thighs. I haven't figured that out yet."

"It's like she was pierced ritualistically. The marks are oddly placed." Nick thought for a moment. "What if it was a fetish thing gone wrong? Those could be hook marks for suspension."

"You think this was sex play?"

Nick shrugged. "It's possible."

"There's a tat on her wrist."

Nick pulled on a pair of gloves and carefully tilted the victim's arm. A diamond had been tattooed on her inner wrist with the old-timey letters NAVAK filling the interior space. He pulled out his phone and snapped a picture. "You ever seen anything like this?"

Soren glanced down at his feet.

"Soren?"

"Maybe, but, uh..." He looked over his shoulder at the rest of the team combing through the scene.

Nick dropped the woman's wrist and peeled off his glove into a garbage bag. "Come on. In here."

He led Soren toward a door that read SUNRISE HOUSE, its letters embossed over the orange face of a rising sun. It was quiet just inside the door, someplace private to talk. He ushered Soren inside. "Spill it."

He froze when the closing door wafted the scent of orange peels and smoke over him. Was it possible the woman from the diner had been here? Rowan. He gave his head a shake.

"Nick? You okay?"

"The tattoo. Where've you seen that tattoo?"

"Look..." He rubbed his jaw. "I love my wife, okay?"

Nick gave him a disappointed look. "Soren..."

"Things have just been a little cold in the bedroom lately. I needed a little something on the side."

Nick groaned, his respect for his coworker flatlining.

"Hey, the guy who doesn't believe in relationships doesn't get to judge me on mine."

Never mind that people like Soren were exactly the reason Nick feared exclusivity. Poor Rhonda. "So where have you seen this logo before? I can tell if you're lying, so don't even try."

"I went to this club with a girl a few moons ago. It was one of those app hookups. Hot as lightning. Hot as lightning, Nick."

"Okay. So you went to a club with a hot girl..."

"The girl had that same tattoo."

Nick's eyebrows shot up. "Did she tell you what it meant?"

His eyes shifted from side to side. "Uh, no. We drank, we hooked up, and she took off."

"Well, get her on the line. Ask her now."

"I, uh, I don't exactly have her number, okay? We connected the one time and afterward, well, her account is, um, gone. We went to a hotel, so, uh..."

"Jesus, Soren. Are you telling me you have no idea who this girl is or how to get in contact with her?"

"Yeah, pretty much."

"Fuck."

"We could try the club again. See if she shows up there."

Nick brightened. "Yeah. Good idea."

"Only, it's hard to get in. Very exclusive. This girl was the only reason they let me through the door. They love beautiful women there."

Nick straightened. "I can clean up."

Soren chuckled. "Can you become a woman?"

That was potentially problematic. "Maybe one of the female detectives can do us a solid."

That idea didn't seem to excite Soren, but then, he wouldn't be crazy about explaining how they connected the body to the club. Nobody liked a cheater.

Nick glanced up the stairs. "Hey, I want to ask some questions here, check if anyone saw anything. See if there's a window overlooking the alley."

"You want backup?"

"No. I got it."

With a nod of his head, Soren returned to the crime scene.

Nick had to be losing it. It was a smell. Just a scent. It probably wasn't even her. But he couldn't help himself. If it *was* her and not someone with the same perfume, he couldn't resist the excuse to speak with her again.

He followed the scent up the stairs and was surprised as hell at what he saw once he got there. At the top, there was a wall of glass with *Sunrise House* etched into the door. It didn't take him long to put two and two together. This was some sort of community center, and he'd come in through the back entrance.

Beyond the glass, his eyes caught on dark hair and red lips. Rowan. His heart skipped. She was surrounded by children painting, drawing, and working with clay. This must be some kind of art studio. She was helping them, her smile as brilliant as the sun. He watched her, entranced as she leaned over one girl's shoulder and pointed at the canvas, then helped another child pour red paint into her tray. Her hands were covered in paint. A particularly vivid red splotch brightened her cheek.

He could have watched her forever. She was like an

angel, and the way the kids looked at her... Kids knew a good person when they saw one. There was nothing but love in those kids' eyes. Everything about the scene brought him back to when he was a kid, when places like this were the only thing keeping him going, when life was dark and seemed otherwise hopeless. A lump formed in his throat.

As if she could hear his thoughts, her gaze flicked up to his and connected through the glass. She knew he was there, watching her. No chickening out now. He opened the door.

"Detective?" The smile faded from her face.

He approached her with as much swagger as he could muster considering the sight of her made his insides turn to Jell-O. "Can I talk to you for a minute? It's about an investigation." He pointed his thumb toward the back entrance.

"I haven't seen a blond man here either," she said, annoyance crinkling her eyes.

He shook his head. "This is a different case."

"Two investigations in as many days. It seems I'm in the wrong place at the wrong time."

"It will only take a minute."

She pushed her hair back from her face and smeared the red on her cheek. He reached out but stopped before touching her when she pulled her head away from his hand.

"You have something there. Paint."

"Oh." She smiled, and he thought the light from it might burn him. She grabbed a clean rag from a pile on the counter and started dabbing at her cheek. "My office is this way."

He followed her into a tiny room with a desk that was way smaller than it should be for an adult. She leaned a hip against the front of it and crossed her arms over her chest.

"What can I do for you, Detective?"

"Do you work here?"

"I own Sunrise House and act as its director."

Owned it. Beautiful, smart, and compassionate. He thanked the good Lord for his rib cage or his heart might jump into her arms.

"What time did you come to work today?"

"Around seven. I don't usually come in that early, but I was helping out with the before-school program. We're understaffed."

"When you came into the building, did you come in through the back or the front?"

"My driver dropped me off in the front. What's this about?"

"Your driver. Did you take an Uber or taxi?"

"Neither. I have a private driver."

Holy shit. Was she some sort of celebrity? A trust fund baby? He cleared his throat. "And you didn't go out the back exit between then and now?"

"No."

"Did any kids mention seeing anything strange out back?"

"No. But they usually come in the front. I unlocked the back door this morning, but I didn't see anything."

He nodded. She wasn't lying, and he doubted she could have seen anything from inside the building anyway. It was the wrong angle, and a construction dumpster was in the way. "Is it okay if I look around the building, ask a few questions?"

She scoffed. "Not until you tell me what's going on."

He gave her his best disarming smile. "Were you here last night?"

"No."

"Where were you last night?"

"I had a showing at my gallery." She crossed her arms over her chest. He was on thin ice here. He'd obviously annoyed her.

"You work at a gallery too?"

"I own Zelda's Folly in Chelsea." She sighed heavily.

His chin dropped. Jesus, who was this woman? Everything about her intrigued him. She was like a puzzle he needed to solve, and he found his mind dwelling on ways to get closer to her. "I don't know much about art. I mean, I like art. It's okay, you know. It's nice on the walls. You don't really notice it, you know, in the doctor's office or whatever. But it's nice. Better than bare walls." God, he was the world's biggest loser right now. Bare walls? He internally groaned. "Thank you for your time, Miss... Rowan. What was your last name? I can't remember."

"I didn't tell you." She stopped talking, and the silence stretched between them. Silence soaked in orange peels and smoke.

She wasn't going to tell him her last name, and he didn't have a reason to require her to. Great. He turned to leave, but an idea, a long shot, made him stop abruptly and pull out his phone.

"One more thing. Since you're the artsy type, maybe you can tell me if you've ever seen this symbol." He brought up the picture of the dead woman's wrist. He wouldn't normally share evidence from a crime scene, but he'd cropped the photo to only expose the logo. On the woman's pale skin, there was no way to even tell the context of the symbol. He turned the screen in her direction.

Then watched all the blood drain from her face.

CHAPTER SEVEN

Rowan stared down at the picture on the detective's phone and tried not to react. The symbol was none other than the logo Adrienne had shown her yesterday for NAVAK. In fact, it was still on her desk, on a sheet of paper halfway under her ass. Her heart beat faster and she forced herself not to glance at the paper that was no doubt sticking out from under her hip. Nick was a detective, and if he was asking her about the symbol, there was likely a good reason, a reason she didn't care to be associated with.

"Have you seen it before?" he asked again, obviously trying to read her reaction.

"Valor. My name is Rowan Valor." She smiled sweetly. "I'm sorry I couldn't be of more help. I have a class to teach. I'll show you out."

She stood up and casually flipped the paper over on her desk. She attempted to escort him from her office by taking his arm and gesturing toward the door. Nick didn't budge. The only thing she managed to do was place her body unreasonably close to him, a result that caused her inner dragon to raise her head.

Only a few inches taller than her, he was nevertheless larger, a man whose arms a woman could get lost in. For a moment she stared at his mouth and the thin white scar that marred his upper lip. It was in the corner. She wondered if the same thing that had chipped his molar had made that scar.

Her dragon shifted under her skin, hot and slick inside her, and she felt her temperature rise. She wanted to kiss that scar. She wanted to close the sliver of space between them and see if he tasted like the spicy sandalwood scent that seemed to follow him everywhere. But Harriet's warning blared in her head. He was human. This was dangerous. For her own protection, she needed to get him out of here, fast.

As if fate were toying with her, he stepped closer, his suit jacket brushing the tips of her breasts. By the Mountain, did he mean to kiss her? He leaned in, his mouth a luscious temptation within reach. But he tilted at the last second, his hand closing around the paper with the logo on her desk and pulling it out from under her hip. She closed her eyes and swallowed. When she opened them again, his expression had morphed from good-humored flirtation to something far more serious. All the muscles around his mouth tightened, pressing his lips into a flat line.

He stared at the logo with an intensity that wrinkled his forehead.

"That's confidential!" She grabbed for the paper and ended up wrapping her hand around his.

Rowan was a dragon. She was strong enough to physically force this human man to his knees. But the buzz that coursed through her when their fingers connected almost brought her to hers. The problem was his presence, his overwhelming masculinity. Her dragon wanted to roll over and expose her belly every time she saw him. Her stomach dropped as their eyes met, her hands went cold, and her breath came out in a shaky exhale. She released his hand.

"Okay." She smoothed the front of her dress and glanced at the toes of her shoes. "I've seen the symbol before —only yesterday actually—but I don't know anything about it." Even to her own ears, she sounded guilty as hell.

"Explain." His voice was low and all grit.

"As I told you, I own Sunrise House. I love these kids. This is my passion. I own this building, but the land underneath it is a land lease."

Nick inhaled through his teeth.

"Yes, I know. Not the smartest investment, but we needed this location. A local church used to own the lease, but they recently sold it to a real estate developer. Based on the guy's MO, we fully expect he's trying to have the place rezoned for commercial purposes."

"Who's the developer?"

"Gerald Stevenson."

Nick frowned.

"You know him?"

"Of him. What does he have to do with this symbol?"

"That's the corporate logo for the corporation who financed the purchase of the land out from under us. Gerald Stevenson was the front man, but my lawyer discovered these guys were behind it. Gerald sent us a letter of eviction. We still have three months until the lease expires, so we have some time, but my lawyer brought this to me because we're trying to buy the land back and this is all the information we have on the company who owns it."

He snapped a picture of the page Adrienne had given her, then stared down his nose at her. "Lying to a detective is a very serious infraction."

He moved closer to her, and she backed up until her ass slapped the desk. She sat on the edge and tipped her head back to maintain eye contact. And oh, her dragon twisted inside her, coiling excitedly at his nearness. What was this? Her entire body tingled.

"I'm sorry I lied to you, but the information on that page is confidential. I wasn't at liberty to share it with you."

"Even if it could help an investigation?"

She placed her hands on her hips. "How would I know that? You still haven't shared a single detail about any crime. Am I a suspect? Are you interrogating me? Did you come in here with a warrant to search my office?"

"No." His eyes narrowed.

"Then I don't think I did anything wrong. And I never lied to you. I simply answered your question by saying I couldn't help you. I can't. Frankly, it's a dead end. My lawyer has tried in vain to connect with a director or administrator, anyone he could make an offer for the land. NAVAK is completely anonymous, and Stevenson is intentionally unhelpful. The closest we can get is the bank they funnel their earnings through. That's the address listed there. He couldn't find anything else."

He quirked an eyebrow, and the corner of his mouth twitched. "I understand your reservations about sharing this with me. However, I've seen this information now. It was in plain sight after all, and you invited me in here." He gestured toward the desk with a hand that was roughly the size of a bear paw. She wondered if it would feel rough against her skin.

"True," she said in a soft voice.

"Well, Rowan Valor, I'm afraid there's only one way I can think of to resolve this situation."

She inhaled deeply, filling herself with his heady,

masculine scent. Her head swam and the tips of her breasts tingled. What was he saying?

Leaning in, she concentrated on his lips. "What's that?"

"You help me find out who is behind this symbol. I have a lead. Someone has linked this logo to a local establishment. I'd like to check it out, but it would help my cover if I had a date. And maybe, if you're with me, you'll get some answers as well."

For a second she took him in, her eyes exploring the highlights and contours of his face. Was this really happening? Was he offering to help her find these people? "Are you allowed to do that? Bring a civilian in on an investigation like this?"

He shook his head. "No."

"Oh."

"But I'm allowed to ask you on a date to a very exclusive club where I might or might not be investigating this symbol and you might or might not find out a few things you need to know."

"Oh."

"Would you like to go?"

Trap set and sprung. She'd walked right into it. She couldn't say no now. Despite Harriet's warnings to stay away from the detective, if she didn't help him with this after evading him, she'd look even guiltier. She had no idea what he was investigating, but the last thing she needed was for him to turn the spyglass on her or Firebrand. "When?"

"Friday. It's fancy. I've been told I need to clean up."

She stifled a laugh. She'd like to see that. "I have a dress."

In fact, she had a closet full of appropriate attire and an oread—a mountain nymph who fed off her magic and in return served her in a domestic capacity—who could make her something new in a matter of hours if she needed it.

"Pick you up at nine?"

"At Zelda's Folly in Chelsea." It was safer. She'd be crazy to give a total stranger her home address, even if it was one of many.

He tipped his head and offered her a full smile. He handed her the paper, his fingers lingering on the back of her hand. "Good. It's a date."

She didn't breathe again until he was out the door.

CHAPTER EIGHT

New Orleans, Louisiana

Tobias stood outside the gates of his brother's Garden District home, feeling dejected. Everything he and Sabrina had worked for, their entire home and existence, had been deconstructed at vampire speed. All his clothes and things had been packed into boxes and hidden in a secret room behind the men's bathroom mirror at the Chicago Theatre, a room that hadn't been used since the days of Al Capone.

For all intents and purposes, everything he had in the world now fit inside the rolling suitcase that had traveled with him from the airport. As instructed, he'd had his taxi drop him off two blocks from the Prytania Street address Gabriel had given him and he'd walked the rest of the way. But when he reached the Garden District home, he checked the address twice and was sure there had been a mistake. This couldn't be the right place.

The gate was locked. Worse, although he'd texted his brother Gabriel to say he'd arrived, the house beyond loomed dark and abandoned. The yard was overgrown, the screens on the windows covered in a thick layer of grime and rust that stained the peeling paint of the siding with orange streaks. Not only did the house look uncared for, it looked unwelcoming, with no lights on inside any of the windows. The New Orleans humidity settled over him like a hot, wet blanket, and everything in him told him to leave, to seek the welcoming air-conditioning of the nearest restaurant or bar.

"I'm going to touch your hand."

Tobias jumped at the sound of his sister-in-law's voice. Although it had seemed as if she'd been whispering in his ear, he couldn't see her. But then her hand landed on his and everything changed. The yard tidied itself, the grass retracting into the earth until it appeared freshly mowed, the bushes' gangly branches becoming perfectly sculpted, and the house's exterior smoothed to a freshly painted, welcoming butter yellow. The gate clicked open.

"To aíma tou aímatós mou," Raven chanted as Tobias stepped across a granite slab that served as the threshold, carved with symbols he couldn't read. She explained, "It roughly translates to blood of my blood. This place is protected with a blood ward, Gabriel's and mine. Anyone who crosses the threshold must be touching one of us or be marked with our blood."

Tobias understood the need for such security. Ever since they'd discovered that their own mother had been part of the coup that resulted in the murder of their oldest sibling and their own exile from Paragon, their lives had been in jeopardy. Only a few short weeks ago, mommy dearest and her sidekick, an evil fairy named Aborella, had sent the captain of the Obsidian Guard to kill them. They'd survived the attack, but none of them were ignorant enough to believe it would be the only one. And that threat was completely separate and distinct from the one Tobias had to now share with Raven and Gabriel concerning his wife's vampire kin.

Raven closed the gate behind them and a ripple warped the air, tinting everything red for a flash before fading to normal again.

"Whoa," he said, placing a hand on his stomach at the place where he felt the spell pass through him.

"Yeah, it's strong. Witch and dragon magic braided together." She rubbed a hand over the small mound of her lower belly. "Pregnant witch. This little guy has made me about twenty times stronger than usual. No one is getting in here without an invitation."

"And no one can see us from outside the gate?"

"Or hear us. Or find us. The house isn't in either of our names. Gabriel has a lawyer friend who set up a trust as owner. There's no way to trace us. You're safe here."

"What exactly did you mean, marked by your blood?"

She flipped over her wrist and showed him a small red tattoo of three wavy lines bisected by an arrow. "We put a drop of our blood in the ink."

He sucked air in through his teeth. "As a doctor, I have to tell you that is not medically advisable."

Gabriel strode through the front door and grabbed his suitcase out of his hand. "The only thing that matters is that it's magically advisable."

"Hello, brother." He accepted Gabriel's hug. "I appreciate your taking me in on such short notice."

"About that, your message was light on the details. Come inside, have a drink, and tell us why you suddenly had to leave your wife." Gabriel ushered them inside, depositing Tobias's bag in the foyer before following Raven into a formal dining room where a tea service fit for royalty was waiting.

Meow. A calico cat leaped down from the bookshelf and rubbed against his legs. He reached down and scratched her behind the ears. "Missed you too, Artemis."

"She's the best cat, Tobias. Honestly, thank you," Raven said.

"No. Thank you. It wasn't like I could keep her."

"Have some coffee or tea. You look exhausted." Raven motioned toward the spread.

"You two didn't have to do all this," Tobias said. He'd been rushed to leave Chicago and hadn't eaten since breakfast, so it was a welcome sight.

"We didn't. Compliments of Juniper and Hazel." Gabriel poured himself a coffee.

That's right. Juniper and Hazel were Gabriel's oreads. Tobias hadn't ever taken one into his service, but only because he'd gone through a phase where he'd tried to deny who he was. He had no problem with them now.

Raven's hand landed on his. "Tell us what happened. Did you and Sabrina have a falling-out?"

"No, nothing like that. It turns out that an ancient vampire named Aldrich saw me shift at Sabrina's coronation."

There was a collective inhale as Gabriel and Raven digested that news. They knew as well as he did that vampires and shifters had a long, violent history.

"As master, Sabrina can control her coven, and all the Chicago vampires have accepted me. But Aldrich is a member of the Forebears, the vampire council of elders.

He's put a price on my head." Tobias frowned and mumbled, "All our heads."

Raven fisted a scone and took a fast, aggressive bite, never breaking eye contact. Her fingers drummed nervously on the table. It took Gabriel longer to connect all the dots.

"Are you saying, brother, that the elder vampires not only know we exist but have explicitly ordered all their kind to... seek out and eliminate any and all dragons that might be among them?"

"More or less. And the words you are looking for are *dead or alive*."

Gabriel leaned back in his chair. "Well now, I'd thought Mother and Brynhoff trying to kill us and finding out my mate was pregnant with a dragon whelp was all the excitement I could expect this year. It seems I was wrong. The vampires want us dead too. My, my, we are popular."

Raven shook her head. "I'm so sorry, Tobias. You can stay with us as long as you need to. But what about the others? We haven't been able to find Rowan or Alexander, let alone your siblings in Europe. How do we warn them?"

"No luck at reaching Rowan then, since I last saw you?" Tobias frowned. When they'd visited Rowan's last known residence, an older human woman had informed them she was dead. They understood that as a dragon, their sister was certainly not dead, but the box the woman had given them held no clues to where she might be. Inside was a small photo of Rowan with Tobias the last time he'd been to Manhattan and run into her, circa 1977. There were some dried forget-me-not flowers, an unopened box of movie-sized Sno-Caps, and the ticket stub to opening night of *Star Wars*. The wooden box itself had been decorated with an ornate dragon inlay on the top.

"Nothing in the box is receptive to my magic," Raven

said. "I believe the box and its contents are enchanted so that they cannot be used to find her."

"Why would she do that?" Tobias asked.

Gabriel gave a low chuckle. "Simple. She wanted you to know she was safe, that she loved you, and that she was disappearing for a while. Everything in that box is about you. She must have thought you would be the only one who might come looking for her."

"I was the only one who knew where to find her."

"She probably planned to contact you once her identity was scrubbed," Raven said.

Tobias groaned. "And now she can't. I sold the house, shut off the landline, and the hospital has no forwarding address for me."

"She never had your cell phone?" Gabriel asked.

"No. The last time I saw her, cell phones weren't a thing."

Raven exchanged a glance with Tobias. "I'm at a total loss. Without something of Rowan's that she's touched recently and hasn't been charmed against my magic, I can't do a locator spell. My last hope is to try to use the dress she brought from Paragon, but it's been so long since she wore it that I don't have high hopes."

Gabriel coupled his hands. "Our siblings have stayed hidden this long. There is no reason to believe that will change anytime soon."

"True," Tobias said. "Sabrina and her father are wiping the minds of the coven. They mean to convince Aldrich that he didn't see what he thought he did. If all goes well, this will work itself out and everything will go back to normal."

Raven poured herself a cup of coffee and slowly stirred in some cream. It was all Tobias could do to restrain himself from lecturing her on the dangers of caffeine to pregnant women. No one said a word over the sound of the clinking spoon. She raised the mug to her lips.

All of a sudden, Raven started to laugh so hard her skin twinkled and the coffee in her mug began to boil. Big rolling bubbles foamed above the rim until she was forced to set it down on the table where it scorched the tablecloth.

"Why are you laughing, Raven?" Gabriel asked.

She stopped, the smile fading from her lips slowly. "Tobias said everything will go back to normal." She laughed again and leaned back in her chair. "Nothing about you dragon siblings is, was, or ever will be normal."

CHAPTER NINE

By Friday Nick had learned a few things about his latest case. The dead girl had a name: Allison Sumner. And she wasn't originally from New York but West Virginia where she'd had a troubled home life. Her parents said she'd moved out when she was eighteen, four years ago, and given them no forwarding address. They hadn't heard from her since. And no, she hadn't had the tattoo the last time they'd seen her.

She'd been killed the night before she was found. Killed and dumped. It was waste management—two sanitation workers—who'd found her beside the dumpster. No one could tell him about the wounds, although his going hypothesis was that she was part of a body-suspension cult—people who got their jollies from hanging themselves from the ceiling with hooks.

He shook his head. This job never got easier.

"Here ya go. Zelda's Folly gallery," the Uber driver said.

It was raining like God had left the spigot on. Giant sheets of water thundered against the windshield and made him feel like they were inside a carwash.

"Wait here while I get my girl," Nick said.

"I don't get paid to wait."

Nick tossed a twenty in the guy's direction. "There. You've been paid."

The rain on the passenger's side of the car let up, and a posh elderly woman's face appeared in the window. Under the sizable protection of a black golf umbrella, she raised her wrinkled knuckles to rap against the passenger-side glass. The driver rolled down the window a crack.

"Mr. Grandstaff." The woman smiled toward Nick. He got the sense she'd been royalty in a former life, or maybe a ballerina based on that straight back and long neck. All he knew for sure was that there was enough cashmere and pearls adorning her perfect posture to warrant her own security guard, and her gray hair was tamed into a perfect twist at the back of her head. "Miss Valor requests that you join her inside and release this driver. She's having her personal car brought around to take you both to your destination."

Nick grabbed the twenty back from the driver.

"Hey!"

"You heard the lady. Take off." He exited the car and hunched to fit under the umbrella.

"I am Rowan's personal assistant, Harriet. Mr. Grandstaff, it's a pleasure."

"Nick." He shook her hand.

"Please, come with me."

He jogged ahead and opened the door for her, thankful for the small awning over the entrance. Harriet shook out the umbrella and angled it carefully beside her. He entered behind her, brushed the mist off his jacket, and realized he was in a different world.

"Oh wow," he said.

Whoever the artist was liked red. Canvas after canvas showcased the color, some depicting a scene entirely in rose-colored hues, others highlighting one important thing in the painting with a shock of red.

"Do you know Able McKenzie?" Harriet asked.

"I read about him in the *New York Times,* but I've never seen his work up close."

She folded her hands in front of her hips. "How does it make you feel?"

Crap. He hadn't expected a pop quiz. He rubbed the back of his neck. "I'm no art critic, but I guess... it reminds me of blood."

"Oh?"

"Like this softer one here, that's like blood as the source of life. And that one over there with the splash of red in that ice-cream cone shape—that looks like poison, like something dangerous. And that one there with the black areas, that's someone bleeding to death." He chuckled. Of course they weren't any of those things. The paintings were abstract. What he'd described as an ice-cream cone was a random grouping of shapes that probably weren't meant to represent anything at all.

But Harriet was smiling. "Very insightful, Mr. Grandstaff."

"Was I close?"

She shrugged. "Interpretation, like beauty, is in the eye of the beholder. But that one you pointed to *is* titled *Poisoned Ice Cream.*"

"Really?"

"No." She shook her head. "It's called *Sunday Afternoon in Central Park.*"

"Ah, but I had the ice cream thing."

She sent him a thin smile.

"Mr. Grandstaff..."

"Nick."

"Nick, I wonder if you might allow me to have a look at your palm." Harriet held out her hand to him.

"My palm?"

Harriet gave him a wide smile and an encouraging nod. He held out his hand. The woman cradled it between her own and inspected his palm as if it were a map she was trying to read.

Until Rowan's voice cut through the room. "Put your hand away, Nick. Harriet, you know better."

Harriet dropped his hand like it was hot. She bowed slightly, turned on her heel, and took off before Nick could even thank her for the umbrella. It didn't matter. When he saw Rowan, he lost all ability to speak.

She was a vision in red that outshone anything in the gallery, her black hair cascading around the lace trim on her shoulders. A goddess in stilettos. He desperately wanted to touch her. It would be transcendent. He needed to tell her. He needed to break open his soul and use his finest words to woo her into his arms.

He swallowed, cleared his throat, and said, "Hi."

THE DRESS WAS WORTH EVERY PENNY SHE'D PAID FOR IT and then some. Nick's stare was a palpable thing that seemed to burn at her neck before tracing its way over her shoulder and around her waist. His mouth hung open, speechless. He was speechless.

Harriet passed her on her way to the office, setting her hand on her forearm to get her attention. "This is a bad idea, Rowan. You're playing with fire," she whispered before disappearing into the back room.

Rowan knew what she meant. The more time she spent with Nick, the more likely he was to remember their first meeting and that she'd stolen the Raindrop of Heaven from the Stevensons. He might be a homicide detective, but she was sure his knowing she had committed grand larceny wouldn't go over well. And if that wasn't enough to make him hate her and potentially arrest her, ruining her most important identity, she was sure the part where she'd forced him to drink the forget-me-juice would.

She didn't want him to hate her. At the moment she wasn't sure what she wanted from him, but it definitely involved him looking at her the way he was right now.

"Hi," he said.

She gave him a warm smile. "Hello." When he didn't say anything else, she added, "Don't ever let Harriet read your palm."

"Why not?"

"She thinks she can tell people's fortunes, and her readings can be disturbing. She's got a penchant for the morbid."

"I'm a homicide detective. I deal with morbid every day."

"Trust me. It's creepy."

"If you say so."

She allowed her gaze to linger on his threads. Perfect clubbing gear. Dark-wash jeans, fitted shirt, jacket. She loved that he wasn't clean-shaven and wondered what his scruff would feel like against her skin.

He puffed out his chest, smoothing his jacket and flashing her a crooked grin. "What do you think? Will they let me in?"

"I'm not sure. Which club?" She grinned.

He deflated. "Ouch."

"I'm joking." She placed a hand gently on his arm and watched his face soften with her touch. His eyelids sank halfway, his stormy gray eyes darkening. Under her skin, her dragon twisted and her heart rate quickened. Odd. It was rare for her inner beast to be so active, but she seemed incredibly interested in this human man. She cleared her throat and removed her hand from his arm, gesturing toward the paintings. "You see blood? I overheard you speaking with Harriet."

He shifted uncomfortably. "Yeah." He winced. "Is that disturbing to you? I promise I don't usually see blood everywhere."

She laughed. "No. Able's work reminds me of blood as well."

"Really?"

She nodded. "Harriet sees fruit, a broken pomegranate to be exact. Others see flower petals. One art dealer I know swore he thought it was representative of fire. One of the things I love about Able is he draws out our subconscious biases."

Nick frowned. "Are you saying you and I have a bias for blood? That's pretty grim."

She shrugged. "It's a grim world."

For a moment he stared at the paintings, growing uneasy and fidgeting with his pocket. She regretted her last comment. It wasn't attractive to let her inner darkness out. She should have said she saw fabric, or paint. She did run a gallery after all.

"What happened to you?" he asked evenly.

"What makes you think something happened to me?"

He turned to her. "You see blood because you've seen

blood. I was a cop—now a homicide detective. It makes sense that I've seen blood. But when did you?"

The kindness in his voice was almost her undoing. She could resist his obvious attraction to her and his charming flirtations, but true kindness was too much. It hit too close to something vulnerable inside her, something she kept walled off from the world.

She cast an eye toward the front window. "We should go. Djorji is waiting."

"Who's Djorji?"

"My driver."

"Oh right." He passed her on the way to the door, using his longer legs and much flatter shoes to his advantage. In a subtle way that made it seem unintentional, he palmed the handle of the umbrella drying in the umbrella stand before opening the door for her and popping it open above her head. He walked her to the car where Djorji stood ready to help her into the back seat.

"You're pretty smooth with that umbrella," she said to Nick. "You should save your chivalry for a real date."

He sighed. "I thought I made it clear this *was* a real date."

"I assumed that was an excuse, a cover for us investigating together." She bent her head and brushed a hand down the front of her dress as if she were smoothing wrinkles that weren't there.

His heavy hand landed in the curve of her back, and her eyes snapped to his. She allowed him to guide her against his chest.

"It's a real date."

His lips were close, and he was big. Big hands, big shoulders. She was a tall woman and she was a dragon, had grown up with dragons. This close, she could tell he was big enough to pass as one, and his nearness sent her inner beast into a frenzy. Muscles deep within her clenched and her skin turned hot.

"I mean, I want it to be a real date. Do you?"

She parted her lips, the heat of his body a sharp contrast to the cool rain pattering against the umbrella and sheeting down around them. His eyes were equally stormy. For a second she was lost in the moment. "I... Yes, I want that too."

"Prove it."

"Excuse me?"

"Prove this is a date."

"How, exactly, am I supposed to prove that to you?"

His throat bobbed as he swallowed. "Kiss me."

Now her dragon writhed, and heat bloomed between her legs. She could barely hold her wings in. Her nipples hardened against his chest. She wanted to kiss him. Wanted to taste him. She placed her hand against his cheek. Rough. Stubbled. Hard. "The kiss comes at the end of the date." She giggled and spent far too long inspecting a dimple in his chin before climbing inside the vehicle.

"Where to, ma'am?" Djorji asked.

She glanced expectantly at Nick, who had folded the umbrella and slid in beside her. She had no idea where they were going.

"Wicked Divine," he said. "Do you need the address?"

Djorji shook his head. He knew Wicked Divine. So did Rowan.

"What?" Nick asked.

Rowan gave him a sideways look. She was a dragon, an expert at keeping secrets. She'd remained completely impassive. So why was Nick studying her? "I didn't say anything."

He leaned forward in his seat. "There's something I

should share with you, Rowan. It's probably not fair for me to keep this from you."

"Oh? You have a secret?"

"I'm not just a detective. I have a certain background... a set of specialized skills. As it so happens, I'm an expert at reading people."

"Uh-huh." She arched an eyebrow. Too bad for him she wasn't "people"—she wasn't even human.

"Your friend Harriet may read palms. I read body language. When you brushed your hands over your skirt, crossed your legs, and then decided to look out the window instead of asking me about Wicked Divine, I knew there was something you weren't telling me. What do you know about this place that I don't?"

Fuck. She looked him directly in the eye and put on her sweetest smile. "I drank too much and became ill there a few years ago. It's a bad memory."

He narrowed his eyes at her. "Riiiight. Liar... liar... pants on fire," he drawled. "How about you try again. What else do you know about Wicked Divine?"

"You're really good at this."

"The best. Government certified. Better than a polygraph."

Rowan rubbed her hands together nervously. What could she tell him? He wasn't ready to learn the truth. As a human, he might never be ready.

"Okay. You're right. I'm not crazy about sharing this, but I used to date the owner, Michael Verinetti." Absolutely true. Nick didn't need to know the guy was a shape-shifter and the head of the largest shifter pack in the Northeast. Michael could be a powerful ally in the hunt for information about NAVAK, or a powerful enemy if he was still pained about their breakup. She'd been the one to end things, and she'd been careful to stay out of the places he frequented since.

Thank the Mountain it seemed to be enough of an explanation for Nick. "Things still awkward between you?"

"Shouldn't be. It's been a number of years since I've seen him."

"I've never been so happy to be carrying a gun." He flashed her a crooked grin that made the scar on his lip more pronounced.

"We probably won't run into him. Unless something has changed dramatically, he's usually too busy managing things behind the scenes to notice what's going on at the front of the house."

Nick leaned back against the leather seat, his gaze sweeping over her. "If all goes as planned, we'll find what we're looking for quickly and be out of there before he has a chance."

Rowan nodded, but inside, her stomach clenched. Nick didn't know it yet, but they'd soon be arriving at a known supernatural hotbed, and the detective was likely in more danger than he realized.

CHAPTER TEN

Good God, the woman was beautiful. A beautiful puzzle full of secrets. She'd lied to him, twice now. He wanted to believe she'd had good reasons, but he was also wary. It didn't make him feel all warm and fuzzy inside to think they'd arrived at a club owned by her ex-boyfriend, a club linked to the logo that was on his murder victim, who was found behind her community center. Coincidence? He didn't believe in coincidences.

Wicked Divine was one of those high-end places in prime real estate. Anyone who owned property here wasn't just loaded, they had connections. Michael Verinetti wasn't someone he wanted to deal with tonight. And he wasn't fooling himself—there was no way they wouldn't run into the guy. Rowan exuded sexual energy in that red dress and heels. Every man within a fifty-yard radius was going to notice her. Word would get back to Verinetti.

Nick helped Rowan out of the car and led her toward the club, distracted by the bare skin of her back under his fingertips. Fuck, he needed to concentrate. He had work to do. A girl was dead and he needed to find Soren's lead, the one with the same tattoo, and investigate if it had anything to do with her murder. That meant he had to resist his desire to not take his eyes or hands off Rowan. A tall order considering every cell in his body was cheering for him to pursue her relentlessly. His libido was on the megaphone and his hormones had formed a pyramid. He was trying to keep his dick from raising the flag.

"Nick, over here." Soren waved to him from across the parking lot, then did a double take when he saw Rowan. Nick watched his jaw drop in a way that would be comical if it wasn't so embarrassingly obvious.

"Everything okay?" Nick asked, fixing Soren with a deadly stare. "You have a little drool there."

"No. Uh, who's your friend?"

"Soren, this is Rowan. She's the owner of Sunrise House." He raised his eyebrow. Soren immediately connected the dots and didn't push it any further.

"Well, all right." He gestured toward the bouncer. "After you."

This was the hard part, getting in without alerting everyone to the fact he was a cop. He took Rowan's arm and led her to the front of the line where a bald and heavily tattooed bouncer gave him a puzzled look.

"The end of the line's back there, buddy." The man gestured with his head, then pointed toward Rowan. "She can go in, but you're gonna have to wait."

"We're on the VIP list," he said. At least he hoped they were. He'd had an analyst in the department working on pulling a few strings all day.

"What's your name?"

"Grandstaff."

The man scrolled through a few screens on his tablet,

barely looking at the names. "No one on my list by that name."

He glanced back at Soren, who stepped forward and said, "Try Averdale."

The man scanned Soren from head to toe. He never even looked at his tablet. "Not on the list."

Nick glanced back at the line. They might be able to interview some of the people who were waiting, but—

"Check again," Rowan said. When had she moved her hand to the man's wrist? And holy shit, that was one hell of a ruby on her finger. It almost seemed to pulse as it glinted in the moonlight. "Try Valor."

The bouncer looked her in the eye, and Nick saw something strange pass through his expression, a subtle widening of the eyes and flaring of the nostrils. Recognition and fear. He was desperately trying to hide it.

"Of course, Ms. Valor." He reached for the rope and unclipped it, letting them through. "Have a good time."

The bouncer hooked the rope behind them and Nick followed her to the door, trying his best to keep his dangling jaw from wagging in her wake. A hostess opened the door for her and the music swallowed them, a pulsing throb that he could feel on his skin and was accompanied by coordinated dancing lights. He had to lean in so she could hear him.

"There is no way that guy isn't going to tell his boss you're here," he said into her ear.

She smiled and leaned in to answer him, her warm breath hitting the shell of his ear in a way that made his cock twitch. "It couldn't be avoided. Did you see that line? We weren't getting in without help. We need to hurry though. As much as I'd like to believe there's no bad blood between us, I'm not sure how Michael will react to me being here. Like I said, we haven't seen each other in years."

If Nick didn't know better, he would have thought he'd come down with an instant case of heartburn, but the ache in his chest had nothing to do with his digestion. He suddenly had an urge to punch Michael Verinetti in the solar plexus, which made absolutely no sense and was completely not like him. He cracked his neck and tried to get his head in the game.

"Let's split up," he said to Soren, who had edged to his side. "Try to find your friend or anyone else with the tattoo. Text if you find anything."

Soren nodded once and disappeared into the crowd. Nick hooked his hand around Rowan's upper arm.

"What exactly are we looking for?"

"Anything or anyone with that logo I showed you."

"Would it be more effective for us to divide and conquer? I could ask around. We might be able to cover more people."

He shook his head slowly. No way did he want her more than an arm's reach way from him. Not in this crowd. Not in that dress.

"It's better if we stay together. Look like a couple. Blend in."

She seemed to agree because she threaded her fingers into his and held his hand. As they entered the crowd, Nick tried to concentrate on scanning the arms and wrists around him for the symbol, but it was hard to think of anything but the feel of her hand in his. He forced himself to focus. Nothing unusual. Expensive suits. More jewelry than he'd ever seen in one place in his life. Botox-tightened skin. Shiny, color-treated hair. Perfectly straight smiles.

Rowan stopped at the edge of the dance floor. "Nothing."

"Me either."

She tipped her head toward the bar, where it took exactly five seconds for the bartender, who looked like he needed surgery to remove the giant chip on his shoulder, to notice Rowan. The guy was an Irish caricature with shocking red hair, freckled skin, and a scrappy physique. Nick could already tell he was going to be a pain in the ass.

"That's Connor. He sees everything," she said. "Whether he'll share it with you or not is a different story."

Nick raised an eyebrow. "We'll see about that."

They sidled up to the bar where Connor served the person he was waiting on, then made a beeline to where they'd pulled up a stool.

"Rowan. There's a face I never thought I'd see in here again," Connor said. "Can I mix you my special Irish jig martini? It's Irish cream, vanilla vodka, and a bit of Irish luck to either knock you on your arse or have you knocking him on his. Whatever suits you."

"No, thanks, Connor," Rowan said. "It sounds delicious, but unfortunately, I'm not drinking tonight. I'm here on business and I need a favor."

Nick felt her gentle nudge at his elbow, and he produced the pictures he had brought with him. The first was Allison Sumner's high school senior portrait and the second was of the symbol tattooed on her wrist.

"Have you seen this girl?" He started with the portrait.

Connor glanced down at the photo. "No."

He caught Rowan frowning at the picture and quickly slipped it back inside his jacket.

"Are you sure? She sometimes went by the name Allison."

"So many girls come in here. I don't remember every face."

Nick analyzed Connor's body language. He was telling the truth.

"What about this?" He slid the picture of the tattoo across the bar between Connor's hands. "She had this tattoo on her wrist. You ever see this tattoo before?"

Connor went absolutely still. *Gotcha.*

"No. Sorry." Connor's eyes shifted away toward the woman three stools down who was motioning for his attention. "I need to get back to work."

That wouldn't do. Nick reached across the bar and grabbed Connor's hand before he could go anywhere, twisting and bending his little finger toward his wrist. It was a little trick of the trade. Uncomfortable. Got their attention. "I have a few more questions."

Connor froze and slowly looked down at Nick's grip on his hand and wrist. His free hand balled into a fist. "Rowan, tell your guest to unhand me or I'll pretty up his mug with a bit of black and blue and a few more scars for his collection."

Locked in eye-to-eye combat, Nick prepared himself for whatever Connor could dish out. He didn't want to fight the guy, but he needed answers. "You're lying about the tattoo. Tell me what you know."

Rowan's manicured hand landed on Nick's, and all his aggression seemed to drain out at her touch. "Let him go, Nick. Connor is a friend. This isn't how we treat friends here."

Ah, hell. He didn't want to burn any bridges with her informant. He released his grip and watched Connor stretch his fingers and massage his wrist.

"Connor?" Rowan moved closer to the bar. "This is important."

Connor shook his head. "Don't get involved in this, Rowan. Trust me on this one. Drop it. I don't know nothing about the girl."

"But you've seen the tattoo," Nick said, catching the nuance in the man's voice.

Rowan squeezed his upper arm and said, "Nick, come on. Dance with me. Connor has things to do."

Nick scowled at the bartender, who vamoosed without another word. He swept the picture off the bar and stashed it in the interior pocket of his jacket with the other one. Rowan led him to the dance floor and slipped her arms around his neck. Thank God for slow songs.

"You know he was lying, right?" he whispered in her ear.

"If Connor's lying to me about something, it's because he has to. It must have something to do with Verinetti."

"Tell me the truth. Did things between you and Verinetti end badly?"

"No, just sooner than he would have preferred. He still occasionally buys art from Zelda's Folly, but Harriet handles those transactions."

"So if Mr. Art Aficionado had a secret that Connor was keeping for him, who in his inner circle would be most likely to crack?" He'd like to crack someone right now. Anything to finish up here and get to the good stuff with this woman in his arms.

She tilted her face up at his, and he had a moment to take in her softly curved nose, smooth olive skin, and amber eyes. "I think the first thing we should do is visit the VIP room."

CHAPTER ELEVEN

Nick was going to be a problem. Rowan hadn't felt her inner dragon roil inside her like that in a long time. Dancing in his arms, his sandalwood-and-spice scent surrounding her, it was all she could do to keep her mating trill from rumbling in his ear. What was wrong with her? This man could ruin her, and she'd do well to remember that.

Had he picked up on the supernatural energy in Wicked Divine? Or did the tattoo of a wolf howling in front of the moon on the bouncer's neck seem like any other tattoo? Connor's red hair and green eyes revealed more than an Irish ethnicity; he was a leprechaun and a magical slave to Verinetti, who held his pot of gold in a vault under this place. He couldn't have told Nick anything even if he'd wanted to. Which meant Michael was hiding something, something about NAVAK.

No, she didn't think Nick had noticed anything strange about the place at all. Although Rowan was rather fascinated by the human's speed and agility. One did not easily snatch the wrist of an adult leprechaun. Odder still, Connor hadn't immediately responded with a blow, which was curious indeed. The leprechaun was an infamous hothead. Which meant something about Nick that had given him pause. Rowan saw it too. Nick was imposing for a human.

The scent of shifters grew stronger as Rowan led Nick up the stairs toward the VIP lounge. The upstairs bouncer recognized her immediately and let her through. She couldn't remember his name, but knew he was a shifter whose animal of choice was a tiger. He winked one yellow eye at her as she passed by.

Unlike the dance floor, which was mostly populated by humans, the VIP lounge was brimming with the most important members of the Manhattan supernatural community. She noticed Eva Hart right away. Her latest single was rising up the charts like it was strapped to a turbo booster. What it was actually strapped to was an *ohrwurm* spell. Eva was a powerful witch, and if you heard one of her songs, you never forgot it.

As Rowan moved deeper into the dim room filled with leather couches, she saw Travellers like Harriet; a slew of werewolves; a handful of fairies, none of whom she'd ever seen before; and a gnome who was a popular fashion designer. Just like the rest of New York, Wicked Divine was a tossed salad of diverse supernatural beings, drawn here by the promise of liberty, the vast natural resources, and the cloak of human weirdness that made it easy for them to blend in and disguise their true nature.

Only one supernatural group wouldn't dare set foot in Wicked Divine: vampires. Vampires and shifters did not, historically speaking, get along. Even from her earliest memories in Paragon, her family's political connections with Nochtbend, the vampire kingdom, were tentative at best. Two different worlds, the same challenges. Luckily,

Manhattan had always been a shifter territory. The New Amsterdam pack had been the preeminent supernatural rule in Manhattan for hundreds of years. For all intents and purposes, Verinetti was king. Not of her, of course. She'd been around long enough to secure her independence from the pack and stake her claim as an equal, but still, her past relationship with Verinetti had elevated her power and influence in Manhattan.

He'd also kept her secret. Most people she interacted with had no idea she was a dragon. They suspected she was some type of were or shifter, but no one would be so rude as to require a demonstration. It was better that way, though the magical energy she put off did not go unnoticed. Even now, Eva turned to look her over, attracted by the power in the air. Rowan kept what she was carefully hidden to all but Harriet and Harriet's people, which included Djorji. She hadn't revealed it to Michael until they'd become physically intimate, a time in her life when she'd thought she might love him. That was before she'd learned that the only thing Michael truly loved was power.

She found a couch in the darkest corner of the room and stopped in front of it. "I need you to wait here for me."

"Huh? Why?" Nick's voice was low and gritty.

She raised her chin and gave him her most disarming smile. "I need to use the ladies' room."

His eyes narrowed and a muscle in his jaw tensed. He didn't believe her. Damn, he truly was a human lie detector. Nevertheless, he didn't push it and lowered himself to the sofa.

"When the server comes, will you order me a fireball mule?"

He sighed. "Sure."

Sensuously, she ran her nails over his shoulder, hoping

the unspoken promise was enough to keep him in his seat. They shared undeniable chemistry, and she didn't mind using that to keep him safe.

She sashayed toward Verinetti's office.

Michael Verinetti always reminded Rowan of a young Al Pacino in *The Godfather*. His face was different: bigger nose, longer hair, and hazel eyes instead of brown, but he had the same Mediterranean complexion and could lie as if he believed every false word that crossed his lips. Although he was known for being loyal to his allies, he could also be ruthless. No one wanted to be on Verinetti's bad side.

He was a true shifter, able to change into any animal he wished, but Michael was a film buff and since the 1980s he'd carried a minor obsession with the movie *Labyrinth*. Since then, his animal of choice was a snowy owl, a preference that was reinforced when Harry Potter's Hedwig became popular. Michael was all about popularity: looks, impressions, trends. When they'd dated decades ago, he'd become annoyed with her involvement in children's charities, not understanding her "obsession with the city's refuse." In the end, that was why things hadn't worked out. Rowan befriended and cared for humans and supernatural beings from all walks of life and backgrounds. Wealth meant nothing to her, nor did the latest fashions, although she tried to dress with the times. What meant the most to her was the heart of a person. Kindness, warmth, friendship. Michael could never understand the joy of painting a picture with a child. Not unless he was planning to sell that picture for big money.

She knocked softly on his office door and found it unlocked. It swung open at the force of her knuckles.

"Looking for me?"

She pivoted to find Michael behind her, close behind

her, his musky scent tingling gamey and sharp in her nostrils. "Hello, Michael," she said. "How have you been?"

He blinked slowly. "Vince said you were here. I thought he was smoking something. I'd heard you were dead."

"One of my identities."

"Does your current identity need a job or to borrow money?" He flashed her a wolfish grin.

"Uh, no."

"So this is a social visit? Lucky me." The corner of his mouth lifted and he stepped in closer, looking at her through hooded eyes.

"I need to ask you something," she said. "In private."

"My luck is getting better. Come on in."

She walked into his office, feeling like a fly crawling willingly into the spider's web. Shifters were strong and fast. Not as strong and fast as dragons, but she was a female of her species and small for a dragon, and she hadn't been trained as a warrior like her brothers. Although she'd never had a doubt she could overpower a human, when it came to other supernaturals, her survival over the centuries had often come down to her wit and diplomacy. It was an uneasy feeling being shut in a room with Verinetti. Between the unwanted sexual energy coming off him and her knowledge that he had once skinned a shifter alive for stealing from him, it took more than a little nerve for her to allow him to close the door.

"What is this important thing that brings you to my club after all these years?" he asked, his voice low and smooth.

Rowan reached into her purse and produced the paper with the symbol. She unfolded it carefully and held it out to him. "Do you know anything about the company with this logo?"

The smile faded from his face. "Where did you get this?"

"My lawyer. This company bought the land under my building. I need to buy it back, but I can't find who to contact to make the offer."

Michael cracked his neck. "Buy a new building, Rowan. That company is unreachable, and even if you could find a contact, they wouldn't take your money."

"Why not? What do you know about them?"

He clucked his tongue. "You'll have to trust me on this one."

She dropped her chin and placed both hands on his upper arms. "Michael, please. I do trust you, but there are children involved. Sunrise House. You know how important those kids are to me. If there's any way, any string you could pull—"

"There isn't."

Rowan's breath caught, and she allowed her surprise to show on her face. "Michael, you practically run this town. What is it about this company that has you rolling over?"

There was a long pause as Michael gritted his teeth and looked at her out of the corner of his eyes. The one thing she could always count on with Michael was the strength of his ego. She'd phrased his inability to help her as a presumed weakness. If her logic paid off, he wouldn't be able to stop himself from countering that presumption.

"You always knew me so well. All these years, I've wondered what happened to you. After things ended, it was like you fell off the planet for a while."

"When you live as long as we do, it's important to change your identity now and then."

"For you it seems like changing your shirt."

"Fair. Is that why you won't help me? You're still angry with me?" She held up the symbol.

"All I can tell you is this... and this is between you and me, not for public knowledge..." He pointed a finger at her face.

"Of course. I won't tell a soul. Who would I tell?" She shrugged one shoulder.

"Not even Harriet."

Rowan shook her head. "Not even Harriet." She wasn't sure she could keep that promise, but she'd say anything to keep him talking.

"This logo represents the corporate front for a growing group of supernaturals from outside Manhattan who are taking up residence on the island for the first time in history. They are... preparing for mass occupation by acquiring property for their members. But as you might suspect, given their nature, they are very secretive about their acquisitions. Just like you and me."

She shook her head in confusion. "What supernaturals have never been on the island?"

He didn't say a word, just walked around her to a bar against the far wall and poured two glasses of something brown and strongly alcoholic by the smell of it. "It's not my secret to tell, and you of all people know I am a man of discretion." He handed her the drink.

She took a sip. Scotch. There was only one supernatural creature she knew of that had never occupied Manhattan. But it couldn't be. It would mean Michael was going against his nature.

"It's vampires, isn't it?" she asked, her eyes widening. "Oh my God, Michael. How are you involved? Are you safe?"

He took a lock of her hair between his first two fingers,

bringing his face dangerously close. "How sweet of you to think of me first."

Actually, her first thought was for the children. They were truly in danger if vampires were coming to their neighborhood. But she was smart enough to know that Michael wanted to be thought of first. Michael came from money and power. His parents had groomed him from the cradle to run their empire. He'd never known anything but privilege. Which meant Michael thought of Michael first and expected everyone else to do the same.

"You know as well as I do that vampires and shifters have a long and violent history. I just worry..."

He wrapped his hands around her waist, and Rowan suppressed the urge to push them away. She needed him to tell her what he knew, and resisting his touch was not the way to accomplish that.

"Not anymore." Michael's chin lifted as if the notion made him proud. She licked her lips and watched his need to stroke his own ego crack his resolve to keep his secret. "NAVAK stands for New Amsterdam Vampire Kingdom, and yes, we've struck a deal. A huge deal."

"You... arranged an accord." She didn't have to fake the look of surprise on her face.

He laughed and shook his head. His hands slid down to cup her hips. "Better."

"It must be brilliant if you came up with it." She was laying it on thick, but she knew she was close. He wanted to tell her. She could feel the truth on the edge of his lips.

"You know I can't tell you everything. The New Amsterdam coven puts a high value on their privacy. I've promised discretion, and I am nothing if not a man of my word." He grinned. "But suffice it to say that the New Amsterdam Shifters have more gold in their coffers than ever before, and we are enjoying the dawn of a new age for Manhattan."

A wave of disappointment and confusion crashed into her.

It must have shown on her face, because he gripped her chin between his thumb and forefinger. "I can't tell you, but I can't stop you from seeing for yourself. Someone like you who has the ability to go... unnoticed."

That got her attention. He knew she could make herself invisible. She locked eyes with him.

"If you should happen to wander downstairs and enter a code that was once familiar to you, I couldn't stop you from drawing your own conclusions. And those conclusions are very impressive. Things have changed, Rowan. You have no idea."

He traced her jaw with his finger and leaned in. This time she did pull away. She slid sideways before his lips could connect with hers and moved toward the door.

"Thanks, Michael. I trust you, and I think I'm going to let this one go."

He frowned. "That would be a wise choice."

Her hand was on the door. She needed to get out of that room.

"How can I reach you?" he said. "I'd like to show you the new Manhattan."

"The gallery. Like always."

"I don't want to talk to Harriet. I want to see you again."

Rowan inwardly cursed. The look in Michael's eyes was one she'd seen before. He was looking at something he wanted, wanted so badly he was willing to do something violent to get it.

She should have stayed dead.

"Now is not a good time." She cleared her throat to hide the crack in her voice.

He didn't look happy, but he nodded his head, his eyes turning as hard and cold as ice. "Be careful, Rowan. I'd hate for your next death to be the real thing."

CHAPTER TWELVE

She'd lied. Nick knew Rowan had lied and he knew why. She'd gone to see this Verinetti guy, risking her pride and maybe her safety to find out what she wanted to know. And she was doing it for those kids. The moment he saw the way she looked at them, he understood she loved them. She wasn't their mother, but they were her children. And didn't that just hit him right in the heart? He'd been one of those kids once and she... she was an angel. He admired the hell out of her drive to help.

Although she'd asked him to wait, he couldn't leave her to face this guy on her own. What if she needed backup? He followed at a distance and watched her slip into an office with a man he presumed was Verinetti. He took cover in the shadows, around the corner of the hallway that led to the men's room. And now he stewed, wondering what was taking so long. Wondering if he should kick in the door and pull her out of there. He had no right to feel this level of possessiveness. She wasn't his wife or even his girlfriend. And he wasn't some sort of stalker who felt the need to control a woman just because he was attracted to her.

Only, every time he looked at her he had this feeling, deep in the core of who he was, that they shared a karmic connection. He wasn't a man who believed in reincarnation, but she was beyond familiar. Something about her spoke directly to the most feral part of him. He desperately wanted to understand why, and the only way to do that was to get closer to her. Was it any wonder then that the thought of her alone in that room with her old flame was like a sliver of wood lodged under his fingernail.

The click of the door opening had him peering furtively around the corner.

Rowan appeared in the doorway. "Be careful, Rowan. I'd hate for your next death to be the real thing," the bastard's voice said from the office.

Next death? Nick didn't understand what that meant, but he understood the tone. That was a threat, and it made Nick grind his teeth.

The office door closed behind Rowan. She looked both ways, then headed straight for him. He flattened himself against the wall and waited for her to pass. She did. He was sure she hadn't seen him. But then she stopped about five feet down the hall in front of him.

"Nick, what are you doing here?" she whispered over her shoulder. She turned slowly and looked directly at him. "I thought I asked you to wait in the lounge."

"I didn't think you'd seen me."

"I didn't. I smelled you... your cologne."

"I'm not wearing any."

"I asked you to wait for me," she said again, more firmly.

"I'm bad at doing what I'm told. What did you find out?"

She frowned. "This isn't safe, Nick. You should go. We can talk later."

He had to stop himself from laughing. "If it's safe for you, it's safe for me. I have training and this." He opened his jacket and showed her his gun.

She scoffed. "You don't have training for this."

"What did he tell you?"

She shifted and released a deep sigh. "You're not going to let this go, are you?"

"No."

"Then be prepared, because you might see some things you don't want to see. And stay close to me. I'll protect you." She turned on her heel and started down the hall.

He shrugged. She was really taking this "I'll protect you" crap seriously. Like she was going to fend off whatever evil they were about to encounter with her bare fists and wearing stilettos. Meanwhile, he was behind her, packing heat and armed with over a decade of experience as a detective. He was also accomplished in martial arts and had grown up in a household where defending himself against near-constant beatings had taught him a thing or two about protecting himself and others. The experience hadn't been a happy one for him. But he was tempted to tell her about it now. If anyone should be out in front, it should be him.

She led him through a set of doors and down two flights of stairs. Subterranean as it was, he encountered stale air and picked up the coppery smell of blood. What he did not hear was the click of her heels. He zeroed in on her stilettos and realized she was walking in such a way that he couldn't hear her footsteps. After concentrating on the phenomenon for several seconds, he shook his head. Maybe he'd underestimated her. Rowan, it seemed, had some skills.

"Do you smell that?" he whispered, inhaling the coppery tang of blood again.

"I suspect it's about to get worse." She paused at a door with a keypad lock. "Take my hand."

He did as she asked and felt a strange ripple flow through him. He seriously needed to control himself. The kind of chemistry going on inside him when he was with Rowan was something that belonged in a high school classroom. He was positively smitten. Smitten like a man who'd never seen a woman before. The feeling was carnal, undeniable, and embarrassing.

He watched her type in a nine-digit code she must have procured from Verinetti. The door unlocked, and they entered a posh, dimly lit hall connecting a series of small booths, each with its own round table of dark wood. Each had a red velvet privacy curtain, but only a few were drawn, blocking the view of who was inside. Most of the curtains were tied back. As they passed, Nick saw both men and women sitting at those tables, eyes turned toward a runway where a fashion model paced. Dressed in a striking ball gown, the woman paused at the end of the stage where the guests seemed to evaluate her.

Hand in hand with Rowan, Nick passed another booth where an important-looking man with gray hair and an expensive suit turned to look at him. Gerald Stevenson. He squeezed Rowan's hand. Hadn't she said Gerald was the one buying up land for NAVAK? *He* wanted to ask the guy some questions, but Stevenson's rheumy blue eyes passed right over him as if he weren't even there, and then he drew his red curtain closed. Typical.

Rowan tugged him along the hall and into an empty booth, closing the curtain. She placed a finger over her lips. It would have helped a lot if she'd briefed him on what Verinetti had told her, but he could play along. She pointed at the woman on stage, then tapped her inner wrist.

He focused on the woman in the ball gown who paced away from them, turned on her heel, and paced back. There it was. He couldn't make out the details of the tattoo from here, but it wasn't difficult to see the placement and shape were the same.

Oh hell no. Nick looked right, then left. Lights flashed in each booth. Everything clicked at once. They were bidding on this girl. *Human trafficking*. He knew the signs, and they chilled him to his soul. All these people were here to buy the tattooed girls. And his dead girl? Probably bought by the wrong person, used up and thrown out. He swallowed down the bile that rose in his throat.

Rowan selected a set of headphones from the wall and handed them to him, then put her own set over her ears. A sultry woman's voice filled his head.

"Once again, the current bid is eighty. She's type B positive, no health conditions, and has fed on only fruits and nuts for the past seven days. Going once. Eight-five to the gentleman in booth six. Once... Twice... Sold to booth six for $85,000. You can pick up your purchase at the back of the auction house."

Nick nudged Rowan and mouthed, "B positive?" Why were they giving out her blood type and her dietary habits? *Oh dear Lord*, he thought, they were auctioning these people for a medical purpose. Were they using them for black market organs? He fisted his hands, but Rowan shook her head and pointed at her headphones. A man walked out on stage, and Nick had no trouble spotting the tattoo on his wrist as well. So it wasn't just women. This guy was big, muscular, not an easy target. It had to be organs.

"Now, a special treat," the voice began. "Male, twenty-seven, type O negative. Blood has been purified of all foreign substances. We will start the bidding at one hundred." A light blinked in one of the booths. "Thank you, booth four. Do I have 110?"

Nick reached for his phone. He needed backup. Human trafficking on this scale was not something he could handle alone. Even though he was careful to keep the thing behind his leg, Rowan's hand slapped over the glowing screen almost immediately. Her face snapped toward the stage. The announcer was staring directly at him.

"Put it away," Rowan whispered, removing her headphones. He slipped the phone back into his pocket and removed his own headphones. But Rowan looked nervous as hell. She took his hand again, and the electric ripple he'd noticed before washed over him. With a tug that pulled him out of his seat, she had them both out of the booth and into the hall before he could say another word. Three large men walked right past them as if they were invisible and burst into their booth.

She tugged harder, and before he could process how weird the entire situation was, he was running to keep up with her, following the bend of the hallway toward the staircase where they'd entered the auction room. Only there was someone blocking the exit, an athletic-looking man in a suit, tall and big as an NBA player. He had a blond woman in a short white dress against the wall, and she was trembling like she was scared as hell. The girl's wrist was marked with a NAVAK tattoo.

Rowan's grip tightened on Nick's hand. He froze. What the hell was going on here? The big guy glanced in their direction but looked right through them. Nick looked over his shoulder. They were standing in the middle of the hallway.

And that's when things went from weird to nightmarish. Nick watched as the man's eyes turned from brown to silver and two sharp canines dropped from his upper mouth. Was this some kind of vampire cult? Jesus, those things looked real. The girl made a high-pitched noise in the back of her throat.

"Relax, little virgin," the man said, and the girl did. Too bad that trick didn't work on Nick. His ticker was pounding out a get-the-hell-outta-Dodge rhythm in his chest in reaction to the Halloween scare fest going on in front of him.

Those teeth landed in the girl's jugular. If the slurping hadn't turned Nick's stomach, the flow of crimson that trickled down between her breasts and stained her dress certainly would. His brain refused to accept what he was seeing. People biting people in some twisted cosplay fetish? Nick could take it no longer.

He shook free of Rowan's hand and drew his gun. "Hold it right there!"

Nick noticed three things at once. One, the man with the prosthetic teeth finally noticed him and reacted with a threatening hiss. He released the blonde, who ran away as fast as her legs could carry her. Two, Rowan disappeared. Like poof from his side into thin air disappeared. And three, the guy was pissed and didn't seem a bit afraid of his gun.

"Who the fuck are you?" The man sniffed the air. "Human, you don't belong here."

"Shut the fuck up and put your hands behind your back."

Big Guy did not comply. The man lunged for Nick and the freak was fast, really fast, but Nick was fast too. He'd spent his childhood dodging his guardian's fists and years practicing jujitsu, and that was before the police academy. He'd had more than enough opportunity to practice in the field too. So when a guy as big as this one came at him, his body knew what to do. He leaned back, watched the guy's fist punch the air over his nose, and at the same time levered his leg up to kick the man in the balls.

The freak hissed like a cat and flew backward, almost like an invisible force had thrown him. Even the biggest guys crumpled when hit in the family jewels.

Nick raised his gun again. "Don't move. I don't want to hurt you." That wasn't exactly true. Nick would love to hurt the dude, and the truth was he could have easily shot the man instead of kicking him in the balls. But he never pulled the trigger unless he wanted his target to die. And he did *not* want this creep to die. He wanted him to answer questions about the tattoo and the dead girl and what was going on tonight.

Where the hell was Rowan?

"Nick, look out!" she said in his ear.

He turned toward her voice but never saw her. At that precise moment, a semitruck plowed into him from behind. Nick's face smacked the floor and his gun skidded down the hall. Fangs pierced his skin before he could twitch. *No one moves that fast*, he thought. *Do all of them have the fangs?*

He ignored the sharp pain and fisted the back of the guy's head. A yank and a thrust and he heard the tear as the man's teeth left his neck. Nick became a flurry of elbows and knees, and then he forced the top of his attacker's head against his chest. With the heel of his palm, he cranked the man's face to the side and brought his entire body weight down on the man's neck. The moment the guy's cervical spine snapped, Nick both heard and felt it. He tossed the body aside. That one wasn't going to be answering questions.

Big Guy was back, and Nick swept his gun off the floor. When he pointed this time, he meant business. But he never had to pull the trigger. The man's feet left the ground of their own accord, his body flying into the wall near the door as if he'd been thrown. His head snapped back on his neck with a sickening crack and he crumpled to the floor. In the blink of an eye, Rowan appeared, standing in front of the door and holding her hand out to him.

"More will come. We've got to go. *Now*!"

CHAPTER THIRTEEN

Rowan cursed. Nick was bleeding. Normally vampire saliva would seal a bite wound like that. Certainly the vampire hadn't spent long at his neck, but when Nick had grabbed the vampire's hair and yanked, a feat she'd never thought possible for a human before she'd seen him accomplish it, he'd torn the delicate human flesh of his neck. There was no way for her to tell how much blood he'd lost or if she should be concerned. At least for now he didn't seem affected.

Nick swept his gun off the floor and grabbed her hand. But far from leaning on her for help, he sped by her and yanked her through the door. That shocked Rowan. Most humans did not handle learning they shared the world with supernaturals well. Up until now, Harriet had been the one exception. Back in 1904 when Rowan had revealed what she was to her best friend and explained why she hadn't aged a day in the thirty years they'd known each other, the old woman had simply pulled out her tarot cards and said she suspected as much. But Harriet was a Traveller; she had been raised to be in touch with the beyond. And that had been a different time, when people had far more faith and a lot less technology.

"Where did you go before?" he asked as he ushered her up the stairs.

She marveled at his speed and agility despite his wound. He really was an exceptional human being. "I made myself invisible, just like I'm making us invisible right now."

He grunted. "What kind of technology are you using? Who do you work for?"

"Work for? I don't understand the question. It's just something I can do." She released his hand to show him and blinked out of sight.

He missed a step and tripped.

"Damn it. I'm sorry, Nick!" She hauled him onto his feet and spread her invisibility over him once more, dragging him through the door and into the alcove where she'd first seen him outside Michael's office. "You're bleeding."

"I'll be okay. We need to get out of here."

"We need to stop the bleeding." She pulled the tail of his shirt from his pants and tore off a piece, pressing the cloth to his neck wound. Covering him with her body, she erected a wall of dragon magic around them. It was ancient and a sister magic to her invisibility, an innate ability that her people historically used to hide their treasure. A vampire burst through the door behind them and ran straight for Michael's office. She thanked all the gods she could think of that her enchantment had worked and the creature couldn't smell the blood. They'd gotten lucky, but they needed to get out of there.

As soon as the hall was clear, she led Nick through the VIP lounge, but the club was packed with patrons now. They'd never get out the way they'd come in. Navigating the crowd, even while invisible, would be difficult if not impossible. She veered left and shoved Nick out onto the crowded terrace.

He looked right, then left. "Maybe we should jump?"

"How much do you weigh?"

"About two fifty."

"Should be okay." She wrapped her arms around him.

"Okay for what?"

"Hang on tight." She spread her wings and lifted him straight up.

Invisibility alone wouldn't hide her scent or the scent of Nick's blood if Verinetti came for them. She needed to put distance between them and Wicked Divine as quickly as possible. And she couldn't keep up the concealing magic she'd used in the alcove while she was moving. It was meant to conceal a place, not a moving object. Quickly, she soared to the car and landed silently beside it, thankful she'd had Djorji wait right around the corner.

As soon as she'd settled Nick and herself in the back seat, she dropped her invisibility.

"Where to, miss?" Djorji asked, starting the engine.

"The penthouse."

He nodded and pulled away from the curb. When she turned back to Nick, his body was tense as a tightly coiled spring beside her. His gray eyes stared straight at her with a burning intensity that had nothing to do with attraction this time. A muscle in his jaw flexed.

"Nick? Nick, are you okay?"

His eyes narrowed to thin slits. She noticed his hand rested on his gun in its holster. "Who do you work for?"

A laugh bubbled from deep within her. "No one."

"Who provided you with the technology and the gear?" His eyes raked over her. "Where are you keeping the wings?"

Her lips twitched. "Technology? What do you think you saw tonight?"

"A fetish cult, obviously. Those people had fangs and were sucking each other's blood. And the tattoos on their wrists, those must be to mark their subs. I doubt they're all willing volunteers. Once we blow the lid off this thing, I expect we'll learn they've been trafficked. So why don't you tell me who you really are and how you just did what you did?"

Rowan frowned. As tempting as it was, she could not let Nick labor under the delusion that everything he'd seen tonight had been human. If he returned with guns and backup, the vampires would retaliate and they would win. Nick could get hurt or killed, and she couldn't have that on her conscience.

"I'm taking you back to my place. We'll get you patched up. Then we can talk."

He didn't protest, but his hand stayed on his gun.

She kept a unit in the Dakota building, which was built in 1884, and Rowan had purchased her penthouse soon after that. If there were any place she'd call home, it would be there. The building was a relic of the gilded age with corner pavilions, stepped dormers, pediments, oriel windows, and decorative terra-cotta paneling and molding. The German Renaissance architecture suited her, as did the internal courtyard and location near Central Park. Not only did her tenth-floor apartment boast double-height ceilings and ten rooms, but her unit had the only rooftop terrace in the building. An oread named Flubell maintained the place like no human could, and when Rowan stayed there, she felt as if she'd turned back the clock to a simpler time.

But perhaps the biggest draws of the property were the security and the fact that the other property owners who lived there were masters of discretion. After all, this was the hotel where they'd filmed *Rosemary's Baby* and also where John Lennon had been shot. The residents were used to a steady stream of tourists and the need for heightened vigilance. She remembered the day Lennon had been murdered and how she'd wished she'd been close enough to make a difference in his fate. She'd adored the musician and his wife. But then, a building like this held many ghosts. Humans were terribly fragile when it came right down to it. Which was why she needed to tell Nick the truth. He needed to know what he was up against.

Djorji dropped them off at the entrance, and Rowan led Nick to the front door.

Brian, the doorman, gave her a concerned once-over. "Are you okay, miss?"

"Oh, the blood, yes." She smiled warmly. "My friend has had the world's worst bloody nose. We're going upstairs to get it cleaned up right now."

Nick nodded, obligingly moving the ball of bloody cloth from his neck to his nose. Fortunately, Brian didn't ask any further questions and Rowan again thanked her lucky stars for the Dakota and its discreet staff. She led the way into her corner of the building and up the elevator where she unlocked her unit and ushered him inside.

Nick's gaze roved over the foyer. "One hell of a place you've got here. I thought you said you were a gallery owner who ran a community center?"

"Gallery owners can't have nice homes?"

"You don't get a place in the Dakota just by being rich. This place turned down Madonna. Fucking Yoko Ono lives here. You have to be a legend to share this address."

She smiled broadly. "Maybe there's more to me than just a pretty face."

He scoffed. "I never thought you were just a pretty face. But once again, I have to wonder who you work for. Are you a spy?"

"No." She winked and gave him her most flirtatious smile, hoping to lighten the mood. "But if you want me to tie you up and interrogate you, you only have to ask." She reached for the bloody cloth he was holding. "You're already bloody. Half my work is done. Let's get you cleaned up."

He gently pushed her hand away. "Bathroom?"

"Down the hall and to the left." She raised her hands and reached for the bloody cloth again, but he drew back. "Let me help you."

He shook his head. "I got it. I'm fine."

NICK WAS NOT FINE. IN FACT, HE WAS FEELING A little tipsy, likely the result of blood loss. On some level, he understood he'd been stupid coming here, possibly walking right into her trap. At least this explained the lies. She had to be a spy. Possibly Russian or Iraqi. If she was, she was barking up the wrong tree. He didn't know anything. He was a homicide detective. That was all.

More likely, it wasn't him she was after but whatever that was he'd seen in the basement of Wicked Divine. She'd saved his life tonight; clearly it wasn't her intention to hurt him. Maybe she was FBI? CIA? Special Ops? Goddamn, he needed a drink.

He found the bathroom and was surprised to find a man's shirt already hanging inside. He stuck his head out the door, looked right and then left. No one. He took a closer look at the shirt. It was his size. What the fuck?

Did she keep a selection of men's shirts on hand just in case?

He stripped out of his jacket and his bloody shirt and used a towel from the counter to clean the excess blood from his neck and torso. Luckily his pants had been spared. He turned to the side and inspected the two puncture wounds still oozing on the side of his neck. Now that he'd cleaned off the old blood, he noted they were barely bleeding anymore. Could've been worse. Thank God the guy missed his jugular.

A box of gauze pads, tape, and related first aid accouterments filled a basket on the counter. That was it; she was definitely a spy. Any woman who kept materials to patch herself up in her guest bathroom had major secrets. He washed the bite out with plenty of soap and water and layered on some antibacterial cream. He'd probably have to see the doctor about this one for some oral antibiotics. He didn't even want to think about the shitload of germs in a human bite. He placed a stack of gauze over the bite and taped it into place.

After washing his face, he rinsed the blood out of his hair and into the sink, scrubbed it with a towel, and ran his fingers through it. There were benefits to wearing it high and tight. By the time he'd put on the shirt—fit like glove—he looked almost as good as new, aside from the pallor from losing a pint or two. He'd live. He tucked in the shirt, then made sure his gun and holster were in place.

When he came out again, he found Rowan sitting in a leather sofa in a room that was bigger than his entire apartment. He couldn't tell if it was a living room or a ballroom. If you pushed the furniture aside, there would be plenty of space for hoop skirts and dancing. In fact, the entire room had a certain historical quality, like he'd walked onto the set of some PBS episode. The walls were lined with fabric, and a fire burned in a fireplace along one wall. The carved mantel looked custom made. It depicted dragons of all things, beautiful and gracefully made to look like they were climbing up the sides and holding up the shelf.

Rowan had changed into a pair of athletic pants and a sleeveless T-shirt. He missed the stilettos and the short skirt but liked that she seemed more comfortable in this. Maybe it was a sign she planned to tell him the truth about who she was.

The fire crackled.

"Would you care for a drink?" she asked. "We have scotch, bourbon, wine. I could find a beer if you wanted one."

"Bourbon." At least he didn't have to worry about her poisoning him. If she'd wanted him dead, she'd had multiple chances tonight.

"Do you want that mixed with anything?"

"More bourbon."

She rose and walked barefoot to a bar in the corner where she poured his drink and a red wine for herself. Damn. He caught himself responding physically to the sway of her hips. Even her bare feet turned him on, perfectly arched, the skin smooth and elegant, her toes painted tulip red. He was doomed. For all he knew, she was some sort of secret agent, but his head kept going straight to the gutter.

As soon as the drink was in his hands, he took a fortifying swig. "Now, can you tell me who the hell you are and where you got the tech to pull that off tonight?"

Rowan looked him in the eye, her face deadly serious. "What we stumbled on tonight was not a fetish group. It *was* human trafficking. You were right about that. Just not for the reasons you think."

"No?"

"NAVAK stands for New Amsterdam Vampire Kingdom. What you saw tonight were vampires bidding on humans supplied to them by Verinetti for a price. NAVAK struck a deal with the local shifter pack to live in Manhattan. I wouldn't expect you to understand the implications as a human, but I can tell you that has never happened before. Vampires and shifters are natural enemies. Verinetti sold out."

He waited for some indication that she was lying, but none came. In fact, all his instincts told him she was telling the truth. Nick laughed. It had to be a joke. "Vampires. Right."

"Vampires, yes. Verinetti and his pack are providing them humans to use for feeding. The tattoos on the human's wrists mean they are part of the vampires' herd. Most of the time, these humans will be kept alive to service the vampires. Vampires in general tend to take care of their humans for the same reasons humans might take good care of their dairy cows. But if one gets out of line, perhaps doesn't want to be used as a blood bag anymore, they won't hesitate to kill them. I'm guessing that's what you were investigating, isn't it? You found that girl you showed to Connor dead with that logo on her wrist."

Nick's knees refused to hold him up any longer, and he sat down on the sofa across from her. His head was spinning. He hadn't told Rowan anything about the crime scene. Aside from the symbol, he hadn't shared any details with her. But now everything she was saying lined up with the facts of the case, and it was just too fucking weird for his brain to process. A chill skittered along his spine.

He took another long drink of bourbon and concentrated on her body language. There was still no indication she was untruthful. For the first time, she seemed open, like all her cards were on the table.

"A-are you saying you believe these are *actual* vampires, like the mythological creatures that drink people's blood?" He laughed nervously, although there was nothing funny about it.

"I know for sure those were real vampires, and I also know they've seen our faces. There were cameras everywhere in that place. And when you released my hand, you lost the protection of my invisibility."

"How... how'd you do that?"

Rowan disappeared.

Nick let out a stream of curses that would make a hardened criminal blush. He blinked his eyes and she was there again. He tossed back the remainder of his drink.

"I know those were real vampires, Nick, because I am a dragon. I can make myself and anything I touch invisible because dragons can become invisible. I can fly, not because of technology, but because I have wings."

Now his head was really spinning. He had to be drunk. Did she just say she had wings? He licked his lips. "You seem like a really nice person, Rowan, but you need professional help."

She stood and crossed to stand directly in front of him, hands on her hips. The look on her face wasn't exactly angry, but she wasn't smiling either. If he had to name her expression, he'd say she was both frustrated and resolved. And she wasn't lying. Nothing scared him more than knowing that as far as all his skills and training were concerned, she was telling the truth. He set his empty glass on the coffee table and stood so that they were face-to-face.

"I like you, Nick. Please don't disappoint me."

With a sound like a flag unfurling, two red, scaled wings spread from her back and arched across the room.

For a second Nick's mind flashed on how really beautiful the wings were, like bat wings but with rose-colored scales that glinted in the firelight. He wanted to touch them, wondered what they'd feel like. But he couldn't. His skin turned clammy, and a tremble took hold of his body. The room tilted and the floor rose up to meet his head. It was easier to fall asleep since he was already lying down.

Everything slipped into shadow, and he gave himself over to total darkness.

CHAPTER FOURTEEN

"Nick? Nick?" Rowan shook his shoulder. When he didn't wake, she scooped him off the floor and carried him to her bedroom, where she positioned him with a pillow under his head. She was relieved when her phone rang. Harriet had arrived and Brian was letting her up. Rowan had texted her to come while Nick was in the bathroom, in the event that his injuries were worse than she'd thought. Now she was glad for the prognostication.

A few minutes later she heard her friend let herself in with her key. "Back here!" she called.

Harriet appeared in the doorway, dressed to the teeth, as always, this time in a lavender suit with a patterned Hermès scarf tied around her throat. Her hair cascaded in straight silver strands to her shoulders. A large black leather bag hung from one elbow.

"For the love of all that is holy, what did you do to him?" Harriet said through tight lips.

"Nothing!" Rowan said defensively. "Why would you assume I did this?"

"Well, what caused it then? Did he remember about the Raindrop of Heaven and pass out from the shock?"

"No... No." Rowan frowned. "Well, actually... he didn't remember, but shock may have been involved. And some blood loss."

"Blood loss?"

"From a vampire bite." Rowan's shoulders slumped as she delivered the news.

Harriet's expression turned horrified. "A vampire? In Manhattan?"

Rowan gave her a quick rundown of everything they'd seen.

"So he's been like this since the bite?"

Shifting uncomfortably, Rowan said, "No, he was fine until I showed him my wings."

"You what?" Harriet's eyebrows inched toward the ceiling.

"He needed to know. I had to prove to him that what he saw tonight was real. They could come for him, Harriet. He has to be ready."

"And you couldn't wait until, I don't know, his body recuperated from the trauma of the evening?"

She scowled. "Sure, that makes sense *now*. In fairness, I didn't think he was badly hurt. He seemed fine when we arrived here."

"This is very irresponsible, Rowan. He's an NYPD detective. Even if he hasn't remembered about the Raindrop of Heaven, you've shown him your identity and Zelda's Folly, not to mention brought him to your true home. Do you realize the risk? You could lose everything you hold most dear. The forget-me potion is still brewing. I can't even make him forget."

Rowan closed her eyes and released a deep breath. "I

don't want him to forget. I want you to heal him. Can you fix him?"

Harriet's steely gaze perused her, her lips twitching at the corners. "Ah, I see now." She flashed a small, knowing smile. Nodding slowly, she said, "I think I can help you. I brought with me my strongest healing elixir. It's not a blood transfusion, mind you. It will only help his human body heal itself, nothing more. But he's strong and his heart is still beating. That's something. There is always risk with humans though, you understand. Fragile creatures."

"I understand. I'll take him to the human hospital if he gets worse."

Harriet reached into her handbag and pulled out a small vial. "Hold his head."

Together, they held Nick's mouth open and poured the elixir down his throat. He made a face, coughed, and rolled onto his side. Harriet dropped the empty vial into her bag.

"Is that a Birkin bag?"

Harriet straightened. "Yes. Why?"

"That's an $8,000 bag." Rowan held the piece of art hanging at Harriet's elbow between her hands, admiring the leather.

"You pay me very well."

"How much do I pay you?"

"Ask your accountant."

"You are my accountant!"

"You pay me very well."

Rowan raised an eyebrow. Even she didn't own a Birkin bag. Not that she couldn't afford one.

Harriet adjusted the bag on her elbow. "Now, we must talk before the detective wakes."

"I told you, Harriet, I wanted him to know. I was ready to tell him. I will deal with the fallout."

She nodded. "I heard you. And I think now is a good time for me to tell you I have read your cards."

Rowan raised a hand. "Stop. I don't want to know. I told you not to snoop into my future."

When Harriet read tarot cards, her readings provided vague guidance that could be interpreted in various ways. Rowan always thought the readings were like a mirror, reflecting back what you wanted to see. Harriet *could* see the present. If she held an object, she could tell you exactly where the owner of that object was or other things about the current state of the object or the owner. But seeing into the *future* was an entirely different and nebulous discipline. While Harriet sometimes experienced premonitions about things that came to pass, a person couldn't count on her visions to be exactly true. More like in the realm of truth. Sort of like buying a ticket to Paris, France, and ending up in Paris, Illinois.

"So you don't want to know about a potential future between you and the human?"

"No. Let it unravel naturally."

"You admit, then, that there is something to unravel? You see or perhaps desire a future with this man." She touched her tongue to her top lip.

"Oh, for fuck's sake. Yes, okay, I have feelings for him. Actually, so does my dragon. Sometimes when I see him, I feel her move inside me as if I'm about to shift. I've never had that before."

Harriet's grin grew even broader and she squealed softly. "Dragon knows best."

Rowan rolled her eyes. "My inner dragon is impulsive and wild. All heart and very little head."

"All heart is the only way to live, darling."

Inhaling deeply, Rowan watched Nick sleep. "He smells so good."

Harriet raised one eyebrow. "He smells like blood and the valerian root in my elixir."

"No he doesn't. He smells like sandalwood and spices. Christmas spices. Cloves and nutmeg." She breathed in again.

The older woman laughed. "That's all you, darling. You have it bad."

Rowan rolled her eyes, then gave in to Harriet's evil scheme. "Okay," she said through her teeth as if her friend had twisted her arm. "What did the cards say?"

Harriet's face lit up. "You're going to be very happy together..."

Rowan did a little dance.

"...after a period of trial where one of you may die."

"Harriet!"

"You know how this works, darling. Death could mean psychological or emotional change. The death card doesn't mean physical death. Well, sometimes it does, but rarely."

"By the Mountain!" Rowan held her head.

Harriet clasped her hands. "I saw many years of happiness—that's the important thing—in at least one possible outcome."

All Rowan could do was close her eyes and take a few deep breaths. It was her own fault for asking. Only temporary insanity could explain why she'd gone against her own rules and asked what Harriet had seen in the cards. Dumb. Stupid. She tried to scrub her brain of the information.

"Did the cards tell you how we could avoid this near-death experience?"

"Oh no, it's coming." Harriet tapped her bottom lip. "Also,

that reminds me... It's probably nothing to worry about, but a magical entity has been testing the boundaries of the *dispărea* charm I have on your person. Someone is looking for you."

"Seriously? When did this start?"

"The past few days."

"Oh, Harriet, why would someone be trying to find me?"

The old woman shrugged. "I assumed it had something to do with the reason your brothers were looking for you. What did Tobias say?"

"I couldn't reach him. He's left his job and moved out of his home."

"Almost like he's running from something." Her rheumy blue eyes widened. "Perhaps that something is looking for you too."

"Perhaps that something is what you saw in the cards that will threaten our lives."

She spread her hands. "But if you live, you will be very, very happy."

"I love you, Harriet, but you're a freak if you think that makes me feel better. Also a freak if you aren't concerned. As my bonded servant, if I die, you die."

"I do not think you will die. I think you will be—"

"Very, very happy. Yes, I heard you."

Harriet's lips thinned and she clasped her hands in front of her stomach. "Well, I find it comforting to be wrapped in the arms of fate and given a glimpse into the beyond. We are all adventurers on this journey called life. The wind is in your sails, Rowan. Can't you feel it? Don't you think it's time to look to the stars to guide you? Even if you can't change your course, they shine quite lovingly."

Nick groaned and rolled over, grabbing his head.

"He's waking up." Rowan hurried to his side.

Harriet worked her fingers under the bandage on his neck and peeled it from his skin. "Voilà! All healed up. My work here is done. I'll see you tomorrow at the gallery. I'm going to be late coming in."

"Why?"

"Traveller council meeting. I hope you won't need Djorji. He's expected around the fire at Ember Fields as well."

"I'll make do. Say hello to the others for me."

Harriet bowed her head before retreating from the room.

Nick's eyes fluttered as he lay beside her in bed, and he let out a groan.

She rushed to his side. "Nick? Are you okay?"

His eyes opened fully and he blinked twice. "What am I doing here?"

"You passed out. You lost a lot of blood at Wicked Divine tonight."

In a burst of movement, Nick thrust himself up and away from her, until his back was against the headboard. He licked his lips. "You had wings!"

She nodded. "Because I'm a dragon."

He blinked at her, staring over her shoulders. Well, okay. If he needed to see them again, she would oblige. She stood beside the bed and again spread her wings.

Rowan might as well have been entirely naked for how vulnerable and exposed she felt showing Nick who she was. She didn't have any more of Harriet's forget-me potion to wipe this from his mind. She was baring her soul to him, trusting that he could accept who she was. And if he rejected her, it would be the worst kind of rejection. No misunderstandings or misconceptions. Nick would have seen what she was and called it garbage. Harriet was right.

It was too risky. She was mad to tell him, but she was also helpless to resist her need to.

He stared at her unblinking, his face frozen in some stony expression she couldn't read. The only thing moving was a vein in his neck that throbbed like it had a life of its own.

"Nick?"

His eyelids fluttered like butterfly wings. Then, slowly, he hung his legs over the side of the bed and stood, straight backed and chin high. He reached for her right wing.

At once she flinched away. "Hey! Ask me before you get all grabby hands." Her cheeks burned. Wings to a dragon were intimate appendages. He might as well be reaching for her breast.

"Oh." His gaze shifted toward the wall.

She took a deep breath. When he didn't look at her again, she asked softly, "Do they disgust you?"

His gaze flicked up to her again, his brow furrowed. "No, Rowan. I think they're breathtaking. Astonishing. Unbelievable. This is all..." He rubbed his head.

"Oh." She searched his face. He wasn't afraid or angry. Just overwhelmed. Perhaps there was a chance that the night wouldn't end in total disaster. "You can touch them now if you want. Gently."

CHAPTER FIFTEEN

Nick's head buzzed like he was in a dream. Maybe he was. He had been sleeping, after all. He moved closer, that smoky citrus scent of hers everywhere in this room. Her room. He was definitely dreaming.

He swallowed hard.

"My wings are intimate to me. I don't usually let others see them or touch them." She licked her lips. "I'm letting you see them because... I like you."

His gaze met hers, and the vulnerability in her eyes melted his heart. "I like you too." He reached for her and slowly stroked his thumb along her jaw, trailing his nail gently beneath her lip before cupping her cheek. "Your wings look like they're made of rose petals," he said. "They're beautiful."

A blush warmed her cheeks. "Thank you."

Sweet. Alluring. If this was a dream, he didn't want to wake up.

She nodded, never looking away from him. He moved his hand from her face and toward the outer bone of her right wing. The tips of his fingers inspected the edge, the texture of scales bumping in smooth regularity beneath his touch.

She giggled, and the sound sent a pleasant shiver along his skin. "It tickles."

"You can feel that?"

"Of course I can feel it. It's my wing."

"Were they... surgically implanted? I didn't think it was possible, but..."

She snatched his wrist, holding his hand between them, and stared him in the eye. "You're not listening. This isn't technology, Nick. It isn't surgery. It's me. My wings are part of me. Of who I am. I'm a dragon from a realm known as Paragon. That's in a different dimension. A different world."

He narrowed his eyes on her, trying to wrap his mind around it.

She groaned. "You said you were a human lie detector. You tell me—am I lying?"

Nick shook his head. "No."

She released his hand. After an awkward moment, he couldn't resist stroking her wing again. She arched and stretched the wing beneath his touch as if it tickled again, and he increased the pressure to long, even strokes that seemed more soothing to her. Damn. He used to think he was a leg man. Who would have thought wings would be his ultimate turn-on?

"How did you come here to this place, from uh, Paragon?" His instincts told him she wasn't lying, but that didn't mean what she said was real, only that she believed it was.

Her brow knitted and she folded her hands between them. "There was a coup. The government of Paragon was overthrown. My mother, an extremely powerful dragon, knowing that I and my siblings were in danger, used her magic to send us all here to Earth, to hide us."

"How many of you are there?"

"Eight. I'm the only girl."

He watched her carefully. Could this be real?

Her lips bent into a nervous smile. "Do you believe me now?"

Nick was a homicide detective in New York. He'd known monsters. Real-life Hannibal Lecters existed in the world. He'd faced them. Seen what they could do. The vampires he'd seen that night were monsters, monsters as evil as the human ones he'd faced. But Rowan... she might be a dragon, whatever that meant, but she wasn't a monster. She was an angel, a goddess, a woman.

He trailed his fingers along her wing, over her shoulder, to the place where the red scales melded into the muscles of her back. Her eyelids drooped and her head tilted to one side. That must feel good. He massaged the muscles there gently, his arms wrapped around her, her citrus scent filling his lungs.

As a detective, he'd thought he'd seen everything. He'd been wrong.

"Nick, tell me you accept that I'm a dragon?" she implored softly. "I need to know."

"I hardly think you need anything from me. After tonight, I think it's clear you can take care of yourself."

She frowned. "Telling you this makes me vulnerable. Can I trust you to keep my secret, even if you can't...?"

"Even if I can't what?"

She took a deep breath and let it out slowly. "Think of me as you did before you knew what I was."

Drawing back, he looked at her through his lashes, scanned her from the tips of her wings to her painted toes.

She was undeniably different, but somehow having her close felt right.

"Nick? Please. Just say it. Whatever you're thinking."

He traced his fingers over her shoulders. So she was a dragon. Everything about her drew him in. Not only the wings but also the way she'd cared for the children of Sunrise House, her invisibility but also her bravery, her speed and also the warmth of her smile. He couldn't wrap his mind around it all right now, but one thing was for certain, Nick had no intention of letting her go until he figured it out.

"I believe you're a dragon," Nick said, his hands circling her rib cage.

Her breath hitched.

"But you must know that I don't fully understand what your being a dragon means yet. I trust you. You're extraordinary; I get that. I see that." He reached again to her wing, petting her along its arc until his fingers hooked in the talon at its crest. It was like holding a bear claw, and he imagined it could be deadly under the right circumstances. He tugged at it gently and was rewarded with the parting of her lips on a pleasured inhale. The slight arch of her back encouraged him. He did it again, his curiosity transforming into deep fascination.

"You're not afraid?"

He gave her a slow, distinctly male grin, his gunmetal-gray eyes growing stormy in the dim light of the bedroom chandelier. "Oh baby, the fear isn't half as strong as the excitement."

She made a sound deep in her throat, almost a purr. Oh, he loved that. He couldn't remember ever being this captivated by anyone, and holding her awakened a long-forgotten need within him, a wild, possessive instinct, purely male and admittedly foolish. He didn't analyze it, only accepted it. He lowered his head and brushed his lips against hers. She was close, soft, and warm in his arms. Rowan might be a dragon, but she melted against him in a way his human body understood.

He lowered his mouth toward hers and paused. Was he doing this? Oh hell yes he was. "It's the end of our date, Rowan. You owe me a kiss."

She gave a nervous laugh and smiled brightly. "Yes. I do. As promised." She rose on her tiptoes and touched her lips to his.

He kissed her then, the way a man kisses a woman when he knows she's actually a hurricane in red lipstick and nail polish. He kissed her thoroughly so there could be no question that he thought of her the same as he had earlier in the day. He kissed her again, deeper, to show her that she was more than he'd ever expected.

A thump came from beyond the bedroom door. Nick tried his best to ignore it and focus on the heaven going on where their lips touched, but Rowan withdrew.

"Did you hear that?"

Internally cursing all manner of man and beast that might have made the offending sound, he looked toward the door. The thump came again. "Yeah, I did." He reached for his gun. It wasn't there. "Where's my weapon?"

She pointed toward the chair next to the bed. "It's there. I took it off you when I put you in my bed. You won't need it. Anyone who can get in here is not someone who will be damaged by a bullet."

He put his shoulder holster on anyway and found his phone underneath it. Fifteen missed messages from Soren. *Shit*! He fired off a quick text. *Safe. Talk later.*

The thump came again.

"It sounds like a bird slapping your window."

Rowan's face drained of all color. "Nick, stay here." She moved into the hall.

"Why? What's going on?"

"Trust me. Stay. Please."

He watched her disappear down the hall. Nick glanced at the mirror in the bedroom and pulled aside his collar. The vampire bite was completely healed. Vampire bite. Vampires were real. *Fuck him.* What a damn day.

Vampires were *real,* and he'd just let Rowan leave to investigate a strange sound. Visions of bats breaking through glass filled his brain. Vampires sinking teeth into that long, graceful neck of hers.

"Sorry, Rowan, but hell no. Not hiding in here," he said under his breath. He crept out of the bedroom. At the end of the hall, he could see the living room, Rowan's back, and two french doors beyond her. A white blur passed beyond the glass. Not a bat. Rowan's head turned, and he ducked into the nearest room to avoid detection.

He found himself in a small library. Or was it an office? There was a mahogany desk, its legs carved to look like winged lions, and a floor globe, all surrounded by shelves and shelves of old books. For a split second, he gaped at the grandeur and beauty of the dark wood, the patina of fine leather, the brass accents on the globe and the leather chair beyond the desk. His eyes trailed over the leather-bound volumes on the shelf and caught on one in particular. *Frankenstein.*

The click of a lock turning reminded him why he was there. He placed his hand on his gun and peeked into the hall again. To his surprise, Rowan had unlocked and opened the glass doors. The white thing—he could see now it was a large white owl—coasted inside and circled past her. Nick's brow furrowed. What was she doing? Letting a wild owl into the house was anything but a good idea. Sure, the thing looked like Hedwig from Harry Potter, not anything sinister, but who knew why it was slamming into her window? Maybe it was rabid or otherwise diseased.

He drew in a shallow breath. The owl was... changing. The feathers swelled and pulsed, the small body morphing as it circled twice, growing larger in the firelight. It dropped behind the sofa, out of sight. Nick jolted when a man stood up exactly where the owl had fallen. A naked man.

Nick pinched himself. Yes, he was awake, although he would have loved to believe this was a nightmare. The guy was buck-naked and looked mad as hell. Even from his current position peeking around a doorway from a room up the hall, Nick could sense the menace rolling off the guy in the way his shoulders and back tensed. The owl-man turned a gravely serious expression on Rowan, the firelight casting deep shadows over his face.

"Michael, what are you doing here?" Rowan said through her teeth.

"Well, well, well." The naked man scanned Rowan, his lips bending into a scowl. "It seems you weren't that hard to find after all. I always knew this place was your favorite."

Michael... Nick knew that voice. He'd heard it earlier that night. This was Verinetti. He gave the guy a quick once-over. *Fuck.* This was Rowan's ex-boyfriend? A shapeshifter with a body like a pro athlete who owned one of the hottest clubs in town and could fly by her window anytime he wanted to? Nick ground his teeth.

"Congratulations, you found me." She shrugged. "I wasn't hiding."

"Do you have any idea what kind of damage you caused tonight?" Michael snapped.

Nick's fingers tightened around his gun. Nobody should talk to Rowan like that. He didn't care who or what this guy was.

"This isn't a good time," Rowan said. "You need to leave." She placed her hands on her hips and spread her wings menacingly. A jealous twinge constricted Nick's chest. He didn't want a jerk like Verinetti to see her wings.

Michael rolled his eyes and swaggered toward the fire without an ounce of shame over his nakedness as far as Nick could see. The shifter took a deep breath through his nose before speaking. "Have I interrupted your playtime with the human? I saw the two of you dancing together on the security video, and then, later, in the auction house. Nick Grandstaff, detective NYPD."

Nick's spine stiffened.

"He has nothing to do with this."

"Then you won't mind if I disembowel him for what the two of you did to me tonight. Four vampires injured. The entire coven thinks Wicked Divine is a security risk. Do you have any idea how much money you might have cost me?"

"Might have?"

He turned cold, dark eyes her way. "I was able to contain the problem. All I had to do was promise the coven master the head of the one who did this."

She growled. "You're fooling yourself if you think I'm going to let you have my head."

"Not yours, Rowan. I hid *your* image on the security feed."

"What about the detective?"

Michael turned from the fire, shadows dancing across his naked form. "Come now. Even I have limitations. The detective was visible for far longer than you. The coven would have noticed. Besides, he's the perfect scapegoat.

Turn him over to me, I'll hand him off to the vampires, and all will be forgiven." His voice was low, soft, and threatening as hell.

"No." The syllable came out through Rowan's clenched teeth.

That seemed to surprise Michael. He tucked his chin and raised his eyebrows. "Interesting. You're protecting the human. Don't tell me that little dance was a sign of a greater affection."

Nick's heart pounded. What would she say? He hoped to God he was more to her than one dance, but he wouldn't blame her for denying it to this asshole. She hadn't known Nick long enough for him to expect her to put herself on the line for him.

"The human is *mine*," Rowan said with a growl that rattled the walls. "My bonded servant. You cannot have him."

Nick's eyebrows shot up so fast it almost hurt. Bonded *servant*? Hers? He caught himself grinning, then pulled his stupid ego out of the stratosphere. They barely knew each other. He certainly was not hers or her servant. He didn't belong to anyone. Although he couldn't deny he'd like to try out being each other's sometime soon.

"Oh? Look at you, all... protective." If the way Michael was baring his teeth was any indication, he was not happy with this revelation. "Someone needs to pay for tonight, Rowan. I must return the man to the coven master or there will be hell to pay."

"Must you?"

"Are you suggesting I lie to the master of the NAVAK coven?"

"You already did for me, didn't you?"

He looked at his nails. "It's a huge risk. Vampires can

smell a lie. It's one thing to make sixty seconds of digital video disappear. An entirely different thing to look Malvern in the face and tell him I have no idea who the human is. I do know who he is: his name, address, job, and, as it appears, his lover." Michael's gaze raked over her in a way that made Nick's skin crawl.

"Tell him you're following up on a lead. That's true and will buy us time."

He lowered his chin. "Diversion will only last so long. Malvern is going to expect results. He won't go away until he has his pound of flesh."

"I'll come up with something. But please do this for me now."

He stepped closer. "Why should I help you?"

"Please... Michael..."

"I'll do it. I'll lie for you—"

"Thank you."

"—*if* you have skin in the game. I want you by my side next time I meet with Malvern, as my date."

Nick's teeth ground together. That fucking slimy bastard. He drew his gun and took a slow, deep breath. Verinetti was dangerous and supernatural. Nick would love to take his head off, but he wasn't stupid. Galloping in there with guns blazing when he wasn't sure what he was dealing with was more likely to get everyone killed than help Rowan. He closed his eyes and returned his gun to his holster.

"You would extort a date out of me in exchange for Nick's life?"

"I'm not requiring you to have sex with me, Rowan, although I wouldn't mind if that was a natural outcome of being close to me again." He flashed her a wolfish grin that turned Nick's stomach. "I'm asking you to appear before the vampire master with me so that he doesn't suspect you and so that you can help me deflect his interest in this matter. Malvern has a weakness for beautiful women. You'll be a distraction, one that will hopefully keep him from asking too many questions. If you want to protect your human, you'll do this."

Nick cringed when Rowan hugged her stomach and tucked in her wings. She couldn't seriously be considering it! He wouldn't allow it. No way would he let her do this to protect him.

"I accept your proposal," he heard Rowan say. "Tell me where and when and I'll be there."

Michael grinned smugly and approached her, reaching for her waist. Nick's eyes widened. Thankfully, Rowan recoiled from the bastard's touch. In the blink of an eye, she'd put the sofa between them.

"This is business, not pleasure. That's over between us, remember?"

Michael swaggered toward the terrace, his smile growing wider. "For now." He opened the door, shifted into the snowy white owl again, and took off into the night.

Nick watched Rowan lock the door behind the owl, then close the drapes. Her chest rose and fell in rapid pants. By the time she turned around, he was there, pulling her into his arms.

"Start thinking of alternate ideas now, Rowan, because there's no way in hell I'm letting you go on a date with that guy just to protect me."

CHAPTER SIXTEEN

"You heard that?" Rowan felt wrung out and exhausted. This was the worst-case scenario. Not only did Michael know who Nick was, the vampires were expecting him to turn over his identity. The only reason Verinetti had hesitated was because of her, whether out of some nostalgia for what they used to have, a sense of guilt for suggesting she investigate the auction, or lingering hope that they might pick up where they left off. Rowan didn't care what Michael's motivation was. Keeping him from turning over Nick's identity to the vampires was her only hope of keeping him safe, and she'd do anything to keep him safe.

"You are not going on a date with that guy to protect me. I can protect myself," Nick gestured toward his gun.

"I told you, the bullets in that weapon are useless against vampires. They'd hardly slow one down." How could she make him realize he was in grave danger? He was a strong man—a strong human man. That wouldn't be enough.

"I seemed to do okay tonight at Wicked Divine. As I

recall, there were a few vampires on the floor when I left. I broke one's neck with my bare hands."

"Yes, you did, and if they were humans, that would be the end. But what you need to know, Nick, is that neither of the vampires you fought are dead or disabled."

"Huh?"

"They healed in a matter of minutes. Woke up, stood up, and probably almost drained someone dry to replenish their strength. There are only a handful of ways to kill a vampire, and breaking their spine is not one of them. It might slow them down, but not for long. You could cut them into pieces and they would eventually heal."

A muscle in Nick's jaw twitched. "So how do you kill them?"

"That's hardly the point! The point is *you* can't kill them. This is a big, powerful coven. Michael knows who you are. Our only hope is to use magic and manipulation to protect you. That means I need to lay new protective wards around this place to keep supernatural creatures like Michael out. I'll need to do your place too. Then I'll ask Harriet to create a charm to hide you. And I will do whatever Michael asks to keep your identity a secret, up until the time the vampires lose interest in you."

"No."

"No what? There wasn't a question in there."

"Michael is using me as leverage to get closer to you. The guy clearly still has feelings for you, and you're playing right into his hands."

"I don't have a choice!"

"Yes, you do. Teach me to defend myself against these things. I'm tougher than I look. I don't kill easy."

"I know you're tough, but—"

"Rowan..." He hesitated, his gaze shifting away from

hers. "If you knew the way I was raised, you wouldn't underestimate me."

"Can't you see this is different?"

He held up one finger, and her stomach tightened under the tension that formed between them. "I am telling you, unequivocally, that I have survived a lot worse than you give me credit for. And if Michael or these vampires expect an easy target, they are in for a rude awakening."

"I didn't mean to offend you." She moved in close and clasped his hands in hers as if her touch might soothe away the hurt and jealous anger she could see brewing behind his gray eyes. "I know you can take care of yourself, but—"

"But nothin'." He pulled her hard against his chest and held her there.

The intensity in his stare didn't soften, but her nearness ignited another element in it. Now she saw desire flickering like lightning in the cloudy gray storm. His gaze trailed to her lips.

There was no hiding her body's response. Her breath came out in a shaky exhale. She melted against him, her skin turning hot as her dragon stirred within her.

"That's more like it." He circled her waist with his hands.

Whatever this was between them, it was strong, unique, and undeniably dangerous. She understood Nick could be her undoing, but she couldn't resist him.

"Considering that in the past several hours, I've learned there are vampires, shifters, and one exceedingly attractive dragon living in Manhattan, I think I've handled things fairly well, wouldn't you agree?"

"Yes," she said breathlessly.

"Good. Because we have more important things to

discuss." He guided her hand to the front of his slacks. "Do you feel what you do to me?"

She did. The considerable size of him pushed hard and thick against her palm. "Yes." A warm ache uncurled deep within her belly.

He kissed her softly, gently teasing her bottom lip with his teeth. Everything in her reacted. Her fingers tangled in his hair, and her body pressed fully against that hard length at her belly.

Much too soon, he broke away, glancing at the sliver of watery light coming in between the curtains. "Is that the sunrise?" He checked his watch. "Aww, crap. It's almost five o'clock!"

"Are you sure you're human?" Rowan mumbled, still affected by the kiss.

He snorted. "Positive. I have to go."

"Hmm?" She couldn't have heard him right. She was falling into his arms, practically throwing herself at him. He couldn't possibly be thinking about leaving.

"Believe me, I'd love to stay. But I have a dog at home who has all four legs crossed by now and is probably taking out his frustrations on my shoes."

"You have a dog?"

"A German shepherd named Rosco. He'd love to meet you. Tomorrow night? My place?"

She shook her head. "You can't go, Nick. It's not safe."

He smiled at her but continued for the door. "Get some rest. I'll call you tomorrow. And you owe me another date. I'm not sure what this was tonight, but it doesn't count."

"A date? You're asking me on a date? Now? No, Nick, I need to—"

But he was already out the door. She ran after him, but he'd caught the elevator. What could she do anyway? If she followed him and tried to force him to accept her protection after what he'd said to her, she'd be crossing a line and violating his right to self-determination. He was a man, a warrior like her brothers. He'd never agree to be treated like a child.

But he didn't understand the danger. Which meant her agreement with Verinetti was the only chance she had of keeping him alive.

CHAPTER SEVENTEEN

As soon as Nick was safely inside an Uber, he called Soren. His partner answered in the groggy voice of someone who'd been awakened from a deep sleep.

"Nick? What the hell happened to you last night?"

"Long story. I'll tell you in person on Monday when I see you at the station." That would buy him some time to decide what he would say. For obvious reasons, telling Soren that a coven of vampires was invading the city under the protective umbrella of a corporate identity didn't seem prudent. But he'd have to tell him something.

Soren cleared his throat. "Listen, Nick. I found Kendra, the girl I told you about. She said the tattoo means she's part of a... club, a sex club, okay? Nothing violent. I think we're barking up the wrong tree on this one."

"We are definitely not barking up the wrong tree."

"So then you did find something."

"Yeah. I can't talk about it now."

"It's just you ignored all my texts and calls. If you found something, why didn't you bring me in?"

Nick rubbed his eyes. Soren was usually more reasonable than this. "I was distracted with the case."

"And with the girl," Soren suggested.

"Yeah. She's a distraction. A gorgeous, lovely distraction."

"Is that right? I want details." There was a pause. "Are you just heading home now? Is this call on your walk of shame?"

"No shame here."

"Well, get some sleep, think about what I said, and call me later."

"Sounds good."

"Oh, Nick, I almost forgot. I ran into Gerald Stevenson last night."

Nick raised an eyebrow and adjusted his phone on his ear. He'd almost forgotten that he'd seen the real estate tycoon in one of the booths during the auction. "How is old Gerald?"

"He's one Raindrop of Heaven short."

Nick sat up straighter. "What?"

"The jewel was stolen along with a set of matching earrings. Camilla opened her safe to try to wear them and they were gone."

Intense pressure squeezed Nick's brain, as if pincers had been applied at his temples and a sadistic madman was trying desperately to crack his skull like a nut.

"Any leads?" He rubbed his head and prayed the Uber would arrive at his apartment soon so he could medicate the hell out of this.

"No. But Gerald mentioned that the last person besides him and Camilla that had access to the safe and was on video surveillance was... you."

"Bullshit," Nick said. "He has housekeeping staff, and his regular security detail would have checked that the diamond was secure after my shift. That's procedure."

His head hurt so bad he thought he might throw up. Images were flashing through his mind, a fragmented zoetrope in black and white with splashes of color. The Stevensons' Hamptons home. A woman's silhouette framed in the light of the moon on the bedroom balcony.

"I'm going to be sick. Migraine," he mumbled. "Later?"

"Sure. Take care of yourself. We'll talk Monday." Soren disconnected the call.

"Here you go," the driver said, pulling up to his apartment building.

Nick exited the vehicle, relieved that whatever had caused the pain in his head seemed to be abating. It was all the stress and exhaustion from the night. There was some dark shit going down in that basement. But real vampires?

And Rowan said she was a dragon. Those wings were part of her and stunning. He couldn't wait to explore them again, run his hands along their edges and learn everything about her anatomy. Could she change into a dragon the way he'd seen Verinetti change into an owl? It didn't really matter. She wasn't human, and although he knew that should scare him, it didn't. He was enchanted. Whatever she was, she rang all his bells and pushed all his buttons. Beautiful, smart, strong, she had it all. He was still thinking about her when he unlocked his door and a gray blur plowed into him.

"Hey, Rosco. Sorry, buddy. You're about to pop, huh?"

He clipped the leash onto the German shepherd's collar and led him out onto the patch of grass behind his apartment building. The sun wasn't entirely up yet, although the sky had taken on that bright lavender quality of coming dawn. The street was quiet, but he remained vigilant as Rosco did his business. Vampires, he supposed, could only come out at night, but Verinetti and his men, they could be a threat twenty-four hours a day. He took comfort in the weight of his gun. Whether or not she approved, he needed Rowan to teach him about the strengths—and, more importantly, the limitations—of vampires.

A bottle rolled across the sidewalk and into the building. In a heartbeat, he drew his gun and whirled, then lowered his weapon when he saw who it was.

"You up early, Mistah Nick," Regine said, hobbling toward him from the alley. He'd never known her to sleep here. She loved her place in the park.

"Rosco needed to do his business." He glanced at the dog, who was sniffing every blade of grass for the right spot, and then looked back at Regine. "I don't usually see you around here. What's going on?"

"Somptin' goin'," she said in a shaky voice, clearly on the verge of tears. "Blood breathers be everywhere. Ne'er like dis before."

"Blood breathers?"

She blew a breath toward her open palm. "Ha. Ha. Blood."

"Their breath smells like blood?"

She nodded, her dark, tangled hair bobbing. "I no wan' dem to bite me. I seen dem bite Alice, and she don' come round no more."

"Where did they bite Alice?" Icy water filled his veins.

She pointed to her neck. "Here. In da park. At night so nobody could see. But Regine sees. I always watchin'."

Rosco nudged his hand and looked up at him with

warm brown eyes, waiting for him to pick up his steaming pile of dog shit. Well, if that wasn't a metaphor for how Nick's life was going, he didn't know what was. He rubbed the dog between his long, pointed ears. Reaching into his pocket, he grabbed his wallet and drew out a twenty. "Here, Regine."

"What dis fo'?"

"Sleep on the bus or go get breakfast."

"Oh, you a sweet man, Nick. Some woman be happy-happy to fin' you."

"Maybe someday. And uh, I think the blood breathers can't come out during the day, so maybe that's when you should sleep."

She nodded her head slowly, then pointed a finger to the sky. "Good. Good." She took the twenty and hobbled off toward the bus stop, and he sighed in relief.

Nick drew a poop bag from his pocket and quickly cleaned up after Rosco, not wanting to linger out in the open. Vampires. Real fucking vampires. He shook his head. Despite what Rowan said about the danger, it wasn't enough for him to hide from this. These things were hurting innocent people. He prayed that Alice wouldn't end up like his murdered girl.

He let Rosco into the apartment and locked up tight, then crawled under the covers, making sure his gun was within reach. He was almost asleep when he grabbed his phone off the nightstand and texted Rowan.

I want you to teach me everything you know about vampires. Please.

Tomorrow? she texted back. For a moment his mind wandered. Was she in bed? What was she wearing? Were her wings out? He ran a hand over his face.

7 PM. Meet me here. He included a contact file with his address.

See you then.

He drifted to sleep to dreams of dark hair, amber eyes, and wings.

CHAPTER EIGHTEEN

New Orleans, Louisiana

This had to work. Raven had tried everything to locate Rowan. Every other spell she could think of. But every time she came close to pinpointing her location, she hit a wall of magic like no other she'd encountered before. What good was being a sorceress if she couldn't even find her mate's sibling to warn her of danger?

Raven stood in the enchanted library above Blakemore's Antiques, dressed in Rowan's red gown, the one she'd been wearing on the day her older brother was murdered by her uncle and their mother cast the remaining eight siblings to Earth. That was over three hundred years ago. Gabriel owned Blakemore's, a store boasting a delightful collection of high-end furniture and decor from the sixteenth through nineteenth centuries. But it was the library on the third floor where Raven had first connected with her power. Gabriel had collected hundreds of grimoires from around the world over his lifetime. Shelves and shelves of books on magic, some of the tomes hundreds of years old, filled the room. Raven couldn't read all the languages they were written in, but that didn't stop them from being useful to her. She absorbed magic. It made her an extremely powerful witch.

The tracking spell she'd employed today to find Gabriel's sister was druidic in origin and combined blood magic with a less complicated location charm. It had required her to push aside the desk in the library in order to make room for a circle of bloodstones whose energy would not only seek out the former owner of the dress but would also use Gabriel's blood to amplify the locator magic, specifically toward his siblings. She wasn't sure of the range of the spell, but she hoped it would be strong enough to reach as far as New York.

"Are you certain about this, Raven? I do not like your doing this here. Why not perform the spell from inside the Prytania house?" Gabriel scowled at her from outside the circle.

He'd been brooding about her trying this all day. He wouldn't be happy unless she was lounging in a padded chair in a padded room and sipping a tepid cup of tea, lest she burn her mouth. That was what you got when you took a dragon as a mate—twenty-four seven protection from a man whose very nature was to hoard the things most precious to him. His mate and his developing whelp topped that list.

"If I did it in our Garden District house, I'd have to fight our own protective blood magic. It would reduce the range of the spell. Blakemore's is protected with a defensive shield but not an offensive ward to repel intruders. It's much simpler and easier to navigate."

"I don't like this. What if Aborella and my mother sense your use of magic? You're drawing on dragon's blood. It will be like a beacon for them."

The thought of Aborella made her shiver. The fairy sorceress with dark purple skin had almost lured her to her doom when Gabriel had taken her to Paragon earlier that year. Aborella was an extremely powerful magical being who worked directly for the evil queen of Paragon, aka Gabriel's mother.

"Aborella scares me as much as she scares you, but if she is watching from Paragon, it will cost her time and magic to get here. We'll be safely home before we're in any danger. Besides, if I do it here, there will be nothing linking us back to Prytania Street. It's safer."

Gabriel chuffed and crossed his arms over his chest.

"Hand me the map. Did you ask Tobias to get the candle for me?" Raven took the rolled parchment from Gabriel's hands and was relieved when Tobias chose that moment to enter with a paper-wrapped package.

"One ginger-root-infused blue candle." Tobias handed it over to her. "Why does Gabriel look like he's going to have a stroke?"

"Ignore him. He's upset that I'm not in a bubble at the end of a leash."

Gabriel growled. "Not true. I'm simply concerned about the risk."

"Do you want to find your sister or not?" Raven yelled, purple sparks rising from her skin.

Tobias waved his hands. "Whoa, cool it, Raven. You're lighting up like a sparkler."

"We're doing this," she said, glaring at Gabriel. "Give me space."

Tobias took three large steps back. Gabriel stayed

exactly where he was. *Fine.* Raven turned in the circle so that her back was to him. Taking a deep breath, she glanced once more at her mate before unrolling the map and pinning down one corner with a wooden toothpick, another with a metal tack, the third under a glass of water, and the last under the candle Tobias had brought her.

"*Fotiá,*" she whispered. The candle blazed to life.

She removed the ruby pendant from her neck and dangled it over the map. "*Virite tórach kin adelphí. Verimas avich drochorus.*" She chanted the spell in the native language it was written in, a language long dead.

The ruby started to spin at the end of its ribbon, and the circle of stones around her produced purple strings of magic that crisscrossed around her until she was standing under a glowing, pulsating dome of power. "Your blood! Now. Both of you."

At least Gabriel didn't fight her on this. He held his palm over the silver chalice she'd left outside the circle and sliced it with her ceremonial dagger. Tobias offered his own hand. One cut and the blood of the brothers mixed in the belly of the cup.

"Bring it here. Pour it over the stones." Raven gestured at the front of the circle.

Eyeing the dome skeptically, Gabriel did as she commanded, his mouth twisting in distaste as the blood left the cup. It never hit the stones. Every drop was caught in the web of magical energy, suspended, thick and crimson along the tracks of power that arced around her. She concentrated, gripping the fabric of Rowan's dress.

All at once, the blood rained down toward the map on the floor near her toes.

"It's happening!" Raven cried.

The ruby in her hand began to spin, so fast she could

barely keep hold of the ribbon it was tied to. Drops of blood rolled across the map like marbles, spiraling under the gem.

"I'm close! I can feel it." The blood rolled toward the state of New York. "Yes. Yes!"

Suddenly, as if she'd opened the door to a moving airplane, a powerful wind howled through the room, blowing back her hair and sending the material of her dress flapping in the gale force. The candle in the corner of the map flickered.

"No. No!" Raven yelled. "It's the defensive magic again. Fuck! The candle! *Fotiá. Fotiá!*"

Raven tried her best to keep the candle burning, but the wind blew so hard through her magical dome she dropped the ruby. The flame extinguished. The purple dome shattered and fell like sand to the floor, where it disappeared.

"For fuck's sake!" she yelled. She had a blister where the ribbon from the necklace had rubbed too hard against her thumb, and she sucked it into her mouth to soothe the burn. Her knees started to shake, and Gabriel rushed to her, gathering her into his arms. "Whoever is protecting your sister is a magical genius."

Tobias stared at the map, tilting his head. "Uh, Raven?"

She detangled herself from Gabriel's grip and followed Tobias's gaze to the map. Although the ruby was cast aside, off the edge of the map, all the blood had stained one specific place in a concentrated red dot that had soaked through the map.

"Sedona, Arizona," Raven said.

"What would Rowan be doing in Arizona?" Tobias asked.

Raven shook her head. "I don't think it's her." She pointed at the ruby. "This is not how the spell is supposed to work. The spell had two parts, the first to find Rowan specifically, using the stone and this dress, the second to find your siblings using your blood. The stone is off the map, deflected by the defensive spell."

"Then who is that?" Tobias pointed at the dot.

Gabriel answered, "It has to be Alexander. He's the only other sibling in the United States."

"Alexander. Of course," Raven said. "There's our answer. We find Alexander first. Maybe he'll know how to find Rowan."

Gabriel groaned and rubbed his forehead. For his part, Tobias made a face like she'd suggested eating something off the floor.

"I know you guys have mentioned that Alexander isn't in his right mind."

A loud scoff came from the direction of Gabriel. "It's more than that, Raven. He's not crazy—he's broken, damaged beyond repair."

Raven drew back at the word *damaged*, but Tobias raised a hand in his defense. "You don't understand because you're applying human logic to dragon psychology. Alexander lost his mate. Once a dragon mates, his soul is bonded to his partner as if wax was melted into wax and cooled into a seal. Life has broken that seal. Maiara is gone, and Alexander..."

"He's the walking dead. Death would be easier than what he lives through every day."

Raven placed her hands on her hips. "What I hear you saying is that your brother is severely depressed, and now that we know where he is, you don't want to deal with him or help him."

Both of them refused to look her in the eye.

"I'm a witch. I have an entire library of magical spells and healing potions at my fingertips. Perhaps I can help him with the proper draught or elixir. Everything you've told me simply makes me surer we need to go to Arizona."

A knock came from the door to the library, and everyone turned to find Raven's sister, Avery, standing just inside the doorway. Raven was struck by how beautiful her sister was, surrounded by dark wood and bathed in the light that poured through the window off Royal Street. Her long hair shone black as polished onyx, and the green dress she was wearing reminded Raven of why Avery attracted so much male attention at the Three Sisters.

"Avery, how nice to see you," Raven said.

"Did I just hear you say you were going to Arizona?" Avery's mouth gaped at the idea. "You are not going to Arizona. Your birthday party is in five days, and everyone is coming. We can't have a birthday party without the birthday girl."

Raven swallowed. "Don't be silly. Of course I'll be here for the party."

"And you still need to tell Dad that you're getting married and that you're pregnant. Mom and I have been trying our best to avoid him since you told us. I don't want to lie, but it's getting harder and harder to avoid his questions about you." Avery tucked her glossy hair behind her ears.

"I know. It's on my to-do list."

"Oh, and may I remind you that we have a wedding and reception to plan, which I seriously think you should consider moving up because you are starting to show. By October your ivory dress is going to make you look like the full moon."

Raven stepped out of the circle of stones and crossed the library to hug her sister. "Everything will get done, I promise. I'm here. I'll talk to Dad... soon."

Drawing back, Avery frowned at the map and the circle of stones. Her gaze roved to Tobias and Gabriel, who stood motionless, as if holding absolutely still would repel her curious perusal. They looked guilty as hell.

Avery's gaze locked on Tobias, her pupils widening as if he were a frosted piece of cake.

"Avery," Raven said. "I don't believe you've met Tobias. His wife had to stay in Chicago for work, but he'll be staying with us for a while."

Awkwardly, Tobias grasped Avery's hand, offering a "nice to meet you" filled with forced cheer. She shook his hand slowly as she took in the rest of the scene.

"What were you three doing in here anyway?" She eyed the red dress Raven was wearing, the map, and the circle of stones. "What's this? Where did you get this dress?"

"Same designer who's doing my gown. It's a prototype. My wedding dress would be white, of course. I was just showing it to Gabriel."

"This... is... a game." Gabriel pointed to the stones. "Tobias and I learned as children."

Tobias raised an eyebrow at his brother. "Right. Just like old times."

Avery's lips parted and her eyes narrowed. "Are you kidding me?" She turned back toward Raven. "You can't show him what your dress will look like before the wedding! This is the type of thing *I'm* here for."

"You're right. I should have called you." Raven grinned stiffly at her sister.

Avery's gaze darted between the three of them. She seemed to guess there was more to the story, but she shook her head like it wasn't worth her time. "Fine. We need to go."

"Go where?" Raven asked.

"The cake tasting! Didn't you get the appointment I sent you?"

Raven shrugged. Was it Saturday already? "Yes. Come help me get changed."

She hooked her hand in Avery's elbow and led her toward Gabriel's old apartment, leaving the boys to clean up the mess.

CHAPTER NINETEEN

She wasn't sure about the wine. Rowan strode toward Nick's apartment building, wearing a little black dress that was a few inches of fabric away from being scandalous and carrying a bottle of her favorite Malbec. Yesterday Nick had said he wanted this to be a date. A real date. But when he'd texted her later, he'd also asked her to teach him everything she knew about vampires. Not exactly date material. Was this a date or an interrogation? She wasn't sure.

Vampire lessons made her far more uncomfortable than the idea of romance. If Nick knew how to kill a vampire, he might try to do it. But chances were he'd get himself killed in the process. As a human, he wasn't fast enough or strong enough to survive if a coven of vampires wanted him dead. Much better if the dress and the wine set the tone for the night.

She walked right into his building and took the elevator to his floor. No security. That wasn't good and was another sign he shouldn't be taking on vampirekind. No, what Rowan wanted was to keep Nick safe. She'd need to ward his place against supernatural threats as soon as possible. If he insisted, she would teach him about vampires, but she planned to do everything in her power to make sure he'd never face one again.

Stopping in front of Nick's door, she heard panting on the other side, a series of sniffs, and smelled the faint aroma of canine. That's right, Nick had a dog. She smiled. A dog was always a good sign. A well-cared-for animal meant a man was capable of loving something other than himself and was a universal sign of trustworthiness. She raised a hand and knocked.

"Move out of the way, Rosco," she heard Nick say. There was a tap dance of dog nails on hard floor, and then the door opened. Rowan had a difficult time keeping her mouth from popping open. Nick stood like some sort of chiseled male art form on the other side of the threshold, his broad chest stretching a plain black T-shirt at the shoulders. *What must it take for a human to attain that kind of physique?* she wondered.

"Wow, you look good," he said to her. Ironic, considering she was thinking the same about him.

He ran a hand across the hard planes and valleys evident beneath his T-shirt. "Maybe I should change."

"Why?" she blurted, then curbed her rabid and embarrassing enthusiasm for the lucky stretch of cotton clinging to his chest. "I mean, I'm the one overdressed." She lowered her gaze to her stilettos. "When you invited me to dinner, I wasn't sure what to expect. Last time I saw you, you said you wanted a date."

He gave her a slow, assessing once-over. "I did... I do..." He rubbed the back of his head. "You look beautiful, and you wore exactly the right thing. I wasn't sure what to wear for vampire-killing lessons."

"Vampire-killing lessons?" She raised an eyebrow. "You

asked me to teach you *everything* I knew about vampires. Believe me, actually trying to kill them is what I know least about, and doing so is a matter of last resort."

He backed up and motioned inside. "Come on in before one of my neighbors hears you talking about vampires or killing. I'd never hear the end of it from my colleagues if someone called the cops."

She stepped inside and was immediately surrounded by his sandalwood-and-spice scent. By the Mountain, her eyes almost rolled back in her head. She braced herself against the wall.

"Are you okay?"

"Fine. It smells good in here."

He pointed his thumb toward the kitchen. "I'm making chicken. I hope you like it."

"Love it."

"Good. I'm just glad it doesn't smell like Rosco." He stared at her for a moment with a smile in his gray eyes that was so sexy she almost lost her balance again. What was wrong with her? He took the bottle of Malbec out of her hands. "Come on in. Make yourself at home. I'll pour this."

Turning, he walked into the kitchen area, a galley style attached to the main room, and dug in a drawer for a corkscrew. The place was simple and small but undeniably cozy. A charcoal-gray sofa was pushed against a wall that was painted a warm blush color. Marigold and navy throw pillows offset a pair of plaid chairs in the same colors across from a glass coffee table. There was a painting of an autumn forest on the wall, the yellow and red leaves seeming to welcome her into the room. The furniture wasn't new, and although the place was clean, Rosco's toys were scattered here and there. Despite being raised in a palace and familiar with luxury, it was possibly the most welcoming room Rowan had ever been in.

She walked deeper into the apartment and noticed another open door. His bedroom. She could see the edge of the bed inside and detect his scent, stronger there.

"See anything interesting?" he asked in a gritty voice.

Her cheeks warmed. "You have a lovely home. It's delightfully cozy."

He popped the cork. "Is that code for small and suffocating with embarrassingly little storage space?" He poured the wine into two short glasses and handed one to her. "Sorry, no wineglasses. Not a lot of room in here for the extras."

She held up her glass and clinked it against his. "Drinks the same. And I was being serious. This place is charming. I love it. And Rosco is the perfect addition." She stroked the dog's head.

"You like dogs?"

"Love them. I have a passion for deerhounds."

"Deerhounds? And I thought Rosco was big."

She leaned down and kissed Rosco between the ears. "Oh no, he's positively purse-sized compared to my last dog, Cerberus. He died a few years ago," she said softly. "I haven't had the heart to adopt another one yet."

On impulse, she kicked off her shoes. With Nick in a T-shirt and sweats, losing the stilettos would make them both more comfortable. Rosco nudged her palm, and she bent over to scratch him vigorously behind his tall, radar-like ears. She was rewarded with a light bump of his nose against hers and then a lick up the side of her face.

"Now I know it's true about you being different. That's the fastest Rosco has warmed up to anyone, ever."

"I have a way with animals. I think they can sense my dragon."

"Your dragon? You talk about it like it's something separate from yourself. I got the sense at your apartment that you were the dragon, you know, with the wings and everything."

"I am." She stood and brushed her hands against each other. "It's a Paragonian expression."

"The planet you're from originally."

"It's another realm, uh, a dimension parallel to Earth."

"Fuck if all my years watching *Doctor Who* didn't just pay off big-time, because yes, I know what you mean. I just never knew they existed in real life."

"We talk about our dragon as if it's a separate and distinct entity because when we shift, we change. We are still us, but our thoughts become less complex. Our dragons are our most unrestrained self, and sometimes, in this form, we can feel that inner animal trying to get out."

"What does that feel like?"

Her cheeks heated. "When you kissed me last night, I felt her move. My inner dragon finds you very exciting."

He finished up in the kitchen and joined her in the living room, so close the intense urge to touch his chest made her fingers twitch.

"You're not like other women, you know."

She smiled wider. "No. I am not." She sipped her wine.

"So, where do we start? How do you kill a vampire?"

"About that. I don't think you should worry about *killing* the vampires, Nick. I can protect you with an enchantment." She gestured toward the window. "We can put a magical barrier around this place, and I have a charm for you that will make you practically invisible to them." She dug in her purse for the sachet Harriet had made for her. When she held up the talisman, he shook his head and frowned.

"Can I ask you something personal? It might seem like a rude question, but it's something I need to know." He swirled the wine in his glass, watching the resulting whirlpool without seeming to see it at all.

"Hmm. You can ask it. If it's truly rude, I may not answer."

"How old are you?"

"Older than you."

"By how much?"

"How old are you?"

"Thirty-eight."

"Approximately 462 years, give or take the gap in time between our dimensions."

He stumbled backward. "Four hundred..."

"I was born about five hundred years ago. Came here to what is now the United States around three hundred years ago. To this realm a few years before that."

"H-how long do you... do dragons live?"

"As long as we can," she said through a smile. "We're immortal. We will live forever unless we are killed. But we *can* be killed." She looked down at her hands. "You asked me once why I saw blood in Able McKenzie's paintings."

"I remember asking. You never answered me."

"My eldest brother, Marius, was murdered in front of me. Decapitated."

"Oh, Rowan..." His brow furrowed. "I'm sorry."

"He was heir to the throne of Paragon. My uncle killed him and usurped the throne for himself before we escaped to Earth," she said. "It was hundreds of years ago, but something like that never leaves you. Although there comes a time when you have to move on from it. Most often, I can hold the memory at a distance. Horrible events are more tolerable at a distance, don't you think?"

His eyes widened. He gulped his wine until the glass was empty, then walked back into the kitchen to pour himself another. A muscle worked in his jaw. Rosco seemed to pick up on his anxiety and followed him, whining softly.

"Something I've said has upset you." She took a step toward him but stopped when she saw his fingers were trembling on his glass. "Does it bother you, that I'm not human?" Maybe he'd changed his mind and the truth was too much for him after all.

"No." He stared into his wine.

"Then it disgusts you that I'm older than you?" She set down her glass and glanced toward her shoes. She could have them on and be out the door in seconds if he rejected her.

"No," he said firmly. He braced himself on the counter and shot her a grave look.

"Then is it because I'm immortal?"

"No."

She stopped short. "Then what is it? Once I told you about my brother, I felt you change. It's like all the warmth left the room. Or can't you admit it bothers you that I'm not human?"

He snorted, then started to laugh darkly in a way that made his big body shake. "Why should it bother me?"

She couldn't tell if he was being sarcastic or trying to make light of the situation, but the longer he laughed, the more her chest ached. She wondered again if she should leave. But then his gray eyes locked onto hers and darkened as if a storm was brewing behind them.

"Human isn't all it's cracked up to be, Rowan." He frowned, his gaze dropping to her chin. "How could it bother me that you're not human when so much about the human race is nothing short of toxic?" He bit out the word as if it stung his mouth.

"I don't understand."

"I've had to do things to survive." He licked his lips. "There's something I need to tell you. I remembered something recently, something that has to do with you."

She cringed. He must have remembered the night she stole the Raindrop of Heaven. Rowan reached for her glass of wine but kept one eye on the door. "You have my full and undivided attention."

CHAPTER TWENTY

Nick didn't like talking about his past. It wasn't the kind of story you could tell among mixed company. Not a nice story. Not something you shared over Waldorf salad at the beach house.

But he liked Rowan. He didn't care that she was a dragon. Maybe that's what he needed, someone with a dark secret as deep and shadowed as his. She definitely wasn't like other women. Everything about her was durable and down to earth, from the way she handled herself with the vampires and with Verinetti to the way she buried her face in Rosco's fur. She was no delicate flower. Beautiful, yes, but in the way of an iron butterfly. If he told her who he really was, would she run for the hills? Or could she handle that he'd come up from the sewer and still carried the stink of it on his soul?

Last night she'd shown him her wings. Tonight he would show her his horns. Let the halos fall where they may.

"My mother left when I was five," he began. "Left me with Stan. I'm not sure if Stan was my father, only that he was living with my mother when she left. I never called him dad, just Stan. What happened to me as a child wasn't the fault of my parents. I didn't have parents. I had Stan."

Rowan traced her finger along the lip of her glass, but otherwise made no indication that his story was disturbing to her. Good. This was about to get much worse, and he wasn't sure he could continue if she looked visibly upset.

"Stan didn't like me, and he certainly didn't like having to care for a child. He was too busy working in a chop shop to worry much about my welfare anyway. His associates would bring in a stolen car, he'd strip it, destroy anything with the VIN, and sell the parts to another buddy of his who would put the pieces on the black market. It was a stressful job because these friends he had, they were the type that might kill you if you fucked up or maybe just because they thought you were dicking around on the clock. Their leader was a guy named Trojan. Big Russian-looking dude. Seemed like he was seven feet tall, but maybe he was six five. Square jaw. Small eyes. The sort of cold eyes that make a guy look dead inside."

He swallowed hard, and Rowan nodded encouragingly for him to continue. "Anyway, Stan would come to the place where we lived. I hesitate to call it home. I don't think it was a home. It was a closet with a toilet and a hot plate, and Trojan owned it. It was one of the ways he controlled his workers. Own where your workers live and you own more than their livelihood. You own their life. Stan would come to the place where we lived at the end of his workday, and the first thing he'd do was take off his belt. Then he'd take out all that stress of working for Trojan on me."

"He beat you... regularly?" Her voice cracked, and disgust peered out of that impassive mask she'd had on. Good. Now he was getting somewhere.

Nick started unbuttoning his shirt. "You never saw. You kept my shirt on last night."

"I had no reason to take it off."

He removed the shirt, and he had to hand it to her for not doing what most people did. She didn't gasp. But there was pity in her eyes and the disgust he'd seen before, stronger now. He hated that look. God, it pissed him off. It was a natural reaction and he didn't blame her for having it, but he hated it. He didn't want pity.

She set down her tumbler and examined his scars. Six on his chest. Two on his right side. Five on his back.

"These are all from his belt?" Her voice cracked.

He pointed to his left shoulder. "This one was a burn. Boiling coffee." He pointed at his chipped tooth. "This? Happened at the same time. Hit in the face with a coffeepot when I was seven. The scar on my lip is from the glass. For some reason, my face didn't burn but my shoulder did. Must have been how the glass broke and the coffee fell."

"By the Mountain."

"This one on my abs, that's from a knife."

She shook her head. "It's so wrong. How can anyone do that to a child?"

The thing about Rowan, she ran a community center. He knew she'd encountered child abuse before. Maybe this was the first time she'd seen an abused child grown up though.

"There's always a reason an adult beats a kid, you know?" Nick said. "The place wasn't clean enough or I'd made too much noise. Like when I got sick and couldn't stop coughing, but instead of taking me to the doctor, he flicked a lit cigarette at my face and told me if I didn't stop he'd make me stop. I spent the rest of the night coughing into my pillow."

Rowan's face changed, morphing from pity to anger. Fire flashed behind her amber eyes. Good. He'd get it all out. If she couldn't take it, he hoped she'd leave now, before he got any closer to her.

"Anyway, I was used to going to school so beaten that the back of my clothes would stick to my healing skin. Every time I'd go to the bathroom, I'd have to peel my pants away from the dried blood and it would rip the scabs and hurt like hell. The nurse knew. The teachers knew. I'm not sure why they didn't do anything. No one cared enough, I guess. But when I was thirteen, I got really sick. Walking pneumonia. I went to school anyway. I never missed school. School was far better than home and the only place I could get a good meal. And that day we had a substitute school nurse. She took one look at me and sent me to the hospital. When they x-rayed my lungs, they saw signs of old injuries, poorly healed bones, cracked ribs. They saw the burns on my shoulder and the scars from Stan's belt on my back."

He paused. She'd moved closer and rested her hand on the scar that ran from his ribs to halfway to his navel. Her full attention was focused on him. That touch shook him to his core. It wasn't what he'd expected. He'd expected her to back away.

"Go on."

"The hospital called DCFS, and I went into a foster home. A couple whose last name was Grandstaff, Judy and Doug, took me in and eventually adopted me. Changed my life. It was great. For the first time I had enough to eat and a safe place to sleep and therapy. Years of therapy that helped the nightmares, the rage." He swallowed hard. "Judy was a great cook. The gentlest, most patient mother. And all those calories she fed me were like rocket fuel. I grew big and I grew up. But the past has a way of refusing to die. I wanted to forget. I wanted to deny I'd ever been Stan's punching bag."

"That's not how it works." Rowan's eyes held ghosts of their own, and he supposed that had to do with her brother's murder. "The only way to master our past is to confront it. When we bury it, the bodies rise."

"Yeah, my buried bodies rose in the form of Trojan. Stan disappeared and his boss found me. You might ask yourself, what did the mob want with a kid like me? I was eighteen when they pulled me off the sidewalk in front of my high school and told me that Stan had been keeping two sets of books. He'd screwed them out of thousands. Trojan figured I was Stan's closest relative and must know something about where they could find Stan and their money. I didn't. They decided I would earn the money back by doing a job for them. I needed to steal a car. A very expensive car."

Rowan shifted. He'd suspected something about her since last night in her apartment, but it wasn't until now, now that he knew she was immortal, that he put it all together.

"I need to tell you something, Rowan. I think we've met before."

CHAPTER TWENTY-ONE

Manhattan, 1998

Rich people lived in a bubble. Nick could always tell the ultrarich because they assumed the world would revolve around them and if it didn't, they could buy themselves out of any mess they wound up in as a result. Take the Aston Martin convertible parked in the alley behind Arnold's grocery. No one parked a car like that in this neighborhood and expected it to still be there an hour later. But what would be devastating for most people was a minor inconvenience for the rich. Whoever owned this thing was asking for it.

If Nick had owned a car, any car, he'd take care of it. That thing would be locked down like Fort Knox. But then, anything Nick had ever owned had been hard-won. He'd once fought another boy over a pair of shoes, taken a hit to the jaw on purpose at exactly the right time to get that boy thrown out of the community center they were in. The pain was worth it to ensure he was wearing those shoes when he left the building. He'd worn them until the toes split.

Whoever had left the car in its current state didn't need it, and that was permission enough for him to use it to save his life. Stan was missing. Fuck if he knew where the asshole had gone, but he'd taken Trojan's money with him. And now Nick had to pay Stan's debt or risk the consequences. He could stand the pain of being tortured himself. He'd been beaten and worse by Stan for most of his life, but he couldn't handle anything happening to Doug or Judy. The Grandstaffs were the kindest, most patient people he'd ever met, and he'd do anything to keep them safe, even hotwire a car and take it to the chop shop in the Bronx where Stan used to work before he'd fallen off the planet.

He hopped behind the wheel and inserted his screwdriver into the ignition. No dice. He pried the plastic cover off the steering column. Everything had to be done quickly, quietly, attracting as little notice as possible. Nick dug out the bundle of wires and sorted out the ones for the battery and the ignition.

"You should be wearing gloves when you do that. You could get the shock of your life," said a voice on his left.

He turned his head and saw a woman standing beside the car. The first thing he noticed was how he could see her thighs. She stood on the sidewalk, wearing a peacock-blue slip dress trimmed with black lace. The kind that was so popular now. No one wore it like this woman did though. His breath caught. Her long black hair cascaded straight to her shoulders, and her round, wire-rimmed glasses shone blue beneath her thick bangs. In her arms was an old leather book. *She had to be* a celebrity or a supermodel. Maybe some billionaire's trophy wife.

"This isn't what it looks like," he said. "I lost my key."

He saw one bushy brow arch above the mirrored lenses. "This is your car?"

"Yeah."

She reached into her bag and pulled out her key fob. The doors unlocked with an electronic chirp. "Funny, I thought it was mine."

He closed his eyes and rested his forehead on the steering wheel. *Busted.* "I'm sorry," he said sincerely. "I don't have a choice." He mumbled the last, sure that she was probably already dialing the cops on her flip phone. He was doomed. Done for. At least he'd be safe from Trojan in prison, if the guy didn't have someone on the inside who'd land a shiv in his gut at the first turn of the guards' heads.

"Hey. Hey...," the woman said softly.

He lifted his head off the steering wheel and looked at her.

"You know, whoever's making you do this, it won't be the last time. These people... they have a way of getting their hooks into you. People like this, they don't let go."

Nick rubbed his palms on his jeans. "You believe me?"

"Yeah. You look scared. Can you tell me who put you up to this?"

He shook his head. It was too dangerous. The last thing he needed was Trojan threatening *her* over this. She was too kind. Too beautiful.

And a great liar. A member of NYPD's finest walked up beside her, his chest straining his blue uniform. So she had called the cops after all. Nick held perfectly still and waited to be arrested.

"Good afternoon," the woman said, her head tilting flirtatiously to the side as her full lips spread into a sumptuous smile.

The cop glanced at Nick and at the small kit of tools he'd left on the passenger seat. "Everything okay here?"

The woman's voice made Nick think she was an angel. She had to be supernatural the way her laugh tinkled like wind chimes and her words dripped like honey off her lips. She drew the cop in.

"Everything's fine, Officer. My nephew's just helping me get the car started." She gently rested her hand on his arm.

Nick's eyes widened at the ruby-red stone shining from the ring on her finger. She had to be the wealthiest person he'd ever met. He'd bet that book in her arms was an antique, probably worth a fortune. *Frankenstein.* It looked like a first edition, the leather having formed a warm, amber patina on the spine where fingers had pulled it from the shelf over decades of use.

"Okay. Okay. Have a nice day." The cop continued on his way.

"Thank you," Nick said.

The woman rested her forearms on the driver's side window and lowered her head so that she was eye to eye with him, those mirrored shades giving him a good look at himself. He needed a haircut and a shave and a new T-shirt.

"Listen to me very carefully."

He gave her his full attention.

"If you are smart enough to steal this car, you are smart enough to figure out how *not* to steal it. You've underestimated yourself. You're better than this."

God, her voice was silky smooth. And her lips. That dress. He was staring at her, and he couldn't look away. "Okay," he mumbled.

"Now get the fuck out of my car and go figure out something else to do with your life." Her smile was gone.

Nick hastily collected his tools and exited the vehicle, holding the door open while she climbed in. She tucked the wires back into her steering column and replaced the plastic panel. A turn of her key and the Aston Martin roared to life. With one last crooked smile over her shoulder, she shifted into drive.

"Don't disappoint me. I hate it when I'm wrong."

CHAPTER TWENTY-TWO

Rowan couldn't believe her ears. Her initial relief at Nick not remembering what she'd thought was their first meeting in the Stevensons' beach house gave way to complete wonder that it hadn't been their first meeting at all. Nick had been the teen who'd tried to filch her car. She remembered how hopeless he'd seemed back then. The scars on his lip and shoulder when she'd caught him red-handed had told her everything she needed to know.

"I remember," she said, eyes narrowing. She removed her hand from his stomach to take him in. "I remember you."

"Last night at your apartment, I was in your library. I recognized a book on your shelf. It's distinctive. A first edition. Leather-bound. It was the book you were holding when I tried to steal your car. *Frankenstein.*"

"I'd just bought it from a pawnshop. I couldn't believe my luck."

"Last night I thought it was a coincidence. I thought the book had made its way to you. It couldn't have been you, after all. That was twenty years ago, and you looked different."

"I change my appearance from time to time. The younger I make a new identity, the longer I can use it."

Nick nodded nervously. "When you told me tonight that you're immortal, the reaction you saw in me was my realizing it *was* you. You saved me that day, Rowan. You changed the direction of my life forever."

She shook her head and scoffed. "I didn't save you. I just gave you a second chance. It was only a car. I could tell you were desperate."

"I applied to college that day to major in criminal justice. That was meant to be my way out. If I could become a cop, I could keep people like Trojan from ever controlling me again. All that time hiding from Stan at school paid off. My grades were good. They let me in. And I worked hard."

"Are you saying you went to college because I didn't have you arrested? I can't take credit for that." Something more was bothering her. "How did you deal with Trojan? I'm sure he didn't give up just because you were admitted to college."

"Trojan came after me, as I expected he would. I kept thinking about what you said to me, that if I was strong and smart enough to steal, I was strong and smart enough to figure out how to get myself out of the situation I was in. I returned to that hole-in-the-wall where Stan and I had lived. It was the same as when I left. Roaches almost as big as the rats. Cigarette butts everywhere. The smell—oh God, the smell. I was hoping to find the money or some clue to where Stan might be. What I found was Trojan waiting for me."

"What did you do?"

"I ran. I was a fast son of a bitch, and I knew all the hiding places around our building, places where I'd hidden from Stan when I was younger. I didn't use the stairwell but instead went out the window at the end of the hall and down the fire escape. Then I jumped the railing into the neighboring parking garage and hid between the cars. Trojan came for me. He caught up faster than I ever expected, almost like he knew where I was going." He shook his head. "I remember crouching between two cars, the concrete stained with oil and grime under my feet. I could hear Trojan's footsteps approaching. He was moving slowly, calling my name, taunting me as if he knew where I was and was just toying with me."

"You must have been terrified."

"I was, and I think that's what he was going for. He flushed me out. I ran to the stairwell and then up to the top of the garage. My thighs were burning and my heart beat so hard in my chest that it hurt. Trojan kept coming. He knew there was nowhere for me to go. I made it to the far side of the garage on the top level, twelfth floor, and I stopped running. Unless I was willing to jump, I had no choice but to stand my ground, and I wasn't suicidal. Despite everything, I wanted to live. I turned and faced him."

The image of the boy he once was cowering in fear from that brute called Trojan turned Rowan's stomach. Her jaw clenched. Had she known, she would have followed Nick and torn Trojan apart.

"How did you get away?"

"My foster dad taught jujitsu. That was his job; he was a martial arts instructor. There was this thing he taught me, that when you face an opponent who is larger and stronger than you, use what he isn't against him. I was tall, skinny, and fast, nowhere near the size I am now. This was before the academy, when I was still catching up from years of neglect. But I had moves. Trojan reached for me. I ducked, put my head and one shoulder between his legs, and popped up. I pushed with everything I had, legs arms... everything. I still don't know how I did it. Adrenaline I guess. I flipped him over the railing."

Rowan inhaled sharply. "He fell from the top of the garage?"

Nick nodded. "I took off before the cops came. For whatever reason, Trojan's men never bothered me again. Maybe they didn't know who I was. Maybe they couldn't find me once I went away to college. Maybe I just wasn't worth it."

Rowan studied him, angry for the abuse he'd suffered as a child but in awe of his perseverance and quick thinking. At that moment, Rowan saw Nick for the first time. Oh, he was human. He'd bleed red if she cut him, and he had a four-chambered heart instead of one made of stone like her own. He couldn't change into anything, and he would grow old and die as all humans did, but he was a survivor and much tougher than he looked. When he'd fought off those vampires at Wicked Divine, he'd shown her who he was.

He truly was a warrior, and any woman would be proud to be his.

"You think differently of me because I killed him." Nick picked at one of his nails.

She started in surprise. "Not at all. You survived. I'm... I'm admiring you."

His eyes lifted to hers and locked. "I don't talk about this often, Rowan. Never. But I told you before that if you knew about my childhood, you would believe me when I say I can protect myself. That I *need* to be able to protect myself." He cast daggers toward her purse and probably at the talisman inside. "I wanted you to know who I am because it's important to me that you see me, really see me, you know. The same way I see you, wings and all. If my past isn't something you can accept..." He didn't finish his sentence because his voice cracked.

"You have a past," she said, moving closer until she could feel the heat from his body through the front of her dress. "All the most interesting people do. We should get along just fine."

He released a relieved breath. "I think plenty of interesting people don't have the little childhood of horrors I had." He exhaled slowly, his palms coming to rest on her shoulders and sliding down her arms to her wrists. "But if it's the key to making you look at me like that, maybe I should have mentioned it sooner."

The fact that he still had a sense of humor after everything he'd been through and had revisited tonight was her undoing. Her dragon roused, and Rowan closed the tiny gap between their bodies, nothing but the thin material of her dress barring skin from skin. He did not disappoint. The long, lean muscles of his arms wrapped around her, his large hands burrowing into her hair. She loved the feeling of being in his arms. He made her feel wanted, adored. Her chest rose and fell quickly, her head tilting back as she circled his neck with her arms. One of his hands pressed into the curve of her back, his touch igniting an electrical storm within her.

"You don't need to tell me stories about your past to win my heart," she said, so close her lips brushed his.

"No? What's the trick then? Knock down three bottles with a single ball? Ring the bottle? Shoot ducks?" His voice was a gritty whisper.

"You can have it for a kiss."

The corner of his mouth twitched. "Lucky me." He brushed his lips against hers.

"Wait."

He stopped, backing off a hair's breadth from her lips.

"Does Rosco need to go out?"

"No. I walked him before you arrived."

"Is the door locked?"

"Yeah... when you came in. Why?"

She looked at him through her lashes. "The last two times I've been in your arms, we've been interrupted."

He laughed, his eyes dancing in the soft light.

"If you kiss me now, I don't want you to stop."

"Deal." His mouth met hers.

Rowan had never been kissed the way Nick kissed her then. Not by a dragon, or a shape-shifter, or another human. His kiss was a free fall, a stomach-dropping descent into madness. A swirling, spinning, star-filled fantasy with fireflies and pounding hearts and heat that threatened to burn her dragon skin.

Nick flipped all of Rowan's switches. He was strong but kind, handsome but genuine, unspoiled and unpretentious. He was everything she'd been denied when she was princess of Paragon. There, she'd been viewed as little more than a designer brood mare. She was courted by every stuffed shirt, power-craving social climber in Paragon, all with their perfectly tailored clothes and perfectly manicured hands. All they'd ever cared about was winning her hand and the power and privilege that came with it. None had cared to win her heart.

Nick was different in all the right ways. He might be human, but his draw for her was anything but. Dragons couldn't combust, but he was a man whose mere presence threatened to consume her. He was her own personal accelerant. She couldn't get enough.

Burn, baby, burn.

Rising on her tiptoes, she licked along the seam of his mouth. He opened for her, lips parting and tongue stroking inside. Deeper. He kissed her like he was claiming her, his big body seeming to completely envelop her. His hand fisted the back of her hair.

Her inner dragon roused and stretched. *Mine.* One hot palm trailed down her back and landed on her ass. He tasted of wine, a hint of mint, and warm, healthy male. And his smell. Oh goddess, his smell was a heady perfume that filled her lungs. It wasn't until he pulled back from her that she realized her wings had extended while they were kissing and had partially wrapped around them.

"Sorry," she said, tucking them behind her.

"I like them," he said quickly. "And I like the sound you make."

"What sound?"

"Like a purr. Like the sexiest fucking purr I've ever heard in my life."

Her face burned. Her mating trill. Her dragon had never bothered to trill with the other men she'd dated. When she'd dated Verinetti, her inner beast rarely even woke up. "It's a, um, dragon thing." She tucked her hair behind her ear and lowered her voice. "I can't control it."

He brushed his lips from her jaw to her ear. "I love it. Let's try to make it happen again."

His mouth trailed down her throat, and then his hands were on her ass, lifting, spreading. She wrapped her legs around his hips.

"I want you, Rowan." He stroked along the place her wing met her back as he held her to him. His touch sent fine tremors through her that seemed to end at the peak of each breast. "It's been a long time for me."

"Me too. But I won't hurt you."

He chuckled. "I think I'm supposed to say that to you."

"I didn't know there was a script," she said into a sliver of space she made between their mouths. With one beat of her wings, she lifted his feet off the floor and moved him into the bedroom.

His eyes widened. "Definitely ad lib," he mumbled breathlessly.

Rosco jumped up from his dog bed, startled by the strange movement.

"Go lie down, Rosco." Nick kicked the door closed behind them.

His scent was even stronger in this room, the navy-blue comforter on his full-size bed seeming to be the source. She desperately wanted more, wanted it all over her.

He backed her toward the bed, and his lips found hers again. Deeper. Hotter. The long, hard length of him pressed into her belly and she ground against him, enjoying the moan she elicited. Drawing back, he grabbed hold of the bottom of her dress and pulled it over her head. Large rough hands stroked along the rose-colored lace that ran from a band around her waist to her breasts. It was backless, all the support coming from the stiff material that ran up and under her breasts at the front of the garment. His thumbs stroked across her hardened nipples.

"This is fucking hot," he said, tips of his fingers playing over the delicate material.

"One of my oread's most ingenious designs. Doesn't get in the way of my wings."

"What's an oread?"

She laughed. "Like a, um, servant, but not human. She's a type of mountain nymph."

His chin lowered. "In that case, let me take a closer look."

His lips trailed down her neck as his hands slid along her sides to the band of the bra. She felt his fingers work at the base of her back, unfastening the clasp. Her nipples hardened at the feel of the cool air when he finally tossed it aside, and then came the slick heat of his tongue flicking against one rosy peak.

Her trill came again, but this time the instincts of her inner dragon exponentially increased her need. Her fingernails scraped along the back of his shoulders. She felt his muscles shift under her fingers and his mouth move to her other breast, drawing her nipple out and sending fire licking the underside of her skin, straight to her core. Every cell in her body was flooded with the desire to mate. He was human. He was vulnerable. She should be wary of any permanent connection that might form between them. But she *needed* to make him hers. It was a deep, carnal need that sent her hands coasting down his abs to his waistband, her nails grazing through the trail of hair that led to... Yes, there he was, heavy and warm in her hand.

"Damn, baby. Take it slow." He nibbled on her bottom lip.

Slow was not what she had in mind. Trailing kisses along his collarbone, she guided his hand to her sex, placing his fingers right where she needed them.

He cursed. "Fast then."

With a thrust of his body, he spun her around and pushed her facedown on the bed. Her panties were off in her next breath. And then he had her by the hips, lifting her onto her knees. His fingers found her core again, but it was his other hand, stroking the underside of her wing, that made her pant in earnest. By the Mountain, she might combust.

"Yeah, like this. You love it when I touch these." His hand stroked along her wing again, and all her limbs trembled. A moan escaped her lips.

She felt him press against her, flesh to flesh.

"Do you want this, Rowan?"

"Yes," she begged, breathless with need.

The sound of tearing paper made her glance back to watch him roll on a condom. He slid into her then, slowly, working himself in and out until he completely filled her from behind. Her body pulsed around him, adjusting to his size, his girth. Deep inside her, he paused to lean over her back, his hands stroking out along her wings.

"What do you like?" He pulled back slowly, then thrust in, hard and fast.

She released a soft mew. He massaged the base of her wing, then reached under and around her waist, up between her breasts, and plucked at one of her nipples with his fingers.

He thrust into her again and again. She could feel the sweet tension build within her, her inner dragon rolling, coming alive. And then he lowered himself across her back and licked along the most sensitive part of her wing.

An orgasm rang through her like a bell.

"Oh yeah, baby. I like that," he whispered into her ear in a deep voice that seemed to stroke her from the inside. "Let's see if we can do it again."

He gripped the edge of her wings with both hands and started to move again. The gentleness he'd exhibited before was gone. He thrust into her hard and fast, finding a rhythm with his body that left her breathless. The pleasure she'd felt before was a shadow of what was building in her now. It flowed from all directions and collided at the apex of her thighs in a supernova of heat and pleasure that made her cry out. Rowan found herself completely lost to it. She rode the aftershocks, her wings straightening, going rigid as one orgasm after another rocked her body.

And then his hands were in her hair and she felt him buck inside her. She reveled in his release. *Mine*, she thought. *Tell me. Tell me I am yours.*

But he said nothing.

They collapsed onto the bed, his arms gathering her against his chest.

"Nick, tell me what this means to you."

He buried his face in her hair. "That was... incredible." He kissed her gently on the temple.

She wanted more. She wanted him to claim her, to say he wanted her and her alone. But she didn't get a chance to broach the subject. Just then, a high-pitched beeping sound tore through the apartment and he pulled away from her.

"Smoke alarm," he grumbled. He bounded off the bed and out of the room.

The pyrotechnics stopped going off in her torso and she blinked rapidly, trying to regain her composure. On shaky legs, she climbed from the bed and pulled her dress over her head, then found him in the kitchen removing a smoking, crispy black chicken from the oven.

Flashing her a sheepish grin, he said, "Dinner's ready."

CHAPTER TWENTY-THREE

This was dangerous. Nick washed down bits of blackened chicken and couldn't stop himself from replaying the best sexual experience of his life in his head. Only moments ago, he'd had Rowan under him. It was all he could do not to throw down his fork and carry her back into his bedroom for round two. She might be willing. God knew the chicken wasn't keeping her at the table. Only, a familiar fear had crept into Nick's thinking, and it curled prickly and cold over his heart.

It would be easy to love Rowan. Too easy. If he were being honest with himself, he might already be halfway along that journey. And he wasn't worth loving. A person whose own mother left him was not a person capable of being loved long term. Committing to someone like Rowan —especially Rowan, who would live forever—was signing up to be left, to experience abandonment all over again. That particular terror ran deep. No, he needed to keep this relationship in the casual zone and not allow his brain to tempt him with this thing inside that wanted a ring on her finger.

"You don't have to eat that," he said to her. "It looks like I pulled it out of a volcanic pit in the earth. We should call it Mount Vesuvius chicken."

"It's not that bad," Rowan said lightly. "Once you scrape the black part off, it's delicious."

He ran a hand over his face. "Okay, so cooking isn't exactly in my wheelhouse, although usually I do better than this. At least you had the cold potatoes and broccoli to keep your charred meat company." He rolled his eyes at himself.

"We were distracted," she said softly. "I think it was totally worth it."

"Definitely." He smiled and looked away, the panicky feeling coming back with a vengeance.

"We have a dish like this in Paragon," she said. "Only we don't use chicken. They don't exist there."

"What do you make it with?"

"It's called krilpon. It's like your pig but with gills and webbed feet. It's traditionally thrown into a fire and eaten after it is completely charred like this. The meat is different though, more like the dark meat."

For a moment Nick tried to picture what she was describing but couldn't wrap his head around it. "Your world is so completely different from this one. It must have been a big adjustment for you to come here."

"It was." She stabbed a piece of broccoli with her fork. "In some ways it's better though. Life for me in Paragon was difficult. I never got along with my parents. If it weren't for my brother Alexander, I would have probably run away a long time before I was thrown out."

"Is that why you run Sunrise House? Because you had a rough childhood?"

She sipped her wine. "Not exactly." She balked, and he got the sense she was hiding something.

"You don't have to tell me. I know the feelings can be complex."

"My childhood was different from yours," she said softly. "I wasn't physically abused, but my parents had unreasonable expectations for my behavior and decorum, and my constant punishment was solitary confinement. My brothers were my only confidants and friends. I wasn't allowed girlfriends. I was rarely allowed beyond the palace walls. Alexander, he's my younger brother, he taught me to paint as an escape from the rigors of palace life. It was my only oasis from a constant desire to slit my own throat."

"Don't say that."

"I wasn't happy." She sighed. "Not at all. To me, my future was a tragedy. Art was my escape. And Tobias. He never failed to lend an ear when I needed one. My brother Gabriel was harder to get close to. He and Marius trained constantly. As the oldest, they were true warriors. A two-man army. Nathaniel, Xavier, Sylas, and Colin were kind enough to me but loved to try my parents. Practical jokers, the four of them. Known for causing trouble. I remember Xavier once made me a small cake for our birthday celebration, and when I bit into it, a live parlor mouse jumped out and hit me in the face."

"*Our* birthday. You and Xavier were born on the same day?"

She shrugged and laughed nervously. "The details of our birth may seem strange to you. All nine of us were born on the same day. Dragons lay eggs. The first male to hatch is considered the eldest and the heir to the throne. That was Marius. After that, succession goes by who hatches next. Gabriel, Tobias, Alexander, Nathaniel, Xavier, Silas and Colin. I, as the only girl, was destined to be queen even though I was born third."

Nick tensed. "What now? You said Marius was the heir to the throne. Wouldn't that make you a princess? Why would you be queen?" He bristled at the idea of her being forced to marry her brother.

"Dragon reproduction is often unsuccessful and females are very rare. In order to ensure there is an heir to the throne, the firstborn male and female rule side by side. Each take a consort outside the royal family. That doubles our likelihood of producing heirs. But because I was the blooded female, my young—we call them whelps—would be first heirs to the throne. That's why it was so important that I be mated. My future pregnancies were the preferred future of the bloodline."

"You talk about it as if they were breeding you? Did you even have a choice?"

"A choice among the highest bidders. I was only allowed to meet men of my station, the ones from wealthy households. When my uncle murdered Marius, my mother cast us all out of Paragon to protect us. That was around three hundred years ago. I came to this world with nothing but the clothes on my back, and to be honest, it was a relief."

"Three hundred years ago," Nick said incredulously.

"Yep—1698. The eight of us arrived in what is now Crete."

"And somehow you all made your way here, to New York."

She laughed. "No. Our mother warned us to split up lest our uncle find us and eliminate us like he'd done Marius. We traveled by boat to Italy, then split up at the port of Genoa. As our knowledge of this world grew, we all agreed it wasn't safe for us to remain in the same country. If we kept moving, we were safe. Even if my uncle found us, by the time he traveled here we would be long gone. But when we settled, we needed to be apart, to dilute our magic enough that he couldn't trace our whereabouts.

"Colin, Nathaniel, Xavier, and Silas hired a guide to take them north by land. I assume they are somewhere in Europe now, but we lost contact soon after. Gabriel, Tobias, Alexander, and I traveled along the coast of Europe for a time. We boarded a merchant ship from the Isle of Wight to the port of Philadelphia in the autumn of 1699. An indigenous guide helped us settle in this new world. I ended up in New York; Tobias, Chicago; and Gabriel, New Orleans. Alexander, well, he's in Sedona now."

Nick shook his head. "So you came here with seven brothers, and you never see them in person. Never hug them. Never share turkey and mashed potatoes and stories around the Christmas tree, ever?"

"I haven't seen my younger brothers or Gabriel in centuries. I met with Tobias once or twice when he was visiting the city at the turn of the century and in the 1970s. We were careful not to stay together long. And Alexander sends me his paintings to sell in the gallery."

"All this because you're afraid your uncle will find you if you are together?"

"Yes."

"Don't you think that after three hundred years, he has better things to do?"

She stared at her knotted fingers. "It's hard to explain how time changes us, Nick. My siblings and I have endured wars, the advancement of technology, new identities, the rise of cities, the fall of empires. We've endured this intimately but also at a distance, our hearts breaking from loss after loss while remaining immortal. We are like stones in a sea of human history. Time and distance have a way of becoming their own beast. Every year, our bond lessened.

Our ways of communicating ended. We lost touch with each other."

"Forgive me for saying so, Rowan, but that is the saddest story I've ever heard. Maybe sadder than having no family at all."

"Do you share turkey with Doug and Judy?"

He smiled. "As often as possible. They live in Arizona now. Both retired. I only get out there once or twice a year."

She sighed. "I wouldn't relive my childhood for anything, but it would be nice to have a real family. I run Sunrise House and am trying to save it because I know the feeling of having no control over your lot in life. I try my best to make things better for those kids."

He played with his fork. "That's an incredible story. Thank you for sharing it with me."

"I'd like to share more with you. I want to know everything about you."

He swallowed. This was getting to be too much, too intimate. All his old insecurities scurried to the surface. If he let her in, he'd be vulnerable. It would destroy him if she left him. She couldn't abandon something that never existed. Casual was safe. Intimacy was war. "First, I need you to teach me how to kill vampires."

The corner of her mouth lifted. "Vampire lessons. You're not going to let that go, are you?"

"No," he said. "I need to be able to protect myself."

She licked her bottom lip. "The first thing you should know about vampires is that ordinary bullets won't do a thing against them. That gun of yours is useless under most circumstances. You can't stab them to death either, and they can't die of hanging or drowning. They don't even need to breathe."

He folded his arms across his chest and leaned back in his chair, studying her.

"Crosses don't work either," she said.

"What does work?"

"Sunlight, always. That folklore is true."

He thanked God. At least he'd given Regine good advice. "Safe during the day. That's good."

"Safe from vampires, but they can compel humans to do their will."

"I can handle humans."

She played with the corner of her napkin, twisting it around her finger. "Silver works, but it's not like in the movies. If you hold something silver against a vampire's skin, it won't do much damage. But if you can trick a vampire into drinking silver or shoot them with silver bullets, it will weaken them. The silver has to be in the bloodstream to do its job. You can sometimes kill a vampire with a silver or wooden bullet directly to the heart or brain. It slows their ability to heal and can kill them if you do enough damage and the vamp is unable to remove it."

He nodded. "Silver and wood, but they aren't reliable. Got it."

She chewed her lip. "There are only two foolproof ways I know of to kill a vampire that don't involve tossing them into the sun: cut out their heart or decapitate them. That goes for all supernaturals. In general, nothing can live without a head or a heart. Even dragons." She rubbed her palms in circles against each other. "Oh, it's also possible to burn vampires to death. That's my preferred choice as a dragon. Everything burns if the fire is hot enough. Everything other than us."

"You're completely fireproof?"

She turned and placed her hand in the candle's flame. It

didn't seem to bother her at all. The hair on the back of her hand didn't singe. There was no smell, no blistering or blackening of her skin. "Which brings me to the most important thing about vampires."

"What's that?"

"You may get lucky and kill one, but they live in covens and will swarm you like ants. Vampires are killing machines, lethal predators. If they come for you, you should run."

"I understand what you're saying, but—"

"I'm glad you understand." A fierce determination narrowed her eyes. "Now, I hope you'll let me do what I need to do." She rose and moved to the window, her ruby ring glowing like a star. He could feel the air spark. The entire place was instantly charged with static electricity. Rowan raised her ring and drew an *X* through the air in front of his window.

Nick got to his feet. "What the hell do you think you're doing?"

CHAPTER TWENTY-FOUR

Rowan swallowed against a rising ache in her chest. What Nick had said was true. Her story was sad, and sometimes she missed her brothers so much she couldn't sleep at night. But it had been a long time since she'd let that sadness in, and part of her resented that Nick had raised those feelings inside her. She channeled that confusing emotional energy into her ring and began muttering her protection spell.

"What the hell are you doing?" Nick asked again.

Rosco had risen from his bed and was hugging Nick's side, panting nervously as the smell of magic filled the room.

"I'm warding your apartment against vampires and others who would seek to do you harm. If Rosco is sensitive, take him outside. I'll be done in thirty minutes." Her ring pulsed with red light.

"Wasn't the point of me learning about vampires so that I could protect myself?" he asked defensively.

She didn't turn her head. "Were you listening to what I said? Your chances of surviving an attack by a vampire are next to nothing. More than one vampire and you're doomed!"

"In your opinion," he said sharply. "Were you listening to *me*? I can take care of myself, Rowan."

"Like I said before, you got lucky. I *need* to do this, Nick. Dragons protect what is theirs. It's in our blood." She drew the symbols in the air and whispered the incantation. Rosco growled.

"I *need* you to stop."

She sensed anger in his voice. She ignored it. "No."

"No?"

"You can try to stop me." She flashed him her most dangerous smile. "We'll see what happens."

He didn't try to stop her, which was good because she would have hated to have to use brute force against him. The spell she was laying down was the same one that protected her treasure room under the gallery. It protected against all supernatural threats. Humans could walk right through it, which was why she would remind him to continue to lock his doors and why her treasure room was inside a vault.

Nick was *hers*, and she would keep him safe. Only he wasn't, was he? He'd never claimed her, not officially. It ate at her, that lack of ownership. She'd felt the bond, but he seemed indifferent to it.

Her mind wandered to Nick's story about his past. Thinking about the abuse he suffered turned her stomach. The thought of anyone treating a child like he'd been treated struck rage into her heart, and she desperately wanted revenge on the evil prick who'd done that to him. But Stan was long gone—probably dead. That demon, for all intents and purposes, had already been slain.

She muttered her spell over and over as she walked the

boundary of his apartment. She should have followed him back then, kept him safe. Now she'd make up for it. She vowed to protect Nick, whether he wanted her to or not.

The ache started in her chest again. She wanted him to be hers. As they'd made love, a bond had formed between them, one she hadn't entirely expected. Her dragon had chosen Nick as her mate. Only, she'd been foolish. Nick clearly did not share her feelings of attachment. If he'd felt the bond, he'd denied it. The physical draw she felt for him was belied by the emotional push he was giving her now. Everything was too confusing. All she had to hold on to was her ability to keep him safe.

"It's done." She turned to him.

Nick's expression was impassive, and he didn't thank her. "I enjoyed myself tonight, Rowan. You didn't have to do this out of guilt or whatever. You don't owe me anything. What happened between us, it doesn't have to mean anything. Maybe it's better if it doesn't."

His words were like a dagger straight to her heart. She physically recoiled from them.

"I mean, you must think I'm damned weak and helpless to feel you have to use magic to protect me."

"I don't think you're weak at all. For a human, you are a remarkable warrior."

"For a human?" He stood up, his face red.

"You *are* human. Supernaturals are faster and stronger. It's not like you can make yourself invisible! You're not a ghost."

Nick grabbed his head as if it hurt and moaned. His eyes squeezed shut and he leaned forward, resting his elbows on his knees.

"Nick? Are you all right?"

Through narrowed eyes, he looked at her. "You become

invisible," he murmured softly as if every word hurt. "Invisible like a ghost."

Her stomach twisted, and bile burned in her throat. "Nick?"

His palms pressed against his temples as if he were trying to keep his head from splitting open. "You're. A. Ghost."

THE MEMORY CAME BACK TO NICK IN A RUSH. "I'M A ghost," she'd said before she'd disappeared, and then an invisible force had wrapped around him, forced his mouth open, and poured a bitter liquid down his throat. His next waking moment, he'd been standing in the Stevensons' kitchen.

"You... You stole the Raindrop of Heaven from Camilla Stevenson's closet. You rumpled the bed when you threw her shoes down on it. Then you used magic to make me forget." He felt like he was going to be sick.

She spread her upturned palms beseechingly. "I'm sorry I had to wipe your memories, but you weren't supposed to be in that room that night. Every other night the guards stay in the guardhouse unless the alarm goes off. How was I to know you'd do rounds?"

"Are you suggesting you had no choice but to drug me?"

"I didn't drug you. Harriet's potions are all-natural and totally safe."

"What about the part where you stole millions of dollars of jewels?"

"You weren't supposed to see me!"

"You weren't supposed to be there."

"Gerald Stevenson had it coming. He bought the land

under my building for the vampires! Those kids are going to be out on the street if I can't find an alternate arrangement. Worse, what do you think the NAVAK vampires will eat when they move in? Huh? Those children's lives are in danger."

Nick dug his fingers into his hair. "Do you even realize that I could be blamed for the theft?"

Rowan frowned, her lips thinning. "What are you talking about?"

"Camilla knows the jewels are gone, and I was the last one in that closet. My partner, Soren, spoke with Gerald at Wicked Divine. He said Gerald is considering pressing charges against *me*. I thought the thief was a member of their cleaning crew or regular security detail. To think it was you all along."

"No," Rowan said. "That's not possible."

He shook his head. "Of course it is. Because you took the jewels!"

"But I replaced them," Rowan said, "with replicas enchanted to look like the real thing. Unless they had a gemologist assess them, there is no way they would assume they weren't."

Nick closed his eyes. "I remember. I checked. I saw them there." He shook his head. "Obviously you fooled no one... No one but me."

Rowan swallowed. "So I'll return them. I'll sneak in and replace them."

A low grunt came up his throat. "Are you kidding me? As soon as I'm accused, the jewels mysteriously appear again? No."

"I just don't understand how they know for sure the jewels are missing and you took them. It doesn't make any sense."

He shook his head. "I think you should leave."

"Nick, you don't mean that."

"I hate lies, and this is the third time you've lied to me. You lied to me at Sunrise House when I asked you about NAVAK. You lied to me in the car about Wicked Divine, and now I find out you wiped my memory."

"I had to. I didn't have a choice."

"We always have choices." He stilled, his hands balling into fists. "Ironically, you taught me that." He shook his head slowly. "I. Can't. *Trust.* You. You need to leave."

Without another word, she grabbed her purse and her shoes. She paused in the open door.

"How many people have you told about your past? That's a lie of omission, Nick. You hide things about yourself because it's not safe to share them." Her amber eyes drilled into him. "Now imagine you had a secret like mine."

She slipped into the hall and closed the door behind her, seeming to take all the air in the room with her. Nick stared at the closed door, rubbing Rosco's head as the dog whimpered softly beside him.

CHAPTER TWENTY-FIVE

New Orleans, Louisiana

"I can't believe Gabriel didn't stay for your birthday party!" Avery said.

The music and the din of partygoers had filled the Three Sisters with life. Raven smiled over her virgin mango mojito and tried to think of something to tell Avery that wasn't a complete lie. Gabriel and Tobias had flown to Sedona to search for Alexander, leaving her behind to meet her familial obligations. Neither Gabriel nor Raven liked the idea of being apart, but Gabriel needed to find his siblings before someone else did, someone like a vampire or another Paragonian guard who wanted him dead. This was the best lead they'd had in weeks.

"Family business," she offered with a shrug. "But he gave me this. We had our own celebration before he had to leave." Raven held out her wrist and showed Avery the bracelet of brilliant-cut diamonds Gabriel had fastened around her wrist.

Avery studied the bracelet, pulling Raven's wrist closer to her face. "Well then..." Her eyebrows slid toward her hairline. She released Raven's wrist and swigged her beer.

The Three Sisters was packed with family and friends. Her mother had gone all out and catered the event herself, complete with a devil's food cake with creamy white frosting. She thought every single person she knew was there, aside from Gabriel and Tobias. But the door opened and in walked the one person she hadn't expected to see.

"Avery?"

Her sister glanced toward the door and grimaced at the sight of their father heading for the bar. "Don't look at me. I didn't invite him. I swear, Raven, I didn't."

Raven slid deeper into their booth and lowered her head. No doubt he was looking for her, but it was dark in this corner of the bar. If she played her cards right, he'd leave without ever talking to her. She was suddenly glad Gabriel was gone. It removed the added complication of Gabriel's protective dragon instincts interfering with what was already an awkward situation. Gabriel didn't like to hide. He liked to breathe fire.

David Tanglewood was a hardheaded pragmatist who had divorced her mother during Raven's battle with brain cancer and stopped coming to visit her when the doctors gave her no chance of survival. He'd tried to reconnect after Gabriel's dragon magic had cured her, but she'd rejected his efforts. She hadn't spoken to her father much since then, mostly because he was an asshole and had never given her the slightest indication of changing his overtly assholistic behavior.

"I didn't invite him," Avery repeated firmly, "but maybe

this is the time to tell him about, you know." Her gaze jumped between her engagement ring and her ever-growing abdomen. "I mean, come on, Raven. He can't find out from a stranger. It's wrong."

Raven swore under her breath. Maybe Avery was right. For the sake of family peace and her mother's and sister's sanity, she needed to at least tell the man that she was getting married and expecting a baby.

"Okay. I'm going to do this, and then I never want to hear about it again."

Avery nodded. "Agreed."

Raven rose from the booth and moved toward the place where her father stood at the bar. His full head of gray hair had thinned since she'd seen him last, and the tanned, leathery skin of his face wrinkled with his smile when he saw her.

"Well, if it isn't my long-lost daughter." He opened his arms. She stood perfectly still, her arms crossed over her chest. He lowered his arms. "Happy birthday."

"We need to talk."

"Do you want something to drink first? I just ordered, but I can call the bartender over again." His voice was a muted roar over the chatter in the bar.

"No. No. I'm fine."

"It's so good to see you. Avery said you were vacationing in Chicago with that guy you've been seeing."

That guy. He knew who Gabriel was. "Gabriel. Gabriel Blakemore."

"Right. The one who owns Blakemore's Antiques. How's that working out?"

The bartender arrived with her dad's beer.

"Let's talk in mom's office. It's loud out here."

"If you're sure your mom will be okay with that."

Raven nodded once. In fact, her mom might be a little pissed about it, but she was working in the kitchen at the moment, and Raven was hoping to keep this short and sweet. He followed her to the small office at the back of the restaurant, past the bartender schedules and OSHA-required posters. She closed the door behind them.

"Should I be worried that you can't talk about Gabriel in public?" Her father sipped his beer.

She rolled her eyes. "I can talk about him in public. Give me a little credit. I just thought this was a better place to..." She flashed her engagement ring, the oversized emerald glinting in the light. "We're getting married."

His face fell. "When did this happen?" He asked it as if she'd just told him someone had died.

"I love Gabriel. This is what I want. I'm very happy."

"What about school?"

"What about it?"

"You never finished your degree. Are you going to do that first before you tie the knot with this guy?"

"Mmm. No. I think that ship has sailed actually. I'm not really interested anymore. I have more important things to focus on."

"Like Gabriel."

"Yes, and other things." She placed a hand on her abdomen, but he didn't seem to notice.

With an exasperated sigh, he lowered himself into one of the nickel-and-black faux-leather chairs in front of her mom's desk, his grip on the beer tightening. Silence uncurled in the room until Raven could hear the clock tick and the distant clanking of workers cooking in the kitchen. She leaned one hip against the desk.

"So, are you shopping for reception halls? The best ones need about a year's notice," he said finally.

She shook her head. "I don't have a year."

Her dad leaned back in his chair, arms crossed, face not even hinting at mirth. In fact, his expression was one of complete vexation, bordering on rage. "Why?"

"Because I'm pregnant." Raven left it at that. Her father could never know that the baby she was carrying was actually a dragon. He'd never believe it anyway. But there would be no hiding her pregnancy. She was already showing.

All the blood seemed to rush from her father's face, and his fingers gripped his beer until his knuckles turned white. "No reason a pregnancy has to mean marriage in this day and age. If it's about money—"

"Stop." She held up a hand. "Before you say something you might regret, Gabriel and I had planned to be married before this happened. In fact, we'd considered eloping. He is exactly what I want, and so is this baby."

He nodded slowly. "So when can I meet this guy?"

Fidgeting with the edge of the desk, Raven decided that honesty was the best policy. "I thought at the wedding would be good."

"At the... Raven, you can't be serious. I can't meet the guy moments before I walk you down the aisle."

"I don't remember asking you to walk me down the aisle."

He stilled as if she'd slapped him across the face. "You don't want me to walk you down the aisle? I know we've had a falling-out, but Ravenna!"

She sighed. "We haven't had much of a relationship since I was sick. It seems like it would be... forced."

He lowered his head and closed his eyes. When he opened them again, he looked like an entirely different person. "I've waited too long to say this. I should have had this conversation months ago. I wronged you, Raven. I am so sorry that I wasn't brave enough—hell, wasn't man enough—to fight alongside you when you were dying and hospitalized. I made every excuse in the book, and I know every word of it hurt you. My absence hurt you. If I could take it back, I would. But I can't. We can only live forward. And all I can say is I accept responsibility for what I did to you, and I am genuinely, truly sorry."

Raven had to stop herself from toppling over. David Tanglewood rarely apologized to anyone for anything. He always had to be right. But just now he looked positively beside himself with regret. Raven didn't know what to do with it.

"Thank you. I'm going to need some time to process that," she said softly.

He sighed. "I understand." He rubbed his palms over the tops of his thighs. "I know I've been difficult. You're a big girl now. You can make your own decisions. You love this guy, and he's clearly well positioned to take good care of you and this baby. I wish you the best."

He stood and turned to leave. Raven felt an immediate swell of relief but also a sudden twang of guilt. He'd apologized, sincerely. Was she a bad person if she didn't accept the olive branch?

"Dad... I don't think we've had a relationship that warrants you walking me down the aisle, but I would like to invite you to come to the wedding. Maybe, over time, things can be different." Her stomach clenched. She might regret this.

"I get it. When is the occasion?"

She winced. "Avery is helping me put something together. I want it to be soon, but we don't know the exact date yet. Once we nail it down, I'll let you know."

"And I'm going to be a grandpa."

"Yes, you are." Raven gave him a tight smile. "I should get going. Avery and Mom will want to cut the cake."

He nodded. "Oh, and Raven, don't worry too much about this wedding. You know, the event isn't half as important as the marriage that follows. I speak from experience."

The force of her father's words hit her straight in the gut. "The marriage" in his case was the one in which he left her mother, the one which she was raised in, believing as children do that her parents were very much in love. She wasn't ready to hear how the family she remembered had all been a big mistake to him.

She opened the office door and ushered him out, gesturing toward the exit. "You know the way."

He hugged her then, and she stiffened in his arms. "Happy birthday, Raven."

Relief flooded her when he finally headed for the door. She hoped to heaven she hadn't just made a terrible mistake.

CHAPTER TWENTY-SIX

Nick showed up at the station the following Monday, feeling like his soul had been torn out, fed through a meat grinder, and then tucked back into his skin. After a day of brooding over beer and nonstop football, he was ready to admit he was completely smitten with Rowan. Too bad he'd basically called her a liar and kicked her out of his apartment. There was probably no coming back from that.

The fact was she *had* lied to him, damn it! And tinkered with his brain. He'd been right to call her out. So then why did everything feel wrong? Everything. It hurt to breathe. He'd completely lost his appetite. And what little sleep he'd had since she left was riddled with dreams of her.

Thankfully, he made it to his office without much contact with other human beings. He rang Soren, and it wasn't long before his partner appeared in the seat across from him.

"So, what's the story? What did you find out about the Sumner case Friday night?" Soren cradled his coffee mug in his hands and blew across the top, breaking apart the curls of steam that rose from the dark brown liquid.

Nick thought for a moment. He needed to phrase this in a way that could be pursued by the department without making him look like a nutcase who thought vampires existed. "There's a secret room, a VIP area on the lower level of Wicked Divine. It appears they're part of a fetish club, some BDSM type of thing. You were right about that. The, uh, submissive partners have those tattoos we saw on the victim's wrist. The dominant partners pretend to be vampires and drink their blood."

Soren laughed nervously. "Vampires?"

"It's as disgusting as it sounds. I couldn't stay long without blowing my cover, but my theory is that the dead girl was the victim of a session that went too far. Worse, I think a lot of the blood donors are there against their will. I saw signs of human trafficking."

"No one is going to believe that." The idea seemed to make Soren oddly jittery. He cracked his neck and sipped his coffee.

"I think a search warrant would be a good start. Take a team into Wicked Divine. See what we can find out."

His partner shook his head. "That's not going to be easy."

"No?"

"Come on, Nick." Soren lowered his voice. "You've lived in New York your entire life. You must know that Michael Verinetti has friends in high places. Maybe we should, uh, focus our energies on leads other than Wicked Divine."

Nick's chest tightened. What the fuck was he hearing right now? He narrowed his eyes on Soren. "I plan to proceed cautiously. There were some wealthy patrons down there last night; I get that. But a girl is dead and someone needs to be held accountable for that. I saw others who may be there against their will. We can't turn our back on that."

"But, I mean, maybe we could pursue it without involving Wicked Divine. I'm just saying you don't want to rock that boat unless you have absolute proof in hand. In fact, you might have trouble getting the warrant." Soren's voice deepened, becoming threatening. "Even if you did obtain a warrant, you might find your life becomes far more complicated once you do."

Nick's jaw clenched until the muscles hurt. He wanted to shake Soren. Why was he protecting Verinetti? He hadn't seemed to have much of a connection to Wicked Divine before. *Fuck*—it had been Soren's tip that had brought him there in the first place.

"What happened last night, Soren? What did that girl say to you?"

Soren's tongue ran along his front teeth, and Nick noticed the way he tightened his grip on his coffee, his eyes shifting around the office. "When I spoke with Kendra, she told me the group was consensual. I didn't know about the biting, okay, but... she mentioned there are some big names in this group. Names we don't want to be on the bad side of, especially you."

"Me?"

He leaned in and lowered his voice. "I told you the Stevensons suspect you in the theft of the Raindrop of Heaven. You might even say they *are* sure and will *make sure* it was you if they need to. They have you on the security tape going into their room. That was the last time anyone saw the jewels in their residence. Nobody wants to have to report you. You're a good detective. But if you keep pursuing these crazy theories of yours, he'll be forced to take action."

Nick's hands balled into fists. Stevenson was there Friday night, at one of the tables in the auction house. He'd acquired land on NAVAK's behalf. Soren worked as security for Stevenson. Soren had hounded him, personally, for weeks about filling in for him at the Stevensons' Hampton beach house because of plans he had with his wife for their anniversary, despite cheating on her with this Kendra person. Soren had been oddly forthcoming with that little tidbit. Now he was accusing Nick of stealing jewels that Rowan claimed she'd replaced.

Nick swore under his breath. He'd been set up. By Soren. *Fuck*, he wanted to kill the guy. He wanted to reach across his desk, grab his damned head, and slam it into his desk until he bled.

He lowered his voice, the tone becoming as threatening as Soren's. "All they have on that video is me walking rounds. And housekeeping and regular security were in that closet after me."

Soren leaned back, his eyes turning cold as ice. "The housekeepers don't have the code, and the regular security guys say they never opened the safe. The next person to check it was Camilla, and the jewels were gone."

"Completely gone? Nothing left in their place?"

"Gone. All the pieces. Necklace and earrings."

Nick thought he might be sick. Rowan hadn't been lying about the replicas, which meant the Stevensons had hidden them, thinking they were the real thing, in order to frame him for a crime that, as far as they were concerned, never really happened.

Soren ran a hand along his desk. "You told me about opening the safe to check on the jewels after you saw the rumpled bedspread. That's a pretty damning piece of evidence, don't you think? You don't want to deal with charges like this. Just let this thing at Wicked Divine go."

Nick's gaze snapped to Soren's.

"Everyone knows who you are," Soren whispered under his breath. "You don't want to mess with these people. They aren't like you and me."

All of Nick's internal warning flares started firing like the Fourth of July. Verinetti had lied to Rowan. Nothing she could do could save him. Verinetti and his crew knew who he was and had planned to blackmail him all along, and he'd bet his life the vampires knew too.

"You set me up," Nick said through his teeth. "Begging me to fill in for you at the Stevensons' summer home. You told me it was for Rhonda, so you could be with her on your anniversary, but you don't care about Rhonda. You've been fooling around on her. No, that was an excuse to get me out there so you could frame me. You're working for him. You did all this because you need detectives who will look the other way when your boss says so, to protect NAVAK."

Soren chuckled under his breath. "You were always so perceptive. Congratulations, you solved the case, Detective. Now, accept the reality that you don't want to be sniffing too close to this flame, you know what I mean? You'll get your nose burned."

Nick tapped his pen on his desk. "I know exactly what you mean. You've made the situation more than clear."

"Good." Soren stood, a shit-eating grin on his face. "Oh, and Nick, keep this conversation between us. I'd hate for others to assume you're hiding something about this jewel theft."

Nick swallowed down the bile rising in his throat and forced himself to remain calm. He'd get this bastard, but he'd do it the smart way. Letting his emotions get the most of him now was not the way to win this game.

"Understood. Uh, I better get to work. Got a ton of email."

Soren nodded smugly and left his office.

Nick rubbed his chest. Rowan had been right, and he understood now why she'd done what she'd done. Manhattan was a city of secrets. When he'd caught her in Stevenson's closet, she had no reason to trust him. Hell, he could have been someone like Soren. She'd taken a risk telling him who and what she was. In the beginning, she hadn't known him enough to trust him. Of course she'd lied. He might have done the same thing in her shoes. Hell, he'd just allowed Soren to believe he'd been bought. That was a lie. Nick had no intention of letting Soren or Stevenson get away with blackmailing him.

But first he needed to warn Rowan that Verinetti was using her. He picked up his phone and texted her.

Need to see you. Tonight?

The important thing was keeping Nick safe. Rowan repeated that to herself as she dressed in the backless red minidress she'd purchased specifically for its ability to be distracting. Michael was taking her to dinner with Malvern, the master of the NAVAK vampires. She needed to keep him from asking questions about the video at Wicked Divine and to redirect his coven's energies away from the man she loved.

Nick. She couldn't stop thinking about him. But he hadn't called her and it was clear from what he'd said the other night, the night they'd made love, the night he'd remembered her stealing the jewel, that he didn't trust her, might never trust her again. She *had* lied to him. All the reasons and excuses she'd given him meant nothing. No reason in the world would excuse her behavior. But she suspected there was more to the story. He might not admit it to himself, but the damage he carried from his past was still with him. Nick had been abused as a child. He'd become a police officer and then a detective to compensate for what he had to do in his youth to survive. Perhaps he didn't want to bond with her, not just because she'd lied but because on some level he didn't think he was worth that sort of commitment.

She wondered if she would ever be the same again or if the unrequited connection she felt to Nick would drive her as crazy as it had Alexander. At least she had this dinner, and the correlating hope that what she was doing was good for Nick, to distract her from her predicament.

A white owl landed on her terrace railing, and Rowan went outside to meet Michael. She'd spelled the boundaries of her home so he could no longer get in without an invitation, and no way would she ruin all her hard work by inviting him in now. She watched him slowly transform to his commonly used and preferred human form, which unfortunately was completely naked.

"Hello, Michael," Rowan said, unable to keep the disgust from her voice.

"Rowan. Aren't you a sight? That dress should be a registered weapon."

"I thought that was the point. Distract Malvern. Keep him from asking too many questions about the attack on Wicked Divine. What about you? Do you plan to show up to this vampire dinner naked?" She crossed her arms over her chest.

"No. I have a car waiting for us downstairs. Far easier to come up this way than to deal with the doorman." He gave her a lecherous grin.

"You just wanted to show me your dick, didn't you?" She made certain that every word was loaded with assurance that she was unimpressed.

"Just thought you might like to see what you've been missing."

She shook her head. "I haven't missed anything about you."

"Careful, Rowan. You're in real danger of losing me as an ally. If that happens, there will be no one standing between NAVAK and your beloved Nick."

She consciously repressed any reaction to that, although her insides squirmed. Michael was a manipulative pig, but she needed to stick this out to protect Nick. "Let's get this over with." She pointed over the terrace railing. "I'll meet you downstairs."

"We could fly down together." He held out his hand to her.

"Can't. I need to lock up." She turned back toward the door.

He didn't move. "I can feel the magic. You've spelled the house against me."

She turned back. "Against all supernaturals. I don't feel safe now that you've invited vampires into Manhattan."

He grunted. "We need to be on our way if we plan to make it to Malvern's on time, but this conversation isn't finished. I don't like being locked out of your life. Makes me feel like you're ungrateful."

"I'm as grateful as I should be. I'll meet you at the car." She rushed inside, her composure giving way as soon as she had flattened her back against the wall out of his sight. She held back the tears, refusing to give him that power over her. He wasn't worth spoiling her mascara. She was a dragon, for the Mountain's sake. She grabbed a tissue from the box on the counter and dabbed at her eyes. One night. For Nick.

Fortifying herself with a deep breath, she locked the doors and grabbed her charging phone from the tray on the table near the door. She'd been so busy today she hadn't checked it. She gasped when she saw a message from Nick. He'd sent it hours ago.

Need to see you. Tonight?

"Nick..." She took a deep breath and texted him back. *Sorry, I'm just seeing this now. I can't tonight. Tomorrow?*

It's important. Please.

Later?

Yes.

How long could a vampire dinner take? *Sure. I'll come by your apartment as soon as I can. It might be late.*

Late's okay

See you then

She hurried out of the building. There was no question which car was Verinetti's. The black Escalade was armored with bulletproof glass. The thing looked like a tank. As she neared, the driver opened the car door for her. She slid in next to Michael and frowned as the doors closed and the windows blackened. A divider rose between them and the driver.

"What's going on, Michael?"

"Malvern doesn't like his whereabouts to be general knowledge. I'm afraid you're going to have to be in the dark until our arrival."

CHAPTER TWENTY-SEVEN

That was it; Nick had officially lost his mind. He sat in an unmarked car across the street from the Dakota building and watched a white owl fly up to the rooftop terrace outside Rowan's apartment. Damn it, he had a feeling when Rowan didn't return his text immediately that there was something going on. Clearly, Verinetti had called in his favor and was forcing Rowan to attend the dinner with that damned vampire, and before he had a chance to tell her what he'd learned from Soren.

But Nick knew what was going on. He didn't trust Verinetti any farther than he could throw his body after punching him unconscious, something he very much wanted to do. And that tank of an armored Escalade he rode in was about as inconspicuous as a five-alarm fire. It was funny—these shifters really underestimated humans. He'd found it all too easy to blend into the crowd and walk right past the monstrosity, pausing to casually press the square-shaped GPS tracker he owned to the inside of the wheel well without garnering a single glance from the driver or the people around him. Hell, the driver never even looked up from his phone. Perhaps he was engaged in a rousing game of *Candy Crush*.

Surprise fluttered in his chest when his phone buzzed as soon as he was back in his vehicle. So she would meet him tonight, late. After her dinner with Verinetti and the vampire. Nick wasn't okay with that. He planned to make certain that Rowan had backup if she needed it. Dragon or not, she deserved that.

The Escalade pulled into traffic. Nick waited a few moments and pulled out too, trailing behind it. He frowned as the Escalade exited Manhattan and drove across the Hudson, heading north. Where was he taking her? He made sure to keep his distance. The red dot on his GPS would tell him exactly where to go. No need to rush.

It was farther than he'd expected. Did Rowan know Verinetti was taking her to BFE? He pulled off the main road onto a winding drive that didn't even register on his GPS. The heavily wooded area made him feel like he'd crossed some magical barrier between the city and rural America. Only a little over an hour from wall-to-wall skyscrapers and he was surrounded by a thick blanket of trees. He cut his headlights.

At the end of that drive, a gate loomed in the distance, lit up bright with security lights. As soon as he saw it, he slowed, then angled the car off the main drive and parked between the trees. Quickly he covered the unmarked car in brush and fallen branches. It wasn't a flawless job, but at night, under the shadows of trees, someone would have to be on top of it to see it.

By the light of the moon he walked along the wall, avoiding the secured gate area. The reflections off security cameras winked at him every few yards. He stayed out of sight until he found a spot between cameras where the forest had overgrown the wall. This would have to do. He climbed one of the trees and shimmied out on a limb to see over the six-foot stone barricade.

The place was a castle. A fucking castle with a watchtower and parapets and guards with assault rifles pacing in front of the front doors and windows. The estate had to be at least twelve thousand square feet, and the wooded acreage around it went on and on, as far as the eye could see. If a vampire bit into you here, no one would hear you scream.

Who the hell was this Malvern guy? This was a fully operational military compound, for God's sake. No wonder they didn't have anyone on this part of the wall; no one in their right mind would go over it unless they had a death wish. Which meant he was stuck on the tree branch, watching helplessly as the Escalade pulled up to the building and Rowan exited it with that piece of shit Verinetti by her side.

It took over an hour to get from Rowan's apartment to Malvern's residence. Over sixty long minutes with Michael dressing reluctantly beside her in a pretentious suit. The length of time they traveled told her nothing. Depending on traffic, it could take sixty minutes to go a couple of miles or it could take them completely out of the city. Once the driver opened the door and Verinetti held his hand out to her, there was no mistaking that it had been the second of those two choices. The grounds were heavily wooded, and the stone castle of a home in front of her loomed on the horizon, a great, glowing mecca under the bright moon.

"Toto, we're not in Manhattan anymore," she whispered as she climbed out of the car.

"No," Michael said, "you are not. And you'd do well to remember that. The NAVAK coven has outgrown these quarters, which is why they are expanding into the city, but very few have relocated yet. Stir up trouble here and you'll have a significant portion of the coven to answer to for it."

"Why would I stir up trouble?"

His eyes lifted to the heavens. "Goddess if I know why you do half the things you do, Rowan." He offered her his arm, but she refused and started up the steps without touching him. "As I was saying."

An extremely tall and lanky vampire, whom she supposed was the butler by the black-and-white uniform he wore, opened the front door for them and showed them to a parlor off the dining room. Her nostrils flared and tingled, the scent of vampire and fresh blood so strong it almost stung her lungs. She followed Michael toward the bar.

"Now that Lurch is gone, can you tell me if we're going to be the only warmbloods at this dinner?" she asked.

Michael shook his head. "The black man in the south corner is one of mine. Werepanther. And those two women and that man over there are blood donors."

Rowan looked at the group of three humans and immediately noticed the NAVAK tattoos on their wrists. All were scantily clad with noticeable bite marks on their necks and thighs. A whiff of medicine-tainted sweat reached her nostrils, and she realized they must also be drugged.

"Will Malvern be serving regular food as well, or should I have had a burger before I came?" she mumbled.

Michael stopped in front of the bar. "Malvern is an excellent host and will see to your every need."

"Drink, miss?" The bartender, whose slightly dropped

fangs gave him away as a vamp, gestured to the cart behind him. "We have a full bar or several types of bagged blood if that's your fancy."

"Vodka and tonic please." She watched the bartender mix her drink and decided the bottles looked untampered with. Still, she gave it a sniff while Michael ordered his favorite Ramos gin fizz. The drink was obscenely complicated, included citrus, egg white, and heavy cream, and required a ridiculous amount of shaking. Who even drank that anymore? For the love of the Mountain, he was a pain in the ass in every sense of the word.

After a few long minutes of listening to Michael ramble on about how he'd bought his fourth nightclub and was expanding the Wicked Divine brand to milk the most out of the human population, Rowan began to wonder if Malvern would show. Where was he? Wasn't this his party? Lurch returned, rang a small bell, and announced dinner would be served.

Michael grabbed her elbow. "Before we go in there, I want to know where we stand. As a shifter, will you finally become a member of the pack?"

She balked. "Why would you ask me that? I've never been a member of the pack. I'm independent and plan to remain so."

"And what about us?"

"There is no us. That's over."

"So, other than protecting this human, there's no other reason you joined me tonight?"

"No. I told you I was doing this to keep him safe. He was only in that position because of me. It's not fair to make him pay for my mistake." She took a different tack when his eyes clouded with darkness. "I'm your friend, Michael. I have always worked with you when you needed me. This is no different. But no, I don't want anything more. Not from the pack and not from you."

The dark clouds remained in his eyes, but he gave her a curt nod and ushered her into the dining room. At the head of the table, the vampire waited. Malvern's hair was platinum white and hung straight down to his jaw. His small eyes were blue, and his complexion was as pale as porcelain. Pale as a corpse. The shape of his face made her believe he was originally from Eastern Europe, or maybe Russia. Based on appearance alone, Rowan had no trouble taking him seriously as the leader of this coven or as the killer she'd heard he was. He looked deadly.

"Michael, you've brought a guest." Malvern's gaze locked onto her and slid down her body before focusing on her neck. "Won't you introduce us?"

Rowan strode around the table and offered her hand. "Rowan. It's a pleasure to meet you."

He stared at her hand as if she'd offered him a roll of barbed wire.

"Vampires don't shake hands," Verinetti whispered. "It's offensive."

She retracted her hand. "My apologies."

"You must not have much experience with my kind," Malvern mumbled.

"No." She added quickly, "How exciting to experience something new. Is there anything more enthralling than the first interaction with a strange and beautiful creature?"

His mouth edged up into a tight-lipped smile. "For those with virginal appetites."

She flashed her most disarming smile. "Even someone ancient can be new to the right person."

"New, yes. But hardly fresh. Any fruit's edibility is limited, even if it is never plucked from the tree."

"Oh, but if that fruit is made into wine, it betters with age, and the first sip is still the most pleasurable."

This time his smile broadened and he flashed a little fang. "True. Sit beside me. I'd like to know you better."

With a wink, he moved her chair back from the table. She'd heard of vampires moving things with their minds. Only the strongest and oldest could do so. Turn off the lights, unlock doors. For him to so casually draw her chair back, Malvern must be old and powerful indeed.

"Tell me, are you the freshly picked grape or the wine?"

She took a seat beside him. "The wine," she said. "Well-aged, full-bodied, and dangerously intoxicating."

Malvern clapped his long fingers together in a creepy way that sent a cold shiver along her neck. She amped up her illusion to hide it.

"Oh Michael, wherever did you find this one?" Malvern asked.

"Rowan has been a member of my pack for years," he said flatly. "I assure you, she can be quite entertaining."

"So you're a shifter?" Malvern asked.

"Yes. I thought it would be obvious given that I am definitely not a vampire."

"Your scent is strange to me. Unlike Michael's."

She glanced back at Michael playfully. "What does Michael smell like?"

"Day-old butchered duck." Malvern laughed and Rowan joined in.

The first course was served, a rocket and radish salad for her and the other non-vampires at the table, a small bowl of blood that gave off the slightest hint of orange for Malvern and his coven mates. She was relieved to be served actual food.

Michael pouted beside her, obviously still offended by

the duck comment. "I wanted to give you an update on our search for that human who infiltrated Wicked Divine the other night."

Rowan stiffened and gave him a dagger-filled glare. Why was he bringing this up now? The entire purpose of their visit was to distract Malvern from this topic.

Malvern sipped his blood and frowned. "Down to business so soon, Verinetti? All right. Tell me, have you found the walking blood bag?"

"We believe he is the father of one of the younger girls in the herd. I have a team of sniffers out tracking him down. He should be dead by morning."

Rowan relaxed. Michael lied so convincingly even she couldn't tell, and she knew his statement wasn't true. She just hoped it wasn't partially true. It wouldn't be beyond Michael to hunt Nick down. Her dragon pressed to the surface. If Michael hurt Nick, she would kill him, with pain. She wrestled herself under control.

"Good," Malvern said. "Stevenson, talk to your friends on the NYPD and make sure we have protection for the auctions. We will pay whatever we need to. My coven must be fed."

Rowan's head turned. Stevenson. That was Gerald Stevenson at the end of the table. The same Gerald Stevenson who had bought Sunrise House right out from under her. The same Stevenson from whom she'd stolen the Raindrop of Heaven. When had he slipped into the room? He hadn't been in the parlor earlier.

"Already done," Gerald said. "We have several integral members of the NYPD on payroll already. They will be avoiding Wicked Divine and squelching any cases that could be problematic for your coven."

Oh no, Nick! Did he know who was on the payroll? If

she knew anything about Nick, it was that he had a good heart. He would never allow that girl's murder to go unpunished. He was probably still investigating it. Not only that, his friend Soren had been at Wicked Divine. Could they trust him? How much about that night had Nick shared with his partner? If Soren was compromised, all her efforts toward taking the heat off Nick would be for naught. She'd have to warn him tonight, as soon as she got back to his place.

"Now to more pleasurable topics," Malvern said, turning his attention back to Rowan. "I mentioned that Michael smelled like day-old duck. Do you know what you smell like?"

She shook her head.

"Nothing I've ever smelled before. You have a smoky scent, something exotic. Alligator? Are you an alligator shifter?"

She wrinkled her nose. "What we shift into is a private matter. We usually don't discuss it."

Malvern frowned.

Focusing on her salad, Rowan hastily filled her mouth. Never had she shared what she was openly with someone she didn't completely trust. It could never end well. Dragons weren't from this planet. Her blood and scales could be used for magical purposes. Every person who knew put her at risk. Hell, at this point, she wasn't happy with herself for telling Verinetti.

Michael's fork hit his plate. "Oh, I don't think we need to keep secrets from Malvern, my sweet. I think he'd be excited to learn there's a one-of-a-kind shifter beside him."

A buzz of fear started between her ears, like wasps had taken up residence in her skull. What did he think he was doing? Surely Michael wouldn't reveal her secret. They had a history, and she'd kept her end of the bargain tonight. Besides, what would he get out of it?

Malvern finished his blood and set the empty bowl down on the middle of the gold charger in front of him. "One of a kind? Now I am intrigued. Does that mean you've never met another shifter like Rowan, Michael, or there are no others like her?"

Michael looked down his nose at her, his expression smug. She felt his hand on her own beneath the table. The touch was a question. It didn't take a mind reader to know what he was thinking. If she returned his touch, he would keep her secret. If she pulled away, he'd tell Malvern she was a dragon. She hated Verinetti in that moment with a red-hot rage that seemed to scald her from the inside out. Defiantly, she ignored his touch.

"I'm not all that special," she said, raising an eyebrow in Malvern's direction.

"Oh, I disagree," Malvern said. "You've already proven yourself to be a unique specimen. Now tell me, Rowan, what are you?"

Michael's touch shifted higher on her leg.

She dug her nails into his skin and shoved his hand away from her. Glaring at Michael, she shook her head. "Nothing worth sharing."

Verinetti's expression turned hard and ice cold. "You're too modest. Rowan is a dragon."

The room went absolutely silent. Malvern's small eyes rounded to the size of saucers before his expression took on the quality of carved marble. He snapped his fingers, and Lurch appeared beside him. He whispered something in his ear. Rowan could barely make out what he said but thought she heard the words *message* and *high priority*.

Once the servant had left his side, Malvern stood from

the table and held his hand out to her. "Rowan, may I speak with you privately for a moment?" He offered her a reassuring smile.

She glanced at Michael, who leaned back in his chair and grinned at her. That bastard. Rowan had to stop herself from openly growling at him. Later, she'd make sure he paid for this. For now, this was a situation that required diplomacy.

She slipped her hand into Malvern's icy grip. With a gentle tug, he led her into a private study. Once the door was secured behind him, he turned to her.

"I hope you will forgive me for interrupting dinner, but you seemed uncomfortable talking about what you are in public. Is it true? Are you a dragon? Or do you mean a komodo dragon?" He tapped his nose. "That is why I smell alligator. You transform into a lizard."

Glancing toward her toes, she said, "No. I am a dragon. The kind that flies." She hated this, but there was something she needed from him, and clearly he found what she was interesting. Perhaps they could make a deal.

"Extraordinary."

"Now that you know, I wonder if we could discuss some business related to your taking up residence in Manhattan."

He raised an eyebrow. "What do you have in mind?"

"As a dragon, I could be of use to your coven. I am very powerful and know Manhattan like no other supernatural. Verinetti isn't the only game in town."

"You are proposing an alliance?"

"I only ask for one thing in return. There's a building in the Upper West Side near Morningside Heights, the home of Sunrise House community center. You've purchased the land beneath it. I'd like to buy it back from you. I'll give you double what you paid if you'll agree."

He rubbed his hands together and seemed to contemplate her offer. "Can I interest you in some wine?"

"Yes, I'd love some." Straightening, she tried to appear as if she made five such deals before breakfast.

"That building is of strategic importance to my coven. Its loss would be a serious inconvenience. How can I be certain you are as powerful as you say?"

She shrugged. "You'll have to take my word for it. I can't shift here. The room is too small."

"Your blood. I can tell by your blood. Give me a taste, and if the magic running through your veins is as strong and powerful as you say it is, I will consider your offer." He didn't wait for her reply before gathering a wineglass and a small knife from the bar.

She offered her arm. There was a fast strike and then a spurt of hot blood. Bright red liquid splashed into his glass before her flesh healed itself.

He held it up and clinked it against her wineglass. "To new acquaintances and powerful alliances."

Overjoyed that her plan had worked, Rowan tipped her head in a gesture of camaraderie, then brought the wine to her lips and took a drink, as did Malvern.

"Goddess, your blood is the most delicious I've ever tasted. No wonder they want you so urgently. It's like drinking pure magic."

"No wonder who wants me?" she asked. But she was having trouble forming thoughts. The room was tilting and it felt like her head might pop off her shoulders. She gripped the back of one of the leather chairs, desperate to steady herself, but it wasn't enough. Head spinning, she collapsed onto the floor, all the air flowing from her lungs in a loud *oomph*.

Malvern's face appeared above her. "Relax, dragon.

Don't fight it. The drug I dissolved in your wine is going to make you take a long nap. When you wake, we'll speak again."

Her vision narrowed as if she were staring down a long tunnel. Then the darkness closed in and she succumbed to unconsciousness.

CHAPTER TWENTY-EIGHT

It had been a long night. Aside from Nick grabbing his binoculars out of his car, he hadn't moved from the branch overlooking Malvern's estate in hours, and his back and neck were officially killing him. But as the darkness slowly faded toward the silver light of dawn, Nick got what he was waiting for. That slimeball Michael Verinetti exited the mansion alone, entered his car alone, and left the property alone.

"Fucking bastard." There was only one thing that had kept him in that tree all night and that was the feeling, down to his bones, that something was not right about this situation. Rowan had promised to come by his apartment that night. If she remained inside, it wasn't of her own free will. Which told him his deepest fear had been realized. Verinetti had never intended to follow through on his end of the bargain. He'd always meant to feed Nick into the jaws of death. Rowan was just a pretty appetizer.

He waited until the sun came up, hoping security would be at a minimum as the vampires all fell asleep. No such luck. If anything, there were more human guards.

More guns. He cursed again. He'd need a small army and plenty of ammunition to get in there. He'd have to do things the smart way if he was going to get Rowan out.

A small army. The light bulb came on in Nick's exhausted brain. He looked at his watch and texted his neighbor to walk Rosco. Then he hopped down from the tree and walked his sore body back to the car.

A little over an hour later, Nick arrived at Zelda's Folly, parked around the corner, and waited in front of the security gate. Harriet didn't strike him as the type of employee who was often late, and he wasn't disappointed to see Djorji drop her off right on time. Dressed in a mint-green suit with a hat that reminded him of something British royalty would wear and a white leather handbag slung across her forearm, Harriet shuffled down the sidewalk toward him.

"Mr. Grandstaff, I was wondering if I'd see you here today. The cards said you were coming, but there's always the element of choice to reckon with."

"Did the cards tell you what's happening to Rowan?"

Her designer pumps clacked to a halt on the sidewalk. "No. Oh dear, this must be serious. Come inside. We'll talk while we wait for the others to arrive."

"Others? What others?"

She didn't answer him but unlocked the security gate and then the glass door. As they entered Zelda's Folly, Nick noticed the art had changed. The room was now filled with abstract sculptures of bent and twisting humanoid forms.

"What do you think of our new exhibit, Mr. Grandstaff?" Harriet asked, removing her hat.

"Uh, the bodies are all distorted. Looks painful. This must be about torture or the Holocaust or something, right?"

Harriet chuckled. "No. Love."

"Oh." Nick shrugged. "I was close."

Laughing under her breath, she led him into the back room and motioned toward a chair. "Please sit and tell me what happened to Rowan."

"Yes, we have to hurry— Oww!" Harriet had grabbed his hand and pricked his finger. He watched a bead of his blood drop onto a square of paper. "What the hell?"

"I need your blood to help Rowan."

"Why would my blood tell you anything about Rowan?"

She smiled at him. "Old Traveller magic. Leave it to me. Now, if you please, tell me your story."

His brows knitted together. He told her everything, from the area the compound was in, to the number of guards, the background with Verinetti and his suspicion that the shifter kingpin had sold her up the river to make amends for what happened at Wicked Divine, all because she wouldn't return his advances.

Harriet removed a large green banana leaf from her purse and placed it on the desk between them. She placed his blood in the center, then sprinkled it with various powders from her bag.

"Are you listening to me?" he asked, exasperated.

She nodded. "Oh yes, Mr. Grandstaff, and I suspect you are right about Verinetti and that Rowan is in mortal danger."

He tossed up his hands. "Well, what are we going to do?"

"What do you think we should do? I doubt very much that you came here believing an old woman like me would be much help. I can give you a few elixirs to aid your efforts, but I'm a horrible shot."

"What about her brothers?" he asked, the secret plan he had been turning over in his brain coming to the surface.

"She said she had family, specifically a couple of brothers whom she called a two-man army. Do you know how to find them? We'll need some serious firepower if we're going to bust her out of that place."

Harriet grinned. "Smart, Mr. Grandstaff. And, lucky for you, Rowan's brothers are on their way here right now."

"They are? But I thought she said they lived far away?"

"Five... four... three... two..."

The front door opened, and the sound of heavy footsteps reached his ears. A deep voice called, "Hello?"

Nick got to his feet and exited the office. Two of the largest men he'd ever seen stood inside the door. Professional-athlete big. One was dark and enormous as a linebacker, the other blond, tall, and exceptionally focused. Nick was used to being one of the biggest people in any room. Not today. At the moment, he felt positively petite.

Harriet shuffled out from behind him and gave a knowing smile. "I was wondering when you two would get here."

"Mrs. Fernhall?" the blond asked, looking utterly confused.

"A white lie. It was Rowan's wish that you not find her. I am Harriet Everwood, bonded servant to your sister. Hello, Gabriel." She shook the dark-haired man's hand, then clasped the blond's. "Tobias."

It was the one called Gabriel who spoke next. "We almost didn't find her. If we hadn't tracked down our brother Alexander's residence in Sedona and put together that the gallery in New York buying all his paintings must be Rowan's, we'd still be searching for her. When Alexander's neighbor said he hadn't been home in several days, we took a chance there was still time to catch up with Rowan here before she moved again."

"I'm afraid your inability to track her was my fault. I've had a concealment spell protecting her for several months. But I must ask, why the sudden urgency to find her?"

"She is in great danger. There's a price on her head. On all our heads. Vampires are hunting dragons by order of their elder council, the Forebears."

"Vampires?" Nick said with alarm. "You're too late. They already have her!"

A collective growl came from the two men, and Nick took a step back.

"Who is this, Harriet?" Gabriel gruffly gestured toward Nick. "And why is he suggesting the vampires have my sister?"

"This is Rowan's bonded mate," Harriet said. "And he's the one who witnessed her abduction."

"Bonded mate?" Gabriel's eyebrows rose toward the ceiling.

The weight of the two brothers' stares bore into Nick. "I'm not sure I would describe us as bonded."

Harriet pointed toward the office. "It's in your blood. I can see it as if you were tied to her with a ribbon."

Tobias held up his hand. "Not that Rowan's love life isn't fascinating, but it sounds like our sister is in trouble. Can one of you fill us in on the details?"

Nick launched into an explanation of what was happening, trying to convey everything he knew about NAVAK all the way back to what happened at Wicked Divine. When he got to the part about Verinetti, he could hear the venom in his voice. He'd never wanted to kill anyone so much in his entire life. And her brothers' reactions did not disappoint. The sheer fury rolling off the two men became a palpable thing.

Tobias glanced at Gabriel and then back at Nick. He

pulled out his phone and started typing furiously. "We should go now, while the vampires are asleep."

"Agreed," Gabriel said. "If this place is as secluded as Nick says it is, one of us can shift and burn it to the ground while the other gets Rowan out."

Nick cleared his throat. "You can't burn the place down. There are humans in there. I saw them last night. They call them the herd. They're all compelled by the vampires and tattooed like chattel."

The brothers groaned. "We both go in then," Tobias said. "Nick, we'll need you to show us where she is."

Nick nodded and started toward the door. "I have a car."

But Harriet held up her wrinkled hands. "I'm afraid that would be a disaster," she said in her high, tight voice. "The spell I performed using Nick's blood says you should attack at twilight."

"But that's when all the vampires will be waking up!" Nick protested.

But Gabriel pointed a finger at her. "She's right. If we attack at twilight, there will be pandemonium. The vampires will be weak. Perhaps they won't have fed yet. And when it comes to the security contingent, the day shift will be exhausted."

Nick couldn't believe his ears. "We can't just leave her there all day! Who knows what they're doing to her!"

Gabriel's hand landed on Nick's shoulder, where he had a moment to appreciate the giant emerald ring the man wore and how it resembled Rowan's ruby one. He noticed Tobias had one too—a sapphire. It must be a family thing.

"Your concern is admirable. You must care for her deeply."

Nick didn't say a word. He was so confused about the

bonded-mate thing Harriet had mentioned. What did it mean? He didn't want to saddle Rowan with a commitment she didn't even know she was making.

Tobias's phone chimed and he thumbed the screen. "Sabrina says the vampires will likely want to keep her alive until the Forebears can talk to her. Although there is a price on her head, they won't want to risk killing her. Not after they taste her blood. And no vampire she knows would pass up a taste."

"Who's Sabrina?" Nick asked.

"My wife and master of the Chicago vampire coven. I've texted her. She'll send help, but her people sleep during the day and it will take her time to get here."

"You're married to one of them?" Nick rubbed the back of his neck.

"She's on our side. We need her. She's the reason we know we are in danger."

Nick closed his eyes and took a deep breath. He'd been awake all night, and exhaustion weighed on his shoulders.

Harriet raised a finger. "Ah. So the magic was correct. Another reason to wait until twilight. And still another, I have a potion brewing that will help you, but you must come with me to Ember Fields to get it. Djorji will drive us." She pulled her phone out of her designer handbag and tapped the screen.

"So, my wife was right. You are a witch," Gabriel said.

"Why would you think I was a witch?" Harriet said. "Do you think witches have cornered the market on magic?"

Nick frowned. "Personally, I'm sick of the 'guess what I am and what I'm married to' game. Can you just tell the human what the fuck is going on?"

Harriet laughed. "I'm a Traveller. What was once called a gypsy here in the old days. My ancient magic is a gift from my ancestors, the earth, and the dragon's tooth that lives within me."

Nick's jaw dropped. "Dragon's tooth?"

Harriet sighed. "Oh dear. I'll tell you the story on the way. Djorji is here. We have work to do."

ROWAN WOKE IN PAIN, ALTHOUGH WHEN SHE TRIED TO adjust her body, she couldn't move but a few centimeters. Her wrists and ankles were bound and she was someplace dark, as dark as the inside of the mountain.

Blinking, she tried to allow her eyes to adjust, but her dragon's vision refused to cooperate. Without it, she was forced to use her exposed skin to gauge her surroundings. Silky fabric brushed her skin. Beside her was... a body. A high-pitched sound came from deep within her throat. She tried to sit up, and the top of her head hit more satin. Thank the Mountain, whatever was above her lifted with the pressure of her head, allowing in a shaft of dim light. The padded and silk-lined walls of a coffin came into view, and Malvern himself lay beside her, dead for the day.

Terror chilled her blood, and she tried to work her knees under her to climb out of the box. Why was she so weak? Every time she attempted to call on her inner dragon, her energy waned, as if opening the connection to her magic was also draining it.

To her relief, a set of hands lifted the lid and helped her out. Her bound feet landed on cold stone, and she looked up into the face of a pale human man whose throat was peppered with puncture wounds and bruises. His dark hair was badly in need of a wash, and his clothing was inadequate for the cold room. She quickly assessed the situation.

Stone walls. One metal door in the back of the room that was worthy of a medieval dungeon.

"Relax. Your bindings are enchanted. If you try to use your powers, they'll only weaken you until you eventually pass out. And the door is locked. They open it from the outside just before twilight, when the vamps wake up."

"You said the bindings are enchanted? Enchanted by whom?"

"Some witch who works for Malvern. I don't know her." He turned and sat down in a chair in the corner of the room where a computer screen glowed. Rowan realized it was the only source of light in the room. "You can sit over there until he wakes up if you want. There's a bucket on the other side of the room if you need to use the toilet. It's not as bad as it sounds. There's a seat."

Rowan swallowed and tested her bindings. As promised, her energy diminished as if she'd gone days without sleep. She slid into the chair beside the human. Despite her predicament, she couldn't help but pity the man who sported the NAVAK tattoo on his wrist.

"What's your name?" she asked softly.

"Barry."

"Do you work for the vampires?"

He blinked rapidly. "I am theirs." There was no other way to interpret his intonation than that he was their property.

She folded her bound hands in her lap and tried to look as casual and unassuming as possible. "So, you spend all day down here, guarding the sleeping vampires."

He looked at her blankly. "All day, all night. I sleep there." He pointed to a nest of filthy blankets on a mat in the corner.

"You sleep there?"

Barry gave her the slightest tip of his head, then turned back toward his screen. He was playing solitaire, and the glow from the monitor accented the dark circles under his eyes.

"When was the last time you were allowed out of this room?" she asked softly.

His hand trembled on his mouse. "I don't remember."

"That's not right, Barry. Fuck, they should at least let you out to see the sun."

He didn't respond. She wondered if he'd really heard her. Rowan watched him click on a card to turn it over and felt a deep sense of dread. This vampire coven had no respect for human life at all. Why should she believe they'd have any respect for hers? The way Malvern had looked at her when she'd said she was a dragon. It was as if she were a butterfly he wanted to collect and pin to his wall. After several minutes had passed, Rowan tried Barry again.

"Do you know what Malvern plans to do with me?" She didn't have high hopes that he would tell her, or that he'd even know, but she had to ask.

Barry frowned at his keyboard. "I overheard them say that the Forebears want you. I think they're on their way here."

"Who are the Forebears?"

He didn't look away from his screen. "Elder council of vampires. They sent a communication a few weeks ago that said any vampire who found a dragon had to deliver it to them, dead or alive."

She inhaled swiftly.

"Don't worry. I'm pretty sure Malvern is addicted to your blood. I've never seen him go to bed with his dinner before."

"He fed on me while I was sleeping?"

Barry snorted. "Like you were filled with chocolate sauce. You heal quickly."

"Barry, if you untie me, I can get us out of here. Both of us. You don't have to live like this anymore."

He smiled weakly. "I can't leave. This is where I belong. This is my purpose."

"Untie me. Set me free."

He shook his head. "Can't. Malvern told me not to."

"Then bring me something sharp so I can do it myself."

Barry closed his eyes tight and rubbed his temples. "I need you to be quiet now. I can't help you. Malvern will be awake in three hours. You can take it up with him."

Rowan leaned back in her chair and closed her eyes. She reached out, trying to follow the magical bond between her and Harriet, the one forged when she'd fed the Traveller her tooth and saved her life. But the more she tried, the more drained she became. Her bindings, it seemed, had stolen even that from her.

She cursed. "Can you at least untie my ankles? I have to use the bucket."

Barry stood and hooked his hand under her arm to help her out of the chair. "No. But I can help you hop."

CHAPTER TWENTY-NINE

Ember Fields was somewhere near Inwood based on the direction Djorji was driving. Nick sat in the back of the black sedan between Tobias and Gabriel, feeling awkward and uncomfortable. Not only was the back seat crowded with him sitting shoulder to shoulder with Rowan's brothers, he was in the unenviable position of them knowing he'd slept with their sister, thanks to Harriet. Either one of them could snap him like a twig. Harriet seemed to be enjoying his discomfort from her roomy seat beside Djorji.

Relief flooded him when the car stopped and the door opened, a waft of cool air breezing through the sedan's interior. He hurried across the seat and out of the car. But when Djorji drove away, he found himself staring at a slender alley between a veterinarian's office and an apartment building. Unless Ember Fields was the name of Harriet's apartment, this was not the place.

"Stay close," Harriet said, "and follow my instructions."

She shuffled into the alley and toward a scrawny tree whose feeble and crooked trunk thrust, seemingly by force of will alone, through a section of concrete that cracked and buckled over the roots. The branches drooped, but then how could it get enough sun or water here, squeezed between two buildings?

Harriet paused before the tree and waited until the three of them were huddled around her. "Good," she said. "Hands on my shoulders please."

They obliged, although there were plenty of shifting eyes and darting glances. She raised her hand and placed it on the tree trunk.

Once, when he was sixteen, Nick had gone on a date with a girl to Coney Island. He'd saved for weeks to have the money to go. Hadn't ever been before. She'd chosen a ride that spun him in every direction—he couldn't remember the name, only that it was horrifying for a first-time amusement park goer. When the ride stopped and they'd walked down the exit ramp, he threw up right between her feet.

He felt the same now. The alley spun, the force of motion drawing him backward so that he needed to grip Harriet's shoulder tighter to hold on. His stomach dropped. Thankfully, he wasn't the only one. Tobias groaned and Gabriel made a noise that sounded like a growl. Seconds ticked by as the surrounding buildings blurred into nothing but shapes and colors. And then the movement slowed. When they finally stopped spinning, Nick couldn't believe his eyes. Harriet's hand wasn't resting on a sapling struggling for the light but on a gigantic oak tree. She removed her hand and wiped her palms against each other.

"Wasn't that fun?" Harriet said. "It never gets old."

Nick took a deep breath to settle his stomach and looked around. All the buildings were gone. In their place were wagons painted in bright colors with wisps of smoke curling from the chimneys. Brightly dressed people came and went from the doors: men, women, and laughing children. Older children danced around a central fire while one played a guitar and sang for them. Others listened, eating some sort of stew from tin bowls.

"Come, my vardo is over there. My gift to you will be ready." Harriet pointed to a particularly large wagon painted red and purple with a green tin roof and a round chimney that spat perfect curls of blue smoke.

"What is this place?" Gabriel asked. His voice was firm, and Nick got a sense he didn't trust Harriet at that moment.

"This place, Ember Fields, was Rowan's bonding gift to me. The fact that it is here and I am too means she's still alive. Both this place and my body rely on her latent magic to exist. Our home has been here since 1887, when Mr. J. Hood Wright invited us to settle here to raise money for Manhattan Hospital. And we did. Lots of money. New Yorkers would come to us to have their fortunes told or play games, and we would donate a portion of our earnings to the cause. But in 1904 the first train came through and with it real estate speculation. We would have been forced to move on. That was the year Rowan saved me from tuberculosis, and when it was clear Ember Fields would get swallowed by the growing urban jungle that had spread across Manhattan, Rowan used her magic to create this slice."

"Slice?"

"This place can't be reached by any means but magic. Her scales protect the four corners and render us invisible and unreachable by anyone without Traveller blood. We come and go as we please, hidden in time. Rowan cut out a piece of the world, just for us."

Nick's chest sank. Rowan was no ordinary woman, and not just because she was a dragon. Sure, she sprouted wings on occasion, but she was also kind and generous to a fault, like no one he'd ever met. Without a doubt, she'd put herself in this position with Malvern to protect him. He had to save her. If he didn't, he'd never forgive himself.

Harriet led them through the door at the front of her wagon, what she called a vardo, and Nick was immediately surrounded by the heady medicinal scent of herbs and dried flowers. There was a cauldron simmering on the cooktop of a potbellied stove inside, its silvery contents giving off the same blue smoke as he'd seen coming from the chimney. The scent triggered a memory, Rowan leaning over him, holding a vial to his lips.

"What is that, Harriet?" Nick asked.

"Forget-me potion. If you make someone drink this, they will forget what you tell them to forget. You can even replace their memory with another."

Gabriel and Tobias filled the tiny space, although Nick could see they'd curled their shoulders forward to try to make themselves smaller in the tiny house.

"Are you saying that if we give this to the vampires, we can make them forget Rowan?" Gabriel asked.

"You can make them forget anything."

Tobias beamed. "If we can wipe the coven's minds, Sabrina might still be able to convince the Forebears that we don't exist."

"How much do we give our target?" Gabriel asked.

"Only a small vial, but the potion isn't done brewing. You must wait. It will be ready by twilight."

"Harriet, did you know Rowan used this potion on me?"

She clutched her pearls and busied herself with a teapot that was magically whistling at that precise moment. "The interesting thing about that is..." She trailed off, digging in her cupboard. She brought him a steaming cup of tea in a floral teacup with a small plate of biscuits that she set on a narrow table in front of the window. "Here you are, Mr. Grandstaff. You must keep your strength up. Cream and sugar?"

"Both." He sat down on the window seat. "So, you were saying."

"About what?"

"Did you know Rowan used your potion on me?"

She waved her hand dismissively. "Don't ask an old woman to speculate on the actions of her friend. I don't know Rowan's mind. I'm not her keeper. If you have questions for her, you'll have to ask her yourself."

Nick grunted.

Tobias and Gabriel glanced toward him in confusion.

"Your sister wiped my brain the first time I met her."

"Oh." Tobias cleared his throat. "I'm sure it was nothing personal."

Nick nodded slowly.

"Mr. Grandstaff," Harriet said. "Why don't you lie down? It's clear you haven't slept all night, and you won't be able to help Rowan if you're exhausted." She pointed out that the padded bench he was perched on was long enough to stretch out on.

"I agree," Gabriel said. "We're going need your help. Get some rest. Tobias and I will wait outside." The giant man made his way out the door, the wagon swaying with his every step.

Harriet again pointed at the bench. "Please."

He stretched out, his head landing on a blue satin pillow embroidered with a red dragon. It reminded him of Rowan.

Help Rowan. Save Rowan. Yes. He needed to do that. Because Nick needed to figure out what this was between them, and goddamn if he was going to let her get killed or stay captured before he got the chance. Frowning, he turned his back on Harriet and shut his eyes. He drifted off to the sound of laughing children.

For all the effort she'd put into making conversation with Barry, Rowan had gotten nowhere trying to convince him to release her from her bindings. She'd drifted to sleep a few times in the chair beside him, only to awake and try again to connect. She'd discovered that Barry had grown up in Oklahoma and wanted to be an astronaut before he'd been trafficked at the age of sixteen. The NAVAK coven had used the fact that Barry was gay and his parents were unaccepting of that to target him on social media. He'd thought he was meeting a boy his age who was also gay, and then he was nabbed by NAVAK, tattooed, and compelled to be their slave. He didn't use those words. Rowan cringed as he made it sound like he was saved by the vampires, but she knew the truth. Poor Barry didn't even know if his parents were alive or dead. He hadn't been free in years.

Her stomach growled.

"Dinner should be here soon."

Silently, she thanked the Mountain they planned to feed her. She needed to keep her strength up if she had any hope of freeing herself. Sure enough, a tray slid through the slot in the door a few minutes later.

He brought it over to her and removed the foil wrapping. "They sent enough for both of us."

Rowan scowled. "Peanut butter sandwiches, chips, and apple juice."

He was already burning through his first half sandwich. Rowan wondered how often he got anything but peanut butter. But she was too hungry to turn her nose up at the food. Carefully angling her bound hands, she chose a sandwich and took a bite. Grape jelly. It wasn't bad.

She was on her second sandwich when a sound from one of the coffins made her stop everything and drop what was in her hands. "Barry, what time do the vampires wake?"

He licked a bit of jelly from his thumb. "Soon now. The sun is still up, so they can't go outside, but they usually wake well before dusk. Malvern likes to eat someone before he starts his day." He rubbed the marks on his neck like maybe they'd started to itch.

Another sound from the coffins, a body shifting against satin, reached her ears, and Rowan was on her bound feet and pressed against the wall.

Barry cleared his throat. "It's better if you don't fight it. Everything is easier if you just obey them."

"Untie me, Barry. This is our chance. I swear to you I can get us out of this if you just untie me." She pleaded with him in hushed tones, her eyes filling with tears. "It's not your fault you're here. You deserved love. You still deserve love. And if you allow me to get us out of here, you can come stay with me. I'll get you back on your feet."

He stared at her, all emotion draining from his face. The gleam went out of his eyes, emptiness filling in where the light went out. "I don't want to leave," he said so quietly she could hardly hear him.

The lid to Malvern's coffin opened with a slow squeak, sending Rowan's heart hammering in her chest. Her eyes darted around the room, but she'd inspected every inch of this place and there was no way out. Malvern's bright blond head rose from the coffin and he turned to face her. She blinked and he was in front of her, his fingers stretching along her cheek and stroking behind her ear, behind her neck.

"There you are, my pet." He pressed himself against her, and she became grateful for her bound wrists now sandwiched between their chests. At least she had that layer of distance between them. "We don't have much time before the Forebears get here and try to take you away. I found you. I deserve you." He leaned toward her ear, his breath smelling of blood. "You would be such a prize in my herd. I bet you fuck like a minx."

She turned her face away from his in disgust and struggled against him, but with her limbs bound, there was nowhere to go. Malvern's teeth extended, and she cried out as he bit the side of her throat. He drank deeply, the sounds of his swallowing filling her ears. Weakness overcame her. And then his hands were on her, turning her to face the wall, and the heavy length of him was pressed up against her ass.

"No. Please, please no."

He pulled her hair to the side and licked up the side of her neck, preparing to bite her again. Her breath came in shallow, shaky jerks. She prayed to the goddess of the mountain for help.

"Let us have a turn," a voice said from behind her.

She turned her head just enough to see the other vampires had woken up and were eyeing her like she was breakfast.

Malvern released an intimidating hiss. "No one touches her but me."

Rowan had a moment to see a redheaded vamp sink his teeth into Barry's thigh before Malvern swept his arm under her legs and caught her. The walls blurred as he raced her from the room and from the hungry gazes of the other vampires. He carried her up two flights of stairs and into a bedroom, this one with an actual human bed.

After a moment of weightlessness, her arms and face slapped against a black velvet coverlet. He gripped her ankles and flipped her over. Malvern's terrifying visage hovered over her like a gargoyle, his eyes wild as if her blood had intoxicated him. His gaze raked down her body. She was still dressed in nothing but the red dress, and she felt naked under the thin material, not to mention filthy from her time in that dungeon where the vampires slept.

"Let me go, Malvern. Whatever you're thinking, don't. You'll be sorry. If you hurt me, I will hurt you. I'll find a way."

"You are in no position to make threats." He flopped on top of her, the full weight of his body pushing her down into the mattress. "Now, where were we?"

CHAPTER THIRTY

Nick dreamed he was floating down a river in a canoe. A very uncomfortable canoe. A bumping, clinking canoe with two men in the canoe ahead of him arguing over where to turn. He came awake in the back of a cargo van to the smell of gun oil and ammunition.

"Gabriel, I'm telling you that was the turn!" Tobias yelled.

Nick sat up, rubbing the knot in his back that had formed from lying on the floor of the van. He got his bearings and stuck his head between the two dragon males, eyeing the setting sun and their surroundings.

"Yep, you passed it," he said. "You wanted that unmarked lane a half mile back."

Tobias scoffed. "I told you. You never listen to me."

Gabriel pulled a U-ey and headed back toward the entrance.

"So, uh, was I unconscious this entire time?" Nick asked, trying to sound casual but feeling every bit inadequate between the two huge men.

Tobias chuckled. "Harriet drugged you. The old bird

gave you some kind of tonic to make you sleep a 'hero's sleep.' She told us to tell you that you may find your natural talents are accentuated tonight, but it will only last until the next time you sleep."

Nick narrowed his eyes. "She drugged me. She fucking drugged me. I've been poisoned by grandma fashionista!"

"Grandma fashionista insisted on reading our palms," Gabriel said. "Felt like I was back in New Orleans."

"You didn't let her, did you?" Nick scratched the back of his head. He was starting to feel weird, hyped up like he'd chugged a thirty-two-ounce espresso.

"We didn't want to be rude," Tobias explained. "Besides, nothing she said made that much sense anyway."

Nick shook his head. "Don't tell me. Rowan told me never to let Harriet read my palm. She said she has a knack for causing self-fulfilling prophecies."

"As a doctor, I feel compelled to inform you that palm reading is a bunch of hooey with no basis in science whatsoever," Tobias said.

"Says the dragon who probably just carried me out of a magical land that can only be reached through a sapling in an alley."

Tobias shrugged. "I was trying to be nice."

Gabriel grunted. "Excuse my brother. He's the compassionate one. It comes from his years of acting as a healer for humans in Chicago. I am not as nice. I will hand your ass to you on a platter if you don't pull it together and help us get our sister back, no matter what our palms say."

Nick nodded slowly, feeling every syllable of what Gabriel had said in his "oh shit!" sensor. Gabriel had turned down the unmarked road, and Nick motioned for him to slow down and pull off between the trees. They rolled to a stop, and he led them to the tree that overlooked the wall.

The sun had started to set, but the level of security hadn't lessened in the least. If anything, there were more humans patrolling the property. The place was absolutely buzzing with security uniforms.

"So what's the plan?" Nick asked. "Where did you get all the firepower anyway?"

Gabriel shot him a dark look. "It's better if you don't know."

"Okay. As a proud member of the NYPD, that makes me really uncomfortable."

"You could be dead soon. Then you won't be uncomfortable." Gabriel handed him a bulletproof vest. The thing was loaded with magazines. More ammo than he'd seen in his lifetime.

Tobias raised a hand. "Hey now, we are not getting our sister's mate killed before we even have a chance to razz her about how she mated a human."

"About this mate thing..." Nick wanted to ask exactly what it meant. What had he signed up for? Clearly he had signed up. People didn't rush forth into a heavily armed fortress knowing they could die for someone they weren't completely sure about. But when he began to ask the question, the looks on her brothers' faces gave him pause. Gabriel especially would doubtless be enraged by any indication that Nick hadn't completely mated his sister. "I... I want to be the one to kill Malvern."

The brothers' smiles were dual images of each other, the way only siblings can be. But then Tobias's expression morphed into an expression that made Nick instantly uncomfortable. He hated pity.

"Did she feed you her tooth?" he asked.

Gabriel raised an eyebrow in Tobias's direction. "Personal much?"

"I'm just trying to assess the potential risks—"

"No," Nick said, trying not to appear appalled at the thought. "She did not give me one of her teeth."

"Feed you—" Gabriel shook his head. "Never mind. You're vulnerable. As much as your instincts make you want to be the one to kill Malvern, I can't promise you anything. Our first priority is to get you and her out of there alive. We are immortal. You are not. I will attempt to allow you to kill Malvern to appease the bond, but I won't let you die to do it."

Nick buckled his bulletproof vest. He preferred not to die. "Sounds fair to me."

"I'm no good at hand-to-hand, Gabriel. You're going to have to take him in." Tobias started stripping off his shirt and pants.

"What's happening right now?" Nick asked as Rowan's brother stripped to his boxers.

Gabriel grabbed Nick's arm and dragged him back toward the van. "Rowan must have told you what we are."

"Of course she did. I just—"

The sound of cracking bones and bursting organs filled his ears, a snap like an overstretched rubber band, and then the clink of metal on metal. Nick whirled to find a brilliant white dragon with piercing blue eyes staring at him from between the trees. The faintest hint of blue radiated between the scales of its chest. The dragon that once was Tobias stretched its wings. Nick tripped while backing the hell up and fell on his ass.

"Holy fuck. What the— Huge. Fucking huge!"

"I take it you've never seen Rowan like this," Gabriel said.

Nick shook his head vigorously.

"By the Mountain," Gabriel said, appalled. "How well do you two know each other?"

"Well," he stuttered. "Real well. I've seen her wings, just not..." He gestured in the general direction of the fire-breathing semitruck between the trees.

Gabriel reached into the van and thrust a CA-415 into his hands. "You know how to use one of these?"

"Stay on the trigger end?"

"Good enough."

"I thought bullets couldn't kill vampires."

"These are silver. Aim for the head. Plus you'll have these." Gabriel strapped a couple of wooden stakes to his thighs and slung a crossbow and quiver of wooden arrows to his back.

All together it was heavy as hell, but Nick sucked it up. There was a reason he worked out. You never knew when you'd need a few pounds of muscle.

Once Gabriel was similarly armed to the teeth, Nick started for the tree, wondering how he was going to climb up its trunk to drop himself over the wall when his every limb was weighted down with weapons and ammo. He paused when a hollow, sonorous flap like unfurling canvas met his ears. He whirled to find Gabriel's green wings glinting black as they shifted in the light. Monstrous wings, the hooked barbs at the arches more pronounced than Rowan's, whose now seemed positively feminine by comparison.

"Hold tight," Gabriel said.

"What?"

There was a rush, and then all the air left Nick's lungs as he was carried straight up, through the leaves and branches of the woods, and over the massive wall. Although Gabriel set him down softly on the other side, it was a long moment until he could catch his breath. He'd never been much for heights, and that ride was like the most intense roller coaster he'd ever been on.

"You okay?" Gabriel squeezed Nick's shoulder, and he forced himself to swallow down the rising urge to be sick.

"Yeah, of course."

The guards in front of the building had already spotted them. A dog began to bark, and men yelled at them in three different languages.

"Tobias," Gabriel yelled. "It's time to clear the way, brother!"

Nick looked toward the sky as branches snapped and a rush of wind blew into him from above. He staggered backward. The airplane-sized white dragon that was Tobias swooped over his head, roaring loud enough that the sound vibrated in his bones. As Tobias rushed toward NAVAK's security contingent, the dragon's chest expanded, glowing bright sapphire blue behind the white scales. The guards fired. *Rat-tat-tat.* But the bullets bounced harmlessly off Tobias's scales. A rushing roar like the working of massive bellows filled the air. The dragon's mouth opened, and its giant teeth flashed in warning. Then a blast of fire left the creature's throat and cut through the twilight, warming Nick's face despite him being a half mile back from the target.

The security guards erupted in screams. Those caught in direct fire were incinerated instantly. Others on the fringes just burned, throwing themselves on the ground to try to extinguish the flames. Those lucky enough to be missed dropped their guns and ran for cover. The few who kept their shit together fired uselessly at Tobias. The dragon flapped his wings, rose and circled beneath the moon, and dive-bombed the fleeing guards, its mighty chest expanding again before raining fire across the front of the building. What resulted was a runway of sorts, a cleared path outlined by two burning strips of fire.

"Don't hurt the dog!" Nick yelled, eyeing a German shepherd that looked a hell of a lot like Rosco running from the blaze.

Gabriel raised an eyebrow in his direction.

"What?" Nick flipped a rude hand gesture. "The dog isn't to blame. He's an innocent animal."

"I assure you, my brother will avoid harming any innocent animals." He raised two fingers and motioned toward the building. "Now, get in there and help me find my sister."

Darkness closed in on Rowan, and she gasped for breath under Malvern's weight. Although her bound wrists were crushed between their bodies, he was still too close, the bite too intimate. The vampire's mouth was sealed around the wound on her neck and he'd been rhythmically swallowing for what seemed like forever but was probably only a matter of minutes. She felt like an antelope caught in a lion's jaws, pinned under the beast with its teeth buried in her flesh, the animal stink of him sinking into her skin.

She wanted to fight him. Desperately, she wanted to. But Rowan's strength had flowed out of her along with her blood. She was immortal, but the enchanted bindings at her wrists and ankles were restraining her magic and keeping her body from recovering. Her skin turned hot, then icy cold from blood loss. Did he plan to drain her completely? It was likely.

"Malvern, you must stop. You're killing me," she rasped.

At last his fangs slid out of her flesh, and she felt his tongue lap grotesquely over the wound.

"You..." His face came into view above her, his ghostly pale features and small, cutting eyes turning her stomach. This close, he looked dead and reeked of old blood. Even with the blush her blood had provided him, he was nothing more than a corpse. He licked his lips and closed his eyes. "Your blood is such a rush."

"You've taken too much," she croaked, her tongue dry as sandpaper. "Release my bindings so that I can heal or there will be no more blood for you to drink."

He frowned and shifted his weight so that he was lying beside her on the bed, his cold, hard body stretched out against her. He ran his long nails down the outside of her arm and hooked his finger in the binding around her wrists. "You want me to remove these?"

"Yes." She sent him a pleading look. She was so weak. Even if he did release her, she wasn't sure she could shift or fight him off in her current state. Not immediately. She shivered as his icy-cold fingers traveled over her hip and down the outside of her leg.

"You are an exceptional specimen. I never knew dragons existed. We all thought you were a myth." His words were slightly slurred and his lids heavy, almost as if her blood had made him drunk.

She shivered with disgust as his nails continued to trace over her skin. "Please. I'm not well." Her voice was barely a whisper, but it was the only weapon she had left. She had to appeal to logic. She must convince him she was worth more alive. "If you release me, I can recover and my blood will last longer."

His hands trailed lower, over the silk charmeuse fabric of her dress, her hip, her thigh. She hated that Malvern was touching her. Oddly, it made her think of Nick, how she was *his* and how only his hands should be allowed on her skin. She hated Malvern and wished she was herself so she could fry him in the fire of her own breath. But she was helpless.

His nails scraped along her calves and then his fingers went to work between her ankles. Once Malvern had succeeded in untying the bindings around her legs, Rowan couldn't help but release a sigh of relief. She stretched her legs and flexed her ankles. The skin was sore, but it would heal.

"Now my wrists. I'll heal. I'll be worth more to you well." She tried to sound sincere and held her wrists out to Malvern.

A wicked smile spread his lips, and he slowly shook his head. "Worth. What are you worth? What could the Forebears ever give me that would adequately compensate me for this?" His eyes raked over her, and he dragged a thumb along the corner of his mouth. "I want you to myself and for myself. And if they will force you from me, I will have you first. I will have you until no one else can. I will be the last to have you."

She shook her head. "No. No, Malvern."

But he had already used the rope he'd pulled from her ankles to thread through the bindings at her wrists and the wrought iron headboard. He forced her hands above her head, leaving her exposed. What little comfort she'd had from the protection of her bindings was now gone.

"You're beautifully pale," he said, grabbing her bottom jaw. "Pale as a vampire. Can you be turned, I wonder? You'd make a lovely vampire."

She stiffened and turned her head away as he leaned down as if to kiss her. He hissed at the side of her jaw, his body coming to rest on top of her again, his knee forcing its way between her own.

"No. The Forebears cannot have you. I will keep you. I will break you."

He squeezed her jaw and forced her to look at him, just as the house shook and the sound of gunfire tore through the dimly lit room.

CHAPTER THIRTY-ONE

The gun kicked in Nick's hands as he sprayed the vampires in front of the mansion with bullets. Thanks to the runway bordered with fire Tobias had laid for them, Nick had made it to the front porch rather easily, Gabriel at his side. But a second wave of security guards had stormed them from both sides. Unlike the coven's human security contingent, these were vampires and more committed.

While Gabriel John Wick-ed his way through the attackers in front of him, a pistol in each hand, his taloned wings working overtime to shred vampires, Nick backed toward the door, shooting anything that snuck by the dragon's killing blows. Rowan hadn't exaggerated; Gabriel was a killing machine. He'd clearly been trained for this.

As for Nick, in all his years in law enforcement, he'd never been in a situation quite like this one. Yes, he'd been shot at, but not like this. This was war. Thank God whatever Harriet had given him was filling in where his skills and abilities fell short. He'd become an excellent shot and was dodging bullets with *Matrix*-like maneuvers he could have never pulled off yesterday. *Pop, pop, pop.* Vampire heads exploded like watermelons under a sledgehammer. A vampire to his left pulled a gun, and Nick finished him in a heartbeat.

Tobias roared and scorched the earth in front of Gabriel, cutting off the vampires who raced in from God knew where to join their brethren. Nick reached the front door and threw it open. A flash of fang dropped from the general direction of the chandelier. He wedged his gun under the creature's jaw and sent its brains into the stratosphere. Two more attacked from the left while one charged straight at him. He put a bullet through the first one's head, kicked the second one in the teeth, and impaled the third one with a wooden stake he drew from the holster on his leg. Number two sat up, a dark-haired male roughly the size of a bear, and Nick got a horrific view of the dining room through a two-inch hole in its abdomen. He aimed for the head, pulled the trigger. *Click.* Nothing happened.

Ejecting the magazine, he reached for another in his vest, only to be plowed over by the charging vampire. The crossbow dug into his back through the vest and his gun slipped from his hand and skidded across the marble floor. The vamp tore the new mag from his grip and hurled it through the window, into the mounting flames. Fangs landed in his shoulder. Nick kneed the vampire in the groin, hard enough to loosen its grip on him. It was enough to free his right hand. He reached down the side of his leg, his fingertips fumbling to grip a wooden stake. *Got it!* Rolling the vampire, he thrust the stake through its heart. Blood sprayed across Nick's chest and then the light faded from its eyes.

Nick scrambled to his feet and drew the crossbow, loading it with a wooden arrow from the quiver. Out of the corner of his eye, he saw Gabriel eviscerate another vamp outside the door before rushing in behind him.

"Watch out!" Gabriel yelled.

Nick saw nothing but a set of blurred shapes. Six more vampires charged at them from the left. His feet left the floor as Gabriel spun him around and lifted him into the air. He easily assessed the situation, pulled the trigger and reloaded, again and again. The arrows pierced eye, head, and heart. All six fell. *Thank you, Harriet.* Nick was good, but he wasn't this good, especially not with a crossbow.

"Drop me," he said to Gabriel, and the dragon obeyed. Landing on his feet, he loaded his last arrow and looked right, then left. Another stream of dragon fire blazed beyond the open door. No more were coming in from that direction.

"Do you have any ammo left?" Nick asked.

"No. A few stakes and a dagger," Gabriel said.

"Me either. Last arrow. One stake."

"Which way is Rowan?" Gabriel asked him. They were back to back in the foyer, scanning every open doorway.

"How should I know?" Nick said. "She could be anywhere."

Gabriel scoffed. "Why do you think we brought you here, Nick? I thought you shared a connection with my sister?"

"I do. I... feel for Rowan... Strongly. I care for her."

Gabriel growled and turned to him, folding his wings away. He pressed a finger into Nick's chest. "Then reach out with your instincts. These vampires stole your *mate*. Are you going to let them have her? Where is she, Nick? *Find* her."

There was that word again. *Mate*. What did it mean? Then again, what did it matter? Rowan was his. *His*. He should have told her so that night they'd made love. He should have thrown her over his shoulder when she'd tried to leave the Dakota, carried her back into her bedroom, and shown her why she couldn't go anywhere with Verinetti that night or ever again. The thought of anyone else touching Rowan made him furious. Heat flooded his face, his chest. Every cell in his body clenched for action. He had to find her. He had to find her now.

Nick's adrenaline soared and something clicked. Whether it was Harriet's tonic or his connection to Rowan, he thought he heard the faintest sound, a buzz or a hum, coming from upstairs. A deep grunt worked its way out of his throat, and he took the stairs two at a time. He glanced back.

"I'll cover you," Gabriel said, backing up the stairs behind him.

Nick raised the crossbow and crept down the hall in the direction of the sound. The floor creaked under his weight, and he tried his best to roll his steps and listen for Rowan. His breath came too quickly. He pursed his lips to try to slow it down. He had to keep his head. Focus. His eyes landed on the last door. She was in there. Somehow he knew.

"No," he heard her whimper, and it was all the confirmation he needed.

He tried to open the door. Locked. Backing up, he threw a kick. Then another. Then put all his weight behind it. The door splintered from its lock and swung open on its hinges. Nick charged in, then came up short at what he saw. Rowan was tied to the bed, her skin pale as snow, her eyes rolled back in her head. He couldn't tell if she was breathing. God, he hoped she was breathing. Her dress had been pushed up her hips, and a pair of fang marks bled from her thigh.

"Oh God, Rowan!" Tears filled his eyes as he rushed to her.

He never reached her. A brutal force swept him off his feet and slammed him to the floor. Nick's head cracked against wood. The crossbow flew across the room and a big, Russian-looking vampire held him down and stared at him through small beady eyes.

The creature laughed wickedly. "It's you! I remember you."

For a moment Nick thought he'd descended into his worst nightmare. The hair was different, but the face hadn't changed. He knew this man. Well, he'd thought he was a man the day he'd thrown him from the parking garage. Clearly he'd been wrong. For twenty years, he'd lived with the guilt of believing he'd killed someone. Now all the events of his past rearranged themselves. No wonder the man had seemed so invincible, so larger than life.

You couldn't kill what was already dead.

"Trojan...," Nick rasped.

"Malvern. You should know my true name before I end you." He dug his nails into Nick's biceps and ran his tongue along his fangs. "I bet you taste sweet, just like your mother."

"My mother?" Nick struggled in Malvern's grip, but he was overpowered.

"She was my whore for years. I lost control one night and drained her dry. Poor little orphan. Did you think she'd abandoned you?"

"You fucking bastard."

"Seems like that label belongs to you. None of us believed Stan was your father. Though who it was is anyone's guess."

Nick thrust his legs and shoulders off the floor, but

Malvern's hold was superhuman. He slammed Nick back into the rug.

"Before we struck our deal with Verinetti for Manhattan, we relied on those like Stan to work for us. True human scum."

Nick's blood pounded in his ears. Trojan was Malvern. It felt like the universe was shaking him, rattling his teeth.

"Did you kill Stan too?" he spat out.

"After you threw me over the rail of that parking garage, we found him and our money. He died soon after."

Nick closed his eyes and forced himself to calm down. He couldn't overpower Malvern. He'd have to outthink him. Gabriel was coming. He'd have a distraction soon. He just had to keep Malvern from killing him until then.

"I don't suppose you'd let bygones be bygones? Let me vamoose with my woman?"

Malvern's fangs dropped and his next words came out on a hiss. "She is mine."

A prickle of hate-filled jealousy climbed his spine. Nick wanted Malvern dead, wanted to see him bleed. Despite his best efforts at remaining calm, he answered Malvern through his teeth. "No. Rowan is *mine*."

"Then I take her from you!"

In a flash of pale flesh, Malvern struck, his fangs piercing Nick's neck where it met his shoulder. He cursed as pain tore through him, like being stabbed with a pair of knitting needles. He struggled against Malvern's hold and managed to wrap his legs around the vampire's hips and squeeze. Was it possible to crush a vampire's bones? He sure as hell was going to try.

His head spun as he felt warm blood trickle down his neck beneath the heat of the vampire's mouth. The worst part was the swallowing, the violation of having his blood forcibly taken and used as energy to take more. As angry and terrified as he was, Nick made himself relax under the vampire's bite. It was the opposite of his instincts but was his only chance of causing Malvern to drop his guard.

It worked. Malvern must have thought the blood loss had weakened Nick, because he loosened his grip and shifted to get a better angle at his neck. Nick used the opportunity to work one arm free, reach over the back of the vampire's head, and gouge his eyes with his clawed fingers.

Malvern gave a strangled moan and dissolved into a dark mist, filtering through Nick's grip. Nick stumbled to his feet and staggered back, drawing the last stake from its sheath on his thigh and pointing it toward the gathering fog.

The dark mist coalesced quickly into the pale shape of the vampire, and one fist shot out toward Nick's head. Nick shuffled right, and the vampire's punch landed in the wall. With speed and dexterity he could only ascribe to Harriet's potion, Nick dodged and stabbed the vampire's side, keeping his grip on the stake as he pulled away.

Malvern staggered back a step, looked down with annoyance at the wound in his gut that was already stitching itself up, and gave him a pitying look. "Oh dear boy, you don't even know how to use that, do you?"

Nick raised the bloody stake between them. "Try me."

An evil little smirk curled Malvern's lip. "You know, I've already had her," he said. "All of her. And she was glorious."

Fury burned through Nick's veins and he tightened his grip on the stake. He wanted to shred the vampire, tear him limb from limb, attack with abandon, bite, claw, and kick. To take out every bit of anger he was feeling on Malvern like his own personal vampire punching bag. But he didn't.

Malvern would expect resistance. He must feign the opposite and wait for him to make a mistake.

Criminals, if observed carefully, always tipped their hand when given enough time and space. It came down to narcissism. Most diabolical minds wanted to be known, they wanted others to be an audience to their dark brilliance. Without even realizing it, Malvern had told Nick his currency. It was Rowan. Her blood. Dragon blood. He forced his mind to steady. Slowed his breathing. Nick backed up against the edge of the bed, putting himself between Rowan and Malvern. He raised the stake.

Malvern swaggered toward him, toying with him. "Put it down. You're human. No match for a vampire."

"I threw you off the top of a building once. I can do it again." He bent his knees and prepared to fight.

A smile spread his lips. Gabriel had appeared in the doorway.

"You think *Rowan* tastes good," he said to Malvern, allowing his eyes to dart over the vampire's shoulder. "Wait until you taste her brother."

Gabriel charged, but Malvern was faster. Nick's feet left the floor and his back slapped against the wall across the room with a resounding crack. He crumpled to the floor. For a moment all he could do was shake his head and try to gather his bearings. It took a second for him to process that Malvern had thrown him across the room before sinking his teeth into Gabriel, most likely believing that was the end of Nick.

His body did hurt and his vision blurred as he got to his feet, but Nick had known pain before. He'd been beaten more times than he could count growing up and had still found the strength to keep going. And all those times as a kid when he was bloodied and hungry, he never had someone like Rowan to fight for. She was far more motivation than he'd ever had before to live, to survive.

His hand closed around the dropped stake as air came back into his lungs in tiny sips. Everything he felt for Rowan channeled into his torso, his shoulder, his arm. He took one step, then two. Then he buried the stake in Malvern's back, up, under the ribs and straight into his cold black heart.

Gabriel pushed the vampire off him with a look of disgust. The coven master's body flopped to the floor and instantly stiffened to the state of a long-dead corpse. Nick spit on his cold gray body.

"For the record, I did not enjoy that," Gabriel said. "But I promised you a shot at taking him down."

"Thank you," Nick said, hobbling over to Rowan. He wished he had a knife to cut the ropes, but he made short work of the knot anyway. He tossed the bindings aside and pulled her into his arms. She was limp as a rag doll and much too pale. He held his ear to her lips and felt the slightest breath hit his skin. Tapping her cheek, he hugged her to him. "Rowan. Rowan, honey, wake up." He turned desperate eyes toward Gabriel when she didn't stir. "What's wrong with her? Why isn't she recovering? She told me she was immortal."

"She is very close to death," Gabriel said. "She needs her treasure room to properly heal."

"Treasure room? Where the hell is her treasure room?" Nick repositioned her in his arms.

Gabriel shrugged. "I haven't seen her in years. Your guess is as good as mine, but it would be somewhere hidden. Somewhere safe."

"Harriet. Let's get her back to the car and pay a visit to the Traveller."

Gabriel reached out to help him with Rowan, but Nick shook his head. No matter how much he hurt, he would not relinquish her. Not ever again. He'd come for her, and he was carrying her out of here.

"All right then," Gabriel said. "Let's find Tobias and get her home."

CHAPTER THIRTY-TWO

Tobias landed on top of the stone mansion and roared down over the burning lawn. Under the full moon, his dragon eyes scanned the grounds. Bodies lay burned and motionless in his wake. Vampires mostly. He'd attempted to avoid the humans and the dog. They weren't the enemy here and were likely compelled to do the vampires' will. Luckily most had fled at the first sight of him. Now there was nothing moving in the circular drive or the rolling yard of the estate. Just the flicker of fire and a soft breeze blowing out of the east and across his scales.

But then the front door opened and Gabriel exited the house. Nick was behind him with Rowan in his arms. Tobias whimpered. His sister was damaged, pale white and limp. He spread his wings, ready to swoop down and fly them to safety, when the distant sound of car engines coming up the drive gave him pause.

Quickly, he made himself invisible and transformed back into his human form. If it was who he expected, he couldn't be seen. The gate opened and a line of three dark SUVs drove toward the mansion, coming to a stop in the front circle. The doors opened. He recognized Aldrich right away. The elder vampire had been at Sabrina's coronation and had been responsible for telling the vampire council about him and his dragon siblings. These were the Forebears, called in by Malvern to get Rowan. Just as he'd thought.

One of the vampires was dressed in a suit that looked like it came straight out of the nineteenth century. He was exceptionally tall and approached Gabriel with an air of entitlement. Clearly this was the leader, Turgun. Tobias remembered Sabrina talking about the ancient vamp, the eldest of their kind.

The master vampire brushed invisible lint off his sleeve and stopped at the bottom of the stairs leading to the front door. "We've come for the dragon," he said, his voice commanding.

Nick placed a kiss against Rowan's temple. "There's no such thing as dragons."

"Who are you? Where is Malvern?" Turgun demanded.

Nick descended the stairs, and Tobias had to give him props. The guy was either incredibly brave or incredibly stupid. "I don't know who Malvern is, but my friend is sick and I need to get her home. Now if you'll excuse me." He started walking toward the gate, passing between the elder vampires.

Tobias knew the moment Turgun smelled Rowan's blood. How could he have missed it? It stained her chest and her dress, and as a doctor, Tobias knew all too well that shit couldn't be mistaken for human. The vampire's nostrils flared, and he held up a hand. The others in his group turned as one to stare at Nick, who was walking as fast as a human who was carrying a dragon could walk.

"Stop, human!" Turgun yelled.

Nick did not stop.

The vampires closed in. With their superspeed, it was almost as if Nick was standing still.

"Leave him alone. He's not what you're after." Gabriel popped his wings and flew over their heads, landing protectively between Nick and the vampires.

The vampires hissed.

Tobias looked up at the moon. "Well, universe, it's been nice knowing you." He spread his wings and prepared to do what he had to do.

Before he had a chance to soar down and help his brother defend his sister and her mate, another group of SUVs peeled into the compound. Five of them. He paused at the edge of the roof as the first one stopped and a familiar face exited the vehicle.

"Sabrina!" Tobias caught the eye of his vampire bride, whose look told him he should stay exactly where he was.

A moment later, the Forebears were surrounded by the Chicago coven's human security contingent, their guns trained on the elder vampires.

"These bullets are soaked in Keetridge Solution," Sabrina said. "Please don't move. I'd hate for any of you to be damaged beyond repair."

"What is the meaning of this?" Turgun snapped, his fangs extending. "You're beyond your coven boundaries, Sabrina Bishop. You'd better have a good reason for this disruption."

Sabrina pulled a snow globe from her bag. Tobias focused in and realized it was of Chicago, the kind you could get at any souvenir stand in his home city. "I do have a good reason," she said, "and all you have to do is look at this to understand it."

The Forebears moved in, staring at the snow-filled orb.

Tobias noticed Sabrina never looked directly at the snow globe. Turgun, Aldrich, and the rest of the vampire council did, however, and each froze in place as soon as they saw it. Sabrina lowered it to the ground between the Forebears, who huddled around the trinket and stared at it, unblinking.

He lifted off the roof and flew down to his mate, pulling her into his arms and kissing her on the mouth.

"Easy, cowboy." Sabrina drew back and winked at him. "I thought you could use some assistance, compliments of Madam Chloe. It won't last. I recommend you make use of that forget-me potion you told me Harriet gave you."

As soon as Tobias had found out about Rowan's capture, he'd texted Sabrina and told her everything. He hadn't expected her to make it to New York as quickly as she had, or with magical reinforcements from the coven witch, but it was like Sabrina to surprise him with her resourcefulness.

"I came as fast as I could. We traveled all day. That's why I only brought humans and a little magic."

"What about the Keetridge Solution? I thought the last of your stores were depleted."

"A lie. Plain bullets. Sue me."

Gabriel joined them, pulling vials of forget-me potion from his vest. "Sabrina, your timing is impeccable, as always."

His wife crossed one foot behind the other and curtsied low. "I live to serve." She took the vials from Gabriel's hands. "Now, not to be rude, but if I'm going to wipe the memories of the Forebears and replace them with a story about an explosion that killed most of the New Amsterdam Vampire Kingdom, I've got to get to work. And it would be helpful if there weren't dragons in the immediate vicinity while I did it."

Tobias kissed her one more time, then watched her

hurry to administer the tonic to the temporarily catatonic vampires. Everyone stopped as the front door to the mansion opened and a crowd of humans stumbled out into the night.

Nick cleared his throat. "It's the human herd. The compulsion is over now that the vampires are dead. Any way we can use some of these SUVs to get them to safety?"

Exchanging glances with Sabrina, Tobias gave him a nod. "My wife will take care of them."

Nick seemed satisfied with that, or maybe he was too tired to object and simply choosing his battles. He stubbornly carried Rowan toward the gate. Tobias was treated to a peek at a serious bruise that was spreading along the back of Nick's neck. The human was injured. He glanced at Gabriel, who looked equally concerned.

"I can carry her for you," Tobias offered.

A growl ripped from Nick's throat. "I got her." The look he shot him was deadly. "No offense. I get you're her brother and everything, but no one is taking Rowan out of my arms until she's well enough to tell me she wants to go."

With mad respect for the man, Tobias gave him an understanding nod, then raced off to retrieve the van.

CHAPTER THIRTY-THREE

The world held a hazy quality, dark around the edges, but it smelled of spices and sandalwood. It smelled of Nick. That's how Rowan knew she was safe. Mouth too dry to speak, all she had the energy to do was turn her face into his chest. His shirt was splattered with blood, but she didn't care. He was her only strength, her only comfort.

"Easy," he whispered. "Hang in there. We're going to get you help. Try some water, baby."

He sat her up against his chest, held her head, and tipped an aluminum bottle to her lips. She gulped too quickly and began to choke, sputtering up as much as she managed to swallow.

He stroked her hair. "Slowly." Lips pressed against her temple, he tipped the water again.

This time she was able to swallow, and the relief was heavenly. Exhausted from the effort, she slumped against him, turning her face to his chest again.

"I know you're tired, Rowan, but there's something I have to tell you."

She didn't say anything. She couldn't. Her eyes drooped

and she leaned heavily against him. All she could give him was a sigh.

"I've been thinking," Nick said, hugging her to him, "that this thing between us, maybe it's bigger than the sum of its parts. Maybe there's something to this idea that people are soul mates. This... bond between us seems like a thing we shouldn't take for granted."

With what was left of her strength, she hooked her fingers in his shirt and tugged. He seemed to understand. Bending his neck, he pressed a soft kiss to her lips. She slipped into unconsciousness once more.

The next time she opened her eyes, she recognized the interior of the art gallery and heard Harriet's voice as she led Nick to the stairwell and then down to the vault. Rowan's heart beat faster. If she were strong enough to speak, she'd insist on going down alone. No man had ever entered her treasure room or seen her shift into her true dragon form. What would Nick think? Would he judge her for the hoard of jewels she kept? Would watching her shift scare him away? And worst of all, would seeing the jewels trigger the anger he'd felt the other night when he'd learned about the memory she'd suppressed of their first meeting, when she'd stolen the Raindrop of Heaven right from under his watch?

But she couldn't speak. Staying awake was enough of a struggle. Everything hurt. Malvern had drained her of so much blood, her veins seemed to rub together like sandpaper. Her internal organs ground out their activities of living without the essence of life as lubrication. If she were human, she'd have died long ago. Only dragon magic kept her alive now. And Nick. The unfinished business between them gave her something to hope for, something to live for.

Harriet's fingers danced across the keypad, and the

vault door opened with the whoosh of its hermetic seal giving way. "Take her inside and set her on the pile."

"Fuck me," Nick said. "Is this all real?"

Harriet made a throaty sound. "It wouldn't be much of a treasure room if it housed cubic zirconia and pearls made of paste, now would it?"

"But... But... Where the hell did all this come from?" Nick's arms held her tighter. If he'd just set her down, the treasure's healing properties would start to work.

"She's a princess and a dragon, Mr. Grandstaff. I'm sure you can imagine the possibilities. Now, if you'd place her there."

Finally he lowered her to the pile in the gentlest way; it made her heart warm to experience the care. He brushed her hair back from her face. "What now?"

"Leave her," Harriet said. "She needs time to heal."

"I'm not going to leave her alone in this... bank vault. What if she needs help? What if this"—he motioned toward the treasure—"doesn't work right?"

Rowan met Harriet's gaze, and the old woman seemed to understand what Rowan couldn't say. This needed to happen. Nick could never be hers completely until he knew the entire truth of what she was.

"Very well. Help me undress her." Harriet pulled the dress over her head and placated Nick's concerns about leaving her naked on a pile of jewels and metalwork. "I'll bring you food and drink. There's a bathroom right outside the vault door. If you think you'll be ill, use it."

"Why would I be ill?" Nick asked.

Rowan concentrated and started to shift, her bones stretching, her organs reordering themselves. Her skin changed, becoming thicker, covering with scales. The process was slower than normal, more deliberate what with her weakness and fatigue. But when she was done, she stretched her wings, yawned, and felt the dragon begin to heal.

"Holy fucking shit balls. I will never get used to that," Nick rattled off, then looked up at her with wide, terrified eyes. "Are you okay?"

She nodded and lowered her head when he reached for her. He stroked along her face and neck. Thank the Mountain, he didn't run away.

"You're beautiful," he said softly near her ear. "Red. I love red."

The purr she released almost hurt, she was so tired.

"Go on. Get some rest. I'll be here when you wake up."

She turned, careful not to sweep him into the wall with her tail, and dove beneath her treasure. Curled in on herself, she fell into a deep healing sleep, one so far gone she didn't even dream.

OF ALL THE SURPRISES LIFE HAD EVER THROWN HIS way, this stole the cake. Nick sat cross-legged, back against the wall, staring at a heap of treasure that now contained his girlfriend. His dragon girlfriend. Not just wings. Not just a barbed tail. She was the dragon and the dragon was her, and somehow, someway, he was okay with that.

In fact, he loved her.

Nick had never believed he could love anyone. No, that wasn't exactly true. He knew he had the capacity to love, just wasn't sure if anyone would or could ever love him. The loss of a mother was always traumatic to children. Nick understood that. But Nick's loss had many edges. His abandonment had come at a time he was most vulnerable and had left no one to protect him from Stan.

Now he understood his mother had never meant to leave him. She'd been wrapped up in darkness and she couldn't get herself out.

Fuck, he hurt. His entire body felt like a fresh bruise, and he was pretty sure the bite mark on his neck was deeper than the last. He lowered himself to the floor and closed his eyes. He wasn't sure how long he slept, but when he opened his eyes again, she was standing there, entirely naked but healthy, as if the horrors of the night before had never happened at all. Unfortunately, he couldn't say the same. He couldn't move.

"You look better," he said.

"You look like hell."

"Fair enough."

She crossed the room out of his field of vision and returned wearing a red robe. She knelt beside him and took his hand in hers. "Thank you for coming for me."

He winked at her, which hurt more than he expected, and squeezed her hand. "Well, I think we had to wipe out most of the New Amsterdam coven to do it, but it will all be worth it if you throw me your handkerchief. Isn't that what princesses did for the winner of the joust?" He chuckled but had to stop when it felt like his ribs might crack.

"You can have more than my handkerchief, Nick."

"Good. Because I want you. All of you."

"I thought you were afraid of relationships."

"I've recently reassessed that fear. Turns out I'm much more afraid of living without you."

She leaned down and pressed a kiss against his lips. It was like an angel floating down from heaven to stab him in the face with a red-hot poker. He groaned.

"We need to call Harriet. You need healing." She began to get up, but he squeezed her hand again.

"Wait, wait a minute."

"I'm here. What's wrong?"

"Do you remember what I said to you in the van, about wanting to try this bond thing?"

She placed her hands on either side of his face. "Yes. I want that too. But I'm worried for you. Let me get Harriet."

"I don't think we should start a new relationship with any secrets between us." He narrowed his eyes on her. He remembered when he saw her in the Stevensons' closet, and there was something bothering him about the memory. "This isn't your true face, is it?"

She shook her head.

"Show me." Nick watched in utter amazement as her face subtly changed. Her nose became more pronounced with a gentle hook, her eyes changed from hazel to bright amber, and her skin darkened to a beautiful shade of creamy bronze. Along the temple beside her right eye was a mark like a double crescent. She tapped it.

"All dragons have this." She pulled up her hair and pointed to a series of V-shaped ridges along her neck. "And this."

Nick remembered now, her face. He hadn't noticed the markings but her hair had been down, the swoop of her bangs covering her temple. But he remembered this face. This gorgeous face. "So this is the real you?"

"As real as it gets."

"Good." He sighed. "You're beautiful as you are."

She smiled and rested her hand on his cheek. "Do you forgive me?"

"I was going to tell you last night when you came to my place that Stevenson was blackmailing NYPD cops right and left. He used my partner, Soren, to threaten to pin the theft on me if I didn't cover for NAVAK."

"That bastard." She bared her teeth.

"Yeah. Now that we've dealt with NAVAK and have over a hundred trafficked humans to reincorporate into society, I think I'll ask your brother's wife, Sabrina, to help us take down Stevenson too, and Verinetti while we're at it. Do you think she'll go for it? Thought we could get your building back if we play our cards right."

She nodded her head, a smile spreading across her face. "You're absolutely diabolical. In a good way."

"Someone's got to pay for what happened to Allison."

"Who's Allison?"

"Allison Sumner, the girl who was murdered. My case."

"You really care about her. I mean, her personally, not just the case."

"Everyone deserves justice. The punishment we doled out to Malvern doesn't make up for what Stevenson did and won't stop him from doing it again for the next highest bidder. And Verinetti is a menace. He has to go down."

A dark cloud passed behind her eyes. "I agree."

"You want to take out Verinetti yourself?"

She nodded. "I owe him one. Besides, the human justice system has a hard time containing supernaturals."

Nick winked at her. "All right. I take care of my kind and you take care of yours. I promise you, I won't cry for Verinetti, whatever you do with him."

Their eyes met and held, and Nick's heart flipped in his chest. His body ached and his head was spinning, but he'd never felt better. Never more at peace.

"Are you okay, Nick? I better get Harriet. You're sweating, and by the Mountain, you're so pale. Nick?" Her cool hand patted his cheek.

God, he was tired. Darkness pressed in at the edges of his vision. He needed to rest, to sleep, maybe for a couple of days.

"Nick?"

"I love you, Rowan," he said. Why not? He felt it. And what did he have to lose anymore that he'd keep something like that a secret? He blinked up at her beautiful face and waited to see if his prayers were answered.

"I love you too." She smiled at him, her cool hands soothing his hot skin. It was odd. She was close but somehow seemed like she was at the end of a long tunnel, as if a circle of darkness was constricting around him.

"I knew it. Who could resist this?"

Then he closed his eyes and gave in to the darkness.

CHAPTER THIRTY-FOUR

"Tobias, what the hell is going on? What's wrong with him?" Rowan crowded around the examination table with Harriet and Gabriel as Tobias examined the love of her life.

Nick had passed out, and Harriet's usual concoction of herbs and magic couldn't rouse him. In fact, her ministrations hardly helped at all. She'd remembered Tobias was a human physician, but they didn't dare take Nick to a hospital. There'd be too many questions. Instead, they'd used Sabrina to commandeer a nearby veterinary clinic so Tobias could examine him.

"He's hypovolemic," Tobias said. "He's bleeding internally. It's a slow bleed, but it's lethal."

"What are you waiting for?" Rowan said. "Stop it!"

Tobias frowned and placed his hands on her shoulders in a way that she recognized was meant to comfort her, but in fact had the opposite effect. Her heart raced in her chest. *Don't say it. Please don't say it.*

"It's too late for human medicine." The words fell between them like glass vases that shattered at her feet.

"No." Rowan's chest constricted from a combination of fear and panic. "I can't... I can't lose him, Tobias. I'll become like Alexander. I won't survive it. I don't want to survive it!"

Gabriel spun her around, pulled her into his chest, and held her tight. "There is another way, sister," he whispered in her ear. "And you've already done it once."

She met his gaze, and his eyes shifted to Harriet, who was staring at her intensely. For over a century, it had just been the two of them, locked in the bond that had formed when she'd saved her friend from tuberculosis with the gift of her tooth. Now the old woman had tears in her eyes, and although her suit was a happy shade of green offset with a gorgeous Hermès scarf in a spring floral pattern, her disposition was nothing if not blue.

"My dragon, my friend," she said. "It will not be easy sharing you. We've endured too much, managed too many escapades, cried too many tears, laughed the laughter of old friends. But I must encourage you to do this thing. My heart, although immortal, is not strong enough to watch you lose him. Don't you dare worry about me. There's enough room in our lives for a man like the detective."

Rowan placed her hand over her heart. "I want him. I want him so much."

"Then take him," Gabriel said.

"Not without his permission. It was a leap for him to accept me as his girlfriend. What if he can't accept me as his forever mate? It's too fast."

Tobias wiped a thumb under her eyes. "Life throws us curveballs, little sister. All we can do is take our best swing. But if you're going to try to hit this one out of the park, you better do it soon. Nick doesn't have much time."

She took a deep, cleansing breath and blew it out slowly. "I'd like the room."

Tobias and Gabriel gave her one last hug each and then exited.

Harriet stayed behind. "If he says no..."

"I won't force him," Rowan said.

Harriet squeezed her arm. "But I will force you."

Rowan raised her eyebrows in question.

"I will force you to go on. I will force you to survive. I will force you to heal. You will not become like Alexander. I won't let you."

Rowan hugged her friend as her tears flowed freely. "I love you, Harriet. Your friendship is a light in the darkness."

The old woman pulled back. "I try. Besides, without you, I couldn't afford to keep myself in Hermès and Chanel. I have quite the habit, you know."

She kissed her on the cheek. "Oh, I know."

Harriet squeezed her arm one last time and left the room, closing the door behind her. It was just Rowan and Nick, his body as still as if he were already dead. She hated it. The tick of the clock on the wall measured out the seconds. Rowan raised her ruby ring and called on the magic that resided in her dragon heart, magic that was her dragon birthright. It was said that in the beginning of time, dragons were slaughtered by other beings searching for the piece of them that embodied immortality. All they achieved was killing those dragons of old and killing their magic with them. For the magic was not in their scales or their blood or even their organs, it was in their souls, their minds, and their ability to love beyond limits.

The clock stopped. Nick opened his eyes.

"What happened, baby? It looks like you've been crying." He reached for her and wiped her tears away with his thumb.

She caught his hand between her own. "We don't have much time. There's something I have to ask you."

"I'm so tired. I don't know what's wrong with me."

"You're dying," she blurted, and the tears came again.

"I am? I'm not in any pain."

"Internal bleeding. It's insidious. We can't fix it. Not a human doctor or Harriet."

"Oh." His face softened.

"I've used dragon magic to stop time and wake you, but I can't do this forever."

"So, this is goodbye?" He rubbed his thumb softly against her cheek. "Don't cry for me, baby. Everyone dies. Well, not you, but humans." His words vibrated at the corners, and she could tell he was trying to comfort her and hide his own fears.

"I can save you," she said, "but it entails bonding you to me, the same way I bonded Harriet. I would have to feed you my tooth. The magic would heal you, but it would also connect you to me for the length of my life."

He inhaled sharply. "Yeah, I heard about the tooth thing from your brothers. Didn't know what it meant though."

"It's forever, Nick. If we do this, there's no going back."

He stared at her for a moment, his eyes wide. "It sounds like you're proposing."

"Marriage is until death do us part. What I am proposing is a commitment far longer and greater still. I'll be able to draw you to me and feel where you are at all times. You will live forever and will have to change your identity as I do. The intimacy this requires is unlike any you've experienced before. At times I will be inside your head. My magic will burn inside you."

She watched his throat bob on a swallow. "You're not doing a great job of selling this thing, Rowan. Jesus."

She ran both hands through her hair, feeling like a feather caked with mud, what beauty and lightness that had existed in her now suffocated under the choice before them. She refused to tell him the rest of it, that she would likely go mad if he said no. She refused to load the weight of her suffering on his shoulders. If he chose this, it must be his choice only, and for no other reason than his deep desire to be with her.

"Rowan... Rowan...," he said softly. "I need to tell you something, and I can't do it with you crying like that. It's tearing my heart out."

She bolstered herself and wiped away her tears.

"Good. Uh, you know, I never really bonded with anyone as an adult. After my mom died and I was left with Stan and he was like Mr. Evil, I just closed off to other people, you know?"

She nodded. She did understand, but it crushed her to hear it.

"I used to think there was something broken in me. Permanently broken, because as a child I'd just never learned to be human like everyone else and there was a hole where my heart should be. A goddamned gaping chasm."

"Oh, Nick..."

"No, wait, I'm trying to tell you something. So I'm walking around all my life with this hole, this weird emptiness that I can't fill with anything or anyone. Drugs don't work, drinking don't work. I can't fill it with anything. And then you come along, and I realize... I realized that the reason I could never fill it with something from this world was because the shape of that hole wasn't of anything worldly. It was the shape of you. Dragon big and as bright as your smile. Being with you, it's the first time I've felt wanted and the first time I've really wanted someone else. It was like a taste of what it was like for other people. Warmth and caring. Feeling... connected."

"Oh, Nick." Her heart warmed at his words.

"I want to do all the things that couples do. Dinner. A show. Fighting over the remote. All of it. I want all of it."

She inhaled a shaky breath. "Then you agree to be mine? To take the tooth?"

"I want to give this a try."

She shook her head. "You're not listening. There is no try. This is forever. There is no room for failure."

He squeezed her arm. "I want the tooth. I want you, Rowan."

Her heart leaped and she would not delay any further. Opening her mouth, she reached into the back and gripped one of her molars. There was pain and a little blood, but with a serious tug she extracted the razor-sharp tooth.

Nick stared at the six-inch molar in absolute horror.

"I can make it smaller." She closed and opened her hand again, and there was a small white pill in her palm. She brought it to his mouth.

He took it from her and tossed it to the back of his throat, then swallowed it down without the benefit of water. "See you on the other side."

His eyes closed and his body went still. The clock began to tick again. Her magic drained from the room as if she'd pulled the plug in an overfilled bathtub. She curled her fingers and ran the back of her nails gently along his cheek.

Now there was nothing to do but wait.

For Nick, waking up after swallowing Rowan's tooth resembled coming back to the surface after a long, deep dive in murky water. The air pressed thick and heavy against his skin, and he held his breath against it, against the darkness. He'd been swallowed by the dark, taken into the belly of a creature of the night and now regurgitated toward a light he could not see yet but whose gravity drew him like the North Star.

He broke the surface with a gasp, his eyes fluttering open to red velvet and candlelight. And her scent like a silk scarf drawn across the inside of his skull, the underside of his skin. He could taste her on his tongue, feel her, or a piece of her anyway, in the deepest corner of himself.

Her face came into view, breathless and waiting. "Nick?"

Filled with a new energy and possessing a body he realized was completely healed, he took her face in his hands and kissed her, kissed her like he could wash away everything dark that had ever happened to her with his own breath. His hands circled her waist, found red silk that slid softly between them.

She was not unaffected. Her nails scraped up his spine and along the muscles of his shoulders.

"I'm naked aren't I?"

Her smile was close and bright. "I had to clean you up. You were covered in blood."

"How long've I been out?"

"Three days. It didn't take as long with Harriet, but Tobias thought it was due to the nature of your injuries. We moved you to my apartment. Hell of a time explaining that one to the doorman." She raised her eyebrows. "How do you feel?"

"I've gotta piss like a racehorse."

She laughed. "The bathroom is there, and Flubell has prepared you something to eat." She grabbed a pair of black sweats off the dresser and tossed them to him. "I also brought you some clothes from your apartment, against my better judgment. I rather like you naked."

"Oh shit—Rosco!"

"He's here and he's fine. He's sleeping in the library. I bought him one of those giant beds."

He backed toward the bathroom. "Don't go anywhere. I'm not finished with you."

"I wouldn't dream of it."

Once Nick had made use of the facilities, he looked at himself in the mirror. Same old mug. Same sandy-brown hair. Same scar that cut through his lip and his eyebrow. But he felt different. He felt awake and alive. Rowan had replaced his batteries. And when he emerged again, he left the pants behind.

Rowan's eyes flicked down his body appreciatively.

"Take off your nightgown," he said, and his voice was all grit.

"Why? What do you plan to do with me naked?" she said through a smile.

He swaggered toward her. "I plan to show you you're mine."

Rowan crossed her arms, fisted the silk, and pulled it over her head. God, she was perfect—lush curves, red lips, and a body filled with dark secrets. His was ready in an instant, hard for her. Only for her. He closed the space between them and took her mouth. His hands explored the soft weight of her breasts, his fingers tugging her erect nipples, drawing them out. Her hips thrust against him and he moaned at the thrill. Their first experience had been good, but now he savored her. He planned to worship every inch of her.

He skimmed his hand down the slope of her waist and slowly, ever so slowly, between her legs.

"Fuck, you're wet. Is this for me? Just for me?"

"Yes," she said, voice husky with need. "I am yours."

He dropped to his knees, hands on her thighs, and looked up at her. "Then let me take care of you. I take care of what's mine."

He kissed her above where his fingers worked and licked up her center. She grabbed the corner of the dresser and hooked one leg over his shoulders, pulling him hard against her. As if he needed any further motivation. She tasted of oranges, of sweetness. He couldn't get enough. His dick twitched, begging to be inside her, but he was a patient man and the sweetest dessert was the one waited for.

Her climax tore through her, and he supported her as her knees gave out and her back arched with pleasure. He rose to meet her, face-to-face, and she wrapped her arms around his neck. Her sigh warmed the skin between his neck and his shoulder.

"You're mine," he whispered to her. "Forever."

"Do you know what forever means?"

He thought about it for a moment. "Maybe. It's an abstract concept for me still."

She hooked her fingers in his and led him from the bedroom to the terrace. "Let me show you."

"Hey, I'm naked here."

"You're also invisible as long as you touch me."

He ran his hands over her ass. "Then I guess I have to keep touching you."

"It's a beautiful night, don't you think?"

"I'm distracted by a beautiful woman and didn't notice."

Her wings unfurled from her back. "Let me show it to you." One arm and then the other wrapped around him, and then her legs. *Standing up*, he thought. *Well, all right.* He grabbed her thighs and slid into her.

"Hang on tight."

"Uh, what?" His eyes widened as she shot into the sky, their bodies locked against each other, coasting toward the moon.

"Jesus, Rowan!" Pleasure traced its fingers around fear as she soared higher and higher, rolling in the air and bracing him against her with her heels. He clung to her, deep inside her. They climbed higher.

"This is forever, Nick. It's not worrying about death or falling. It's knowing that you're hard to kill. It's the sun and the moon and us."

He trailed kisses up her neck and whispered, "I like us."

"Me too."

She turned in the air and thrust against him. It took him a second to find the rhythm, bracing himself against her shoulders, her heels. They were tangled together as tightly as woven vines.

And then, as he felt her body climb again toward that golden peak, she folded her wings and dove. Nick's stomach dropped as his climax rocked through him and his body rushed headfirst toward the Dakota building. He felt her orgasm again. She bucked against him. The roof rushed toward him. Closer. Faster.

"Rowan!"

Her wings unfurled without a moment to spare, and they swooped and coasted gently back to her rooftop terrace. Nick's heart pounded so hard he could feel it in his skin. She landed softly, setting him on his feet, their bodies parting. She ran her nails through the hair behind his ears and held him close. His brain replayed the feeling of flying, of dropping, of shattering inside her.

Against her cheek, he whispered, "I think I'm going to like forever."

CHAPTER THIRTY-FIVE

It had been centuries since Rowan had spent any time with Gabriel and Tobias together, but as they reunited over a few slices of pepperoni pizza at Lombardi's, she realized what she'd been missing. Family was a treasure that could never be replaced. Comfort and connection surrounded her, and she slipped back into the ways of her childhood, looking up to Gabriel and leaning on Tobias as they discussed what had happened with the vampires and how Sabrina, Tobias's vampire bride, had wiped the minds of the Forebears and sent them back to Romania thinking all the talk of dragons had been disproven. What Aldrich had seen had been nothing but an illusion produced by a very talented witch.

So it was soul crushing to learn that her mother had collaborated with her uncle to kill their brother Marius and that Paragon was now under their rule. But she believed her brothers, believed that they had stayed apart for no reason other than her mother's desire to keep them weak, to make them forget where they came from and their responsibilities to the world they left behind.

"Scoria was here," Tobias said. "With orders to kill us all."

Rowan gave a shrill inhale. "Mother sent Scoria himself?"

Tobias nodded. "In March. Chicago. We had to eliminate him."

Rowan brought her fingers to her lips. Scoria was the captain of the Obsidian Guard. Sending him was the equivalent of waging war.

"It's no longer enough to allow us to live out our existence in another realm. Now she and Brynhoff want us dead," Gabriel said.

"But why?"

Gabriel fixed Tobias with a steady stare. "My mate, the one who returned to Paragon with me when I discovered our mother's treachery, she is a witch."

"Oh, Gabriel." Rowan tried not to judge. She loved her brother, and she of all people now understood the undeniable nature of finding one's mate. But witches were forbidden.

"Believe me, I felt the same way," Tobias said. "But I'm more convinced than ever that Raven was sent by the goddess of the mountain herself. I think the same prophecies that warned us about witches may actually be promising us a way to save Paragon."

Rowan leaned forward and said through her teeth, "Before we go any further, there is something I need you to understand. I will never go back to Paragon. I have a life here now with Nick, one I prefer to what I left behind. I will never be a Paragonian queen. I will never marry another dragon or birth a bunch of whelps to propagate the race. Do you understand me?" That was that. She'd raised her voice to her brothers, something she'd never done in her five hundred years. But she was no longer a Paragonian princess. She was the captain of her own ship, the ruler of her own life, and she would live it on her own terms.

"Never," Gabriel said, the fire in his dark eyes burning. "I would never do that to you, Rowan. But mother sent Scoria for a reason, and she will send others. Next time she may come for you herself, or—"

"Alexander. We have to warn Alexander! He's unwell and he can't protect himself."

"We know." Tobias took her hand in his and squeezed. "He's how we found you. Through the paintings."

"You saw him?"

"No. His apartment was empty. But we were in his apartment, and it looked like he had been there recently." Gabriel rubbed the back of his neck. "Judging by his rooms, he's not in a good place."

"We're concerned he's suicidal," Tobias said.

Rowan frowned. "I've seen it in his art. He's getting worse. Darker."

"A suicidal dragon who suddenly has an easy way to kill himself...," Tobias said.

"We have to find him," Rowan said, "before someone from Paragon does."

Gabriel placed a hand on hers. "So we can count on your help, Princess?"

"Don't call me that, Gabriel. Honestly."

He winked at her.

"Yes. Yes, you can count on me. You saved my fucking life and the life of my mate. I owe you. And I owe Alexander. I will help you."

Gabriel took her other hand. "Together again."

She grinned and offered a deep chuckle. "What could possibly go wrong?"

~

THE CHIEF OF POLICE STOOD NEXT TO NICK AS HE arrested Soren. They'd already raided Gerald and Camilla Stevenson's homes and found several links proving the real estate developer was the mastermind behind NAVAK and the largest human trafficking ring ever busted in New York. Nick had no problem proving Soren was Stevenson's accomplice. It seemed Gerald had hours and hours of recordings on their relationship, probably meant to use against Soren if he ever turned on him. Pretty damning stuff.

"You're a fucking bastard," Soren yelled, spitting as Nick handcuffed him and read him his rights.

"Yeah, I'm a bastard. But I'm an honest bastard who gives a crap about integrity." He handed Soren off to a fellow cop to process.

"Great job, Nick. This bust is a record breaker. You've saved hundreds of trafficked victims."

It meant a lot to Nick to hear those words from a superior. This job, these people, they'd become like a family to him. But they weren't his family. This was a job. And he'd given far too much of his life to it.

"While you're feeling pleased, maybe this would be a good time to ask you for some time off."

"A vacation?"

"Longer. Administrative leave."

The chief grew serious. "Fill out the paperwork and we'll see what we can do."

Nick did exactly that and left the moment his shift

was over. He needed to stop at the jewelry store. He had a ring to buy before he met Rowan for dinner and more important things to do than could be found in a police precinct.

ROWAN SIGNED THE PAPERS ADRIENNE PLACED IN front of her, her heart overflowing with joy. The land under Sunrise House was hers. With the signing of these papers, she owned it. No lease. Bought and paid for.

"How did you pull this off?" she asked, shaking her head.

Her lawyer, Adrienne, grinned and collected the stack of paperwork from her desk. "I didn't. Stevenson offered it to me of his own free will, and I bought it on behalf of your company. I've been pursuing him for months. I have no explanation."

She inhaled deeply as a fine shiver ran along her skin. Nick had entered the building. A moment later, he appeared in her doorway, a shiny black bag dangling from his fingertip.

"You wouldn't know anything about Stevenson selling me the land under this building, would you?" She gave him a welcoming smile.

He crossed the room and pecked her on the lips. "It seems Stevenson is capable of doing the right thing when given the proper motivation."

"What motivation could that be?"

"Selling the building or death? I'd sell the building too, under those parameters."

"Nick, you didn't!"

"After the deed was done, I gave him some of Harriet's

potion and made him forget we'd ever had the conversation. I think it worked out just fine."

Adrienne closed his attaché case and stood. "I have to agree, and I think the kids who come here every day will think so too." He held out a hand to Rowan, who shook it, and then to Nick. "Always a pleasure. Enjoy your evening."

"Say hello to Sally for me," Rowan said.

He gave her a wave before slipping into the hall.

"Stevenson and Soren were arrested today; your building is yours. I'd say this was a good day," Nick said.

Rowan grinned. "One of the best."

"What's left on our to-do list?"

"You mean Verinetti? Harriet helped me with something. It's only a matter of time before it takes effect."

"I don't want to talk about Verinetti on our date tonight."

"Good, neither do I. What do you want to talk about?" They were going to see *Cursed Child* and then having dinner at Eleven Madison Park. She couldn't wait.

His brows pinched together. "There's just one hanging thread we need to tie off."

"What's that?"

He reached into the bag and popped the top on a ring box. "Will you marry me, Rowan?"

Her mouth dropped open. The diamond inside was lovely and surrounded by rubies. "A princess cut?"

"No longer a princess of Paragon, but my princess instead." He looked at her through his lashes.

She withdrew the ring from the box and tried it on.

"Is that a yes?"

"Hold on a minute!" She held it up to the light and started laughing. "I need to fully assess my options here."

"Oh? Is it a hard decision?" He tugged her from her

chair, spun her around, and landed her in his lap where he tickled her furiously. "Fine then. I will live out my days as your servant. I think you should buy a pool so that I can officially be your pool boy."

She turned the ring in the light. "Naaaah. I'll marry you."

He laughed. "You've decided?"

She stopped laughing and looked him in the eye. "But not because of the ring. Only because I love you more than I ever thought possible."

"Sounds like a good reason to me." He sealed it with a kiss.

Rowan scooted off his lap and pulled him from his chair. "Let's go. Djorji's waiting, and we don't want to be late."

They locked up together and danced their way to the car and their first real date.

HARRIET WAITED ON THE TERRACE OF ROWAN'S Dakota-building home, dressed in a camel-colored suit with the most deliciously patterned nautical Hermès scarf, her favorite Birkin bag slung over the crook of her arm. The thick falconry gloves she wore did not match her outfit, but some things couldn't be avoided.

She'd been there a while. Now it was just a matter of waiting.

He would come. He always did.

Especially today of all days, when Nick had busted Gerald Stevenson and ended all hope he might have had of gleaning any more money from the man.

Sure enough, lit only by the streetlights below, a white

owl flew toward her and landed on the wrought iron rail. The bird looked at her and flapped its wings, growing more agitated as it realized its feet were stuck. Harriet calmly walked to it and clamped a metal tag around Verinetti's leg.

"You're probably confused about why you can't shift or fly away," she said to the bird, who was snapping at her and flapping its wings furiously. "I can't take credit for this one. It was an idea someone named Madam Chloe had, a witch out of Chicago, very powerful. I made the salve you are standing in. A simple concoction of herbs with a nerve agent that temporarily makes it impossible for your feet to release the rail. Madam Chloe made you the tag around your ankle, an enchanted metal alloy that makes it impossible for you to shift."

The owl looked at her in horror and struggled more furiously.

"Ironically, it's made of the same stuff Malvern bound Rowan with. He almost killed her, you know."

The owl screeched and flapped.

"Your feet will relax in a few more minutes and you'll be able to fly away, but I'm afraid you will be an owl for a very long time, Michael Verinetti. Unless you can find someone to cut that off you. They won't be able to cut the tag itself. That's impervious. They could cut off your leg, but be advised, you'll want medical personnel nearby because when you shift back, you'll have one less leg to stand on."

Harriet backed inside the open door, knowing the owl could not follow. The space was still warded against him.

"I suggest you get comfortable in your new skin," Harriet said. "If Rowan has to deal with you again, she won't settle for a life sentence. It will be the death penalty." She closed the door between them and watched through the glass as the owl's feet finally released the rail and it flew off toward Central Park.

Rosco nudged her hand with his nose, and she rubbed the German shepherd between the ears. "There's my good boy. You have my permission to eat that bird if you ever see him again. Now, let's go get a treat."

EPILOGUE

June 9, 2018
New Orleans, Louisiana

Raven stood at the head of the aisle, wearing a dress that was as unique as the creatures who had created it. Juniper and Hazel had outdone themselves with this one. She'd already received questions about who the designer was and had said she'd designed it herself, a lie her sister Avery clearly did not believe.

The dress was made of a light, airy fabric and embroidered with diamonds that shimmered when she moved. Of course, anyone who saw it would assume they were crystals. The oreads had designed the gown backless with strings of diamonds swagged from shoulder to waist. No one in their right mind would assume they were real either. The dress draped over her every curve and was cut with an empire waist that completely hid her small but growing baby bump.

"You don't seem nervous at all," her mother said beside her. "That's a good sign."

"How could I be nervous? I'm making the best decision of my life."

Her mom smiled. "Speaking of life decisions, good or bad, I see you invited your father, and he brought a date."

Raven gave her side-eye. "See what you get for hounding me to talk to him?"

"I wanted you to tell him you were expecting, not invite him back into the fold."

"Meh, don't get too excited. I don't plan to make involving him in my life a habit."

Her mother nodded appreciatively.

The music started, and Avery took her first steps down the long aisle in front of her, a bouquet of lilies in her hands.

"Here we go," her mom whispered, squeezing her arm.

Raven watched Avery reach the front of the church where Tobias met her and escorted her to the side of the aisle. It was sad that Sabrina couldn't join them, but it was a day wedding, and although she could tolerate the sunlight, it weakened her. Raven understood.

Gabriel's sister, Rowan, proceeded down the aisle after Avery. Raven had enjoyed getting to know Gabriel's sister and her new mate, Nick. She was overjoyed that the princess had agreed to be in her wedding and thought she looked flawless in the off-the-shoulder emerald gown that Avery had chosen for the occasion.

Once Rowan reached the head of the aisle, her fiancé, Nick, ushered her to the side behind Avery and Tobias. That's when Gabriel stepped into view in front of the priest, looking even bigger and darker than usual in a black tuxedo. Raven released a happy sigh.

"Ready?" her mother asked her.

"Absolutely."

"This doesn't mean you're going to break with tradition and change your name from Tanglewood to Blakemore, does it?"

She scoffed. "Absolutely not. I can be as good a wife as a Tanglewood than as a Blakemore."

Her mother laughed. "You make me proud."

The music changed, and they started down the aisle.

Raven continued, "Men have had the privilege of keeping their names for centuries. I'm certainly not going to spoil the Tanglewood legacy and bow to the patriarchy now."

Her mother's eyes wrinkled at the corners with her smile as they reached the front of the church, and she leaned forward to give Raven a kiss on the cheek. "Thank you for letting me do this, Raven. You don't need me, not anymore, but I'm here for you."

"I need you, Mom. I'll always need you." Her hands trailed from her arm and she turned to Gabriel. His eyes misted at the sight of her. Her love, her dragon, her immortal mate. She felt exactly the same way.

The ceremony itself seemed to play out in fast-forward, their vows a string of pretty syllables that all reiterated what she already knew for sure—he was her soul mate, they were bound for life, and she would go to her death for him and for their child.

"I now pronounce you husband and wife," the priest said. "You may kiss the bride."

Gabriel bent to meet her halfway. She rose up on her tiptoes and captured his mouth. She was careful to keep it appropriate for church, but she couldn't wait to get him home. She already wondered at the delights she'd find in his bed tonight, just as she did every night. Loving Gabriel was an adventure in slick heat, soft kisses, and the throes of magic that brought with them their own pleasures.

Gabriel took her hand. "Come, my wife. We must greet our guests."

He led her back up the aisle where they lined up next to Avery, Tobias, Rowan, and Nick to shake hands and greet attendees as they left for the reception. There were several people Raven didn't know well, distant relations that her mother had invited and past neighbors whom she hadn't seen in years.

Her father kissed her on both cheeks and offered his congratulations, but he did not introduce the woman who accompanied him. She was auburn-haired and freckled, and when she shook Raven's hand, her touch sent a shiver of power up her arm. Raven went rigid, a strange taste filling her mouth, her hand turning cold as ice.

The woman released her and slipped into the crowd, arms linked with her father's. They left the church before Raven could question what had happened.

"What's wrong," Gabriel asked, rubbing her back with a steadying hand. "All the color just drained from your face."

"Did you recognize that woman who was with my father?"

He squinted after her, but she was long gone. "No."

"She had power. I felt it. And it was somehow familiar."

"Familiar how?"

She shook her head. "I'm not sure."

He massaged the base of her neck. "Maybe a natural witch," he said. "Try not to worry. If she'd wanted to make mischief, she would have done so."

Raven tried to comfort herself with that thought and gave Gabriel a grateful kiss. "Thank you. You're right. I'm not going to think about it. Not tonight. Tonight is about you and me and our future."

"David, please excuse me. I need to use the powder room," the stranger said.

The man she knew was Raven's father smiled at her, although she was sure there was nothing going on behind his blank stare. She'd had him entranced for most of the day. She'd told him to call her Charlotte, but other than that, he knew nothing about her. Exactly as she wished.

She ducked into a bathroom and closed and locked the door, examining her reflection in the full-length mirror. The auburn hair and pale skin were quite ugly, but one mustn't get lazy when using illusions. The last thing she wanted to do was stand out. She'd been so close to the witch, but principles were principles. She'd let Raven have her wedding. There would be time enough to take her, the right time, when she could use her father to gain access to her without the threat of three dragon heirs to deal with.

Until then, she needed to bide her time, to be patient. She cast off the illusion in the privacy of the small room and watched her reflection turn dark purple in the large mirror. Much better. She unfurled her gossamer wings, stretching one, then the other, and sighed in relief. Aborella was a powerful and patient fairy sorceress, and she wouldn't be leaving Earth without Raven and the whelp she carried in her womb. And if she played her cards right, she'd take the treasure of Paragon with her.

Thank you for reading Rowan and Nick's story. Both are anxious to find Rowan's brother, Alexander, before the Empress of Paragon does.

Alexander exists on the edge of insanity after the loss of his beloved Maiara. But when his family arrives on the scene, details about the dragon sibling's early history in America may hold a promise and a secret to healing his heart. ***Turn the page to read an excerpt.***

Get your copy of Dragon of Sedona today!

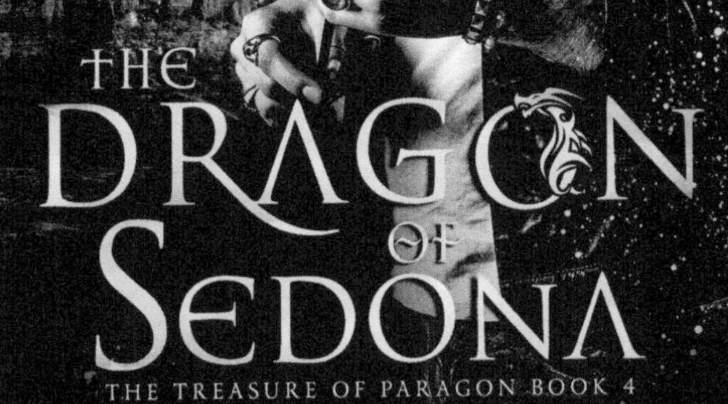
THE
DRAGON
OF
SEDONA
THE TREASURE OF PARAGON BOOK 4
USA TODAY BESTSELLING AUTHOR
GENEVIEVE JACK

PROLOGUE

October 1699
Appalachian forest, North America

"Run, Maiara, run!" Her father shoved her along the path, tugging their horse's reins behind him. The weary beast could move no faster, laden down as she was with pelts and supplies. Prickling fear raised the hair on Maiara's nape, and she desperately tried to incite the animal to move, joining her father in his efforts, but the mare dug in her hooves. The headstrong beast won the battle of wills.

Maiara's moccasins slipped on the slick mud, flinging her to the forest floor. She broke her fall with her bare hands, the earthy scent of decaying leaves filling her nose. Above them, her hawk circled, the bird's shrill screams a warning as their pursuer closed in. Crushing pain throbbed within her rib cage, more from her pounding heart than from the fall.

She couldn't think about the pain. Not now. With a single-minded focus, Maiara scrambled to her feet and clutched her father's arm. "Leave her!" She pried the reins from his hands despite his protests.

An arrow whizzed past her ear and lodged in the tree behind her. Her father's blue eyes widened over his ruddy cheeks. Finally he saw reason. Abandoning the mare, he grasped for her hand. His was large, burly and pale. Hers was small, dark and smooth. There was comfort in that hand. Trust. He'd saved her life before.

"Run," he commanded. She did.

They wove among the trees, the monster haunting the edge of her vision. At first, the thing appeared to be a man, in the image of a warrior from the Mohawk tribe, bald except for a roach of black hair decorated with porcupine quills, bones, and feathers. War paint striped his cheeks. Despite the bracing chill, he wore only his breechcloth and a pendent, an orb the size of a human eye that winked at her as it pulsed a soft blue light at the base of his throat.

The monster may have looked like a man, but if what followed Maiara and her father had ever been human, he was no longer. Now, he was a *wendigo*, a demon sent from the netherworld to rid this land of her kind, a relentless shadow, disappearing when the sun was high only to stretch toward her again. He would not rest until every one of her people was dead. The blue wink of the stone around his neck turned her blood to ice. Whatever that was, it was unnatural, perhaps a remnant of the evil curse that had made him.

Another arrow flew and she ducked, narrowly avoiding its barb. The *wendigo* stopped at the place their mare blocked the path and roared. Its eyes glowed as red as burning coals, and its mouth opened wide enough to swallow her entire head. All illusion of its humanity melted with that bone-chilling roar.

Now the mare moved, tried to gallop away, but the *wendigo* snared its haunches with a set of razor-sharp claws that sprang from its hands. In a flurry of flashing teeth, the hell-spawn tore through the pony, ignoring its equine shrieks. Blood sprayed. Maiara pressed her hand to her mouth as the scent of death reached her, and her stomach threatened to spill its contents. She averted her eyes, but the crunch of bones echoed through the woods long after the horse's squeals abated.

Maiara strained to put more space between them and the demon. She gripped her father's arm tighter and forced him forward. They both knew the meal wouldn't be enough for the *wendigo.* The savage beast had an insatiable appetite.

"You must protect yourself." Her father stumbled. He could not keep up with the pace of their run. She used every muscle in her diminutive frame to help him to his feet. "It's the only way." He was pleading with her now as if she were a petulant child.

Another arrow, another roar. As she'd feared, the creature had already resumed its hunt. It would never quit. Never stop. Not until Maiara was dead.

"Now, Maiara. Go!"

The demon's gaping maw drooled only yards behind them. Her father's gray hair was slick with sweat. Through a throat raw from panting she rasped, "No! Try harder."

His feet gained purchase and they were off again. "How did it find us?" he muttered more to himself than to her. They were fools to think the *wendigo* wouldn't pursue them, not after everything. He stopped short, clawed at his chest as if it hurt. "Maiara! You must leave me."

"I won't," she screamed, shaking her head. She would not abandon her last living family.

"You have no choice." He squeezed her hand again. Her father had raised her. Her father had saved her. He'd always been wise, and now the truth in his gaze cut straight to her heart. "Don't let your mother's death be in vain."

Above them, her hawk cried out another warning, this one sharper than the last. She heard the bowstring snap, the whoosh of the arrow. Her father's eyes widened and, in a final burst of speed, he shifted in front of her. The arrow, meant for her, landed in his back. He collapsed against her. Her scream was silenced by a sharp bite of pain. The tip of the arrow that had passed through her father's body pierced her chest.

Trembling, she thrust with all her might, tearing the arrowhead from her flesh and allowing her father's dying body to fall from her arms. A sob caught in her throat.

"Go," he whispered. His eyes turned unblinking toward the heavens.

Too late now. Too late. She raced down the path, breathless, thighs burning. Blood from the wound in her chest blossomed like a rose on the front of her deerskin tunic. The *wendigo* closed in at alarming speed.

She had no choice and no reason now to stay behind. At a full run, she scanned the trees, extending her arms. Desperate prayers to the Great Spirit tumbled from her lips. With a last glance toward her faithful hawk above, she did what she had to do.

She escaped.

CHAPTER ONE

2018
Sedona, Arizona

Alexander felt like Wile E. Coyote, only instead of blowing himself up trying to kill the Road Runner, his efforts to free himself from the purgatory he suffered were repeatedly thwarted by a different sort of bird.

His personal vexation was a red-tailed hawk hundreds of years past its natural expiration date, yet far too stubborn to die. Unlike the cartoon Road Runner, the hawk made no attempt to run from him with a resounding *meep, meep!* and leave him in its dust.

On the contrary, this bird rarely left his side. Despite his many attempts to separate himself from the winged creature, it remained an obsessive, magical pain in the ass.

"You're not going to stop me this time, Nyx," he said, meeting the hawk's intelligent amber eyes. Ironic that she resisted so thoroughly when his motivation revolved around her. The two were cogs in a never-ending wheel of pain. He only wished to throw a wrench in the gears and save them both.

He called the bird Nyx after the Greek goddess of the night. Red-tailed hawks weren't nocturnal animals, but this one had ushered darkness into his life. The kind of darkness that lived on the inside of a man that no amount of desert sun could ever reach.

At one time, the bird had belonged to his mate Maiara. She'd called the hawk Nikan, the Potawatomi word for "my friend." The two had been inseparable until the night Maiara was brutally murdered. After her death, after her body was burned, the hawk attached to him like a tick burrowing for blood, presumably bound to him by the grief they shared.

He refused to call her Nikan after that. She was no friend of his. She was a ghost. A demon. She was Nyx, the night, and her darkness had been with him ever since.

A stab of longing cut through him. Thanks to Nyx, not a day passed he didn't think of Maiara. The bird was a constant reminder of his loss.

"You have to let me do this," he pleaded with her. He wasn't beyond begging. Anything to end this horror-go-round of an existence.

The early morning sun was blinding as he scanned the horizon from the top of one of the massive red mesas Sedona was known for. In his hand, he gripped a roll of thin, sharp wire. In his mind, he held an appetite for death. No, that wasn't entirely true. It wasn't that he wanted his life to end, just the pain.

For a dragon, losing a mate was like having a thin flap of skin scraped from their body. Everything was painful, stinging, astringent. His body and soul were raw nerves, left with no protection against the elements, no shelter from the burning sun. He hurt. Everywhere.

With a deep breath, he took in the beauty of his surroundings one final time. The landscape's signature red color, courtesy of iron oxide that veined like blood through the stone, provided a sharp contrast to the cerulean sky. The topography was roughly as dry and coarse as the surface of Mars, yet brimming with life, the occasional grouping of desert trees or cactus growing from the stone. Survival in the bleakest of circumstances.

There'd been a time he'd found its mystique comforting. Not anymore. A clear indication the time had come to end this madness.

"You don't want to go on like this, do you?" He stared at Nyx as if to will an answer from her. She let out a shrill cry that let him know exactly what she thought of his plan. "I will never understand you. This has to be as much a nightmare for you as it is for me. Whatever Maiara did to you to make you immortal has bound you to me. Never able to live as a wild bird. Never able to mate with your own kind."

He shoved his hands in the pockets of his jacket. "Have you ever stopped to think that if I died, perhaps you could be free? Truly free."

She flapped her wings and leapt to his arm, her talons digging into the black leather. Not that her grip was a threat to his dragon skin anyway. He might have looked human with his wings tucked away, but he was far tougher and healed much faster than any man. The hawk rubbed its head against his bearded cheek, its soft russet feathers ruffling at the contact. She brushed her beak against his nose.

As he stared at her, he saw his reflection in her tawny eyes. By the Mountain, he looked like shit. Even in silhouette, he could tell he badly needed a haircut and to trim his beard, and he knew the rest of him wasn't any better. He was emaciated and likely smelled of liquor and self-loathing.

He gently nudged her back onto the branch of the juniper tree. "That's enough. Wait there. This will be over soon."

It was hard to kill a dragon. Technically, he was immortal. Poison wouldn't work. Walking in front of a semitruck wouldn't work. If alcohol could've done him in, he'd already be dead. By the Mountain, he bought tequila by the case. It would be easier to run his motorcycle off a bridge, but a fall for a dragon wasn't much of a threat. Dragons couldn't drown or burn to death.

There was only one foolproof way to kill a dragon: decapitation. He checked that the wire was properly fastened around the base of the tree and placed the noose around his neck, then backed up to get a running start.

This was going to hurt.

Glancing toward Nyx, he was relieved to find her gone. Maybe his lecture had gotten through to her after all. She'd left him. It was a sign.

He ran for the edge.

Three steps from the brink, Nyx flew straight up, sheering the side of the cliff. He cried out. Her wings fluttered against his cheeks and talons scraped his neck. Unable to stop his momentum, his feet slipped out from under him and he became a baseball player sliding into home, only the plate was open air beyond the cliff's edge. His dragon's wings tried to punch out but got caught in his leather jacket, store bought—not part of the specially designed wardrobe his oread had made him to accommodate his extra appendages. *Fuck.* For a second, he seemed to hang in the bright blue sky, Nyx with his noose in her claws hovering over him.

"You mangy-feathered, slimy-beaked, bit—" He dropped like a stone.

His back collided with the gravel in front of his motorcycle. *Oww.* Immortal or not, it hurt when bones broke. Perfectly still, he stared at the hawk as she banked and circled down toward him, her cries echoing off the cliffs.

"I really hate you," he whispered. It came out as a squeak. He worked to pull breath into his aching lungs as a sickening slurp indicated his bones were already healing. Not too much damage, then. Slowly, he raised a hand and ran his fingers through his hair. The back of his head was sore, but there wasn't any blood. He was fine. Depressingly whole.

The crunch of wheels on gravel turned his head. A minivan had pulled off the highway and parked next to his bike, and a tall white man wearing dark socks and sandals was climbing out of the driver's seat.

"Hey, are you all right?" The man hurried to him and leaned over Alexander, the floppy brim of his hat casting shade over his face and blocking his view of Nyx.

"I'm fine."

"What are you doing lying on the side of the road?"

He glanced toward his bike. "I'm, uh, just resting."

"Buddy, this is not the place. Someone could run you over."

He cleared his throat. If only that would be enough to do him in. "Hmm. Right. I'll be on my way then." He allowed the man to help him up and gave his neck a good crack.

"Hey... Hey! Are you that guy? You know, that guy who

paints the desert scenes with the bird." The man turned to the van and yelled, "Honey, it's that guy!"

Alexander groaned. Oh dear goddess, please open the earth and swallow him down to hell pronto. This was the last thing he needed today.

A woman in a Minnie Mouse T-shirt, jean shorts, and a green visor hopped down from the passenger seat of the minivan.

"My word, it is him. Alexander! We just bought one of your paintings. You're so talented."

"Thanks," he mumbled. "I really have to go."

"Oh wait, can we get a picture?"

"I, uh..."

The woman had already pulled one of his paintings from the back of the van. He recognized it—a piece he'd done a few years ago of Nyx, the red rock, and the blue sky. It was a money piece. It meant nothing to him; he'd just painted it for the money. It was the Thomas Kinkade of his work, beautiful and meaningless.

She held it in front of his chest, her husband holding the other end of the canvas, and then popped her arm out to take a selfie. He did not smile.

"One, two, three..." she prompted.

The glare from the cheesy grins on either side of him was almost blinding. Out of sheer guilt, he popped the corner of his closed lips a quarter of an inch. A series of clicks later, she slid her phone back into her pocket.

"Thank you! What a special moment," she squealed.

She loaded the painting into the van and the two waved their goodbyes. He watched them drive away from the seat of his motorcycle.

Once they were gone, Nyx landed on the handlebars of

his Harley-Davidson and cooed her apologies. He glared at the bird. "So, that's how it's going to be? No way out."

She chirped and lifted into the clear blue sky.

He revved the engine. "What a fucking Monday."

ALEXANDER EXISTS ON THE EDGE OF INSANITY AFTER the loss of his beloved Maiara. But when his family arrives on the scene, details about the dragon sibling's early history in America may hold a promise and a secret to healing his heart.

Get your copy of the Dragon of Sedona today!

MEET GENEVIEVE JACK

USA Today bestselling and multi-award winning author Genevieve Jack writes wild, witty, and wicked-hot paranormal romance and fantasy. Coffee and wine are her biofuel. The love lives of witches, shifters, and vampires are her favorite topic of conversation. She harbors a passion for old cemeteries and ghost tours thanks to her years attending a high school rumored to be haunted. Her perfect day involves a heaping dose of nature and a dog. Learn more at GenevieveJack.com.

Do you know Jack? Keep in touch to stay in the know about new releases, sales, and giveaways.

Join my VIP reader group
Sign up for my newsletter

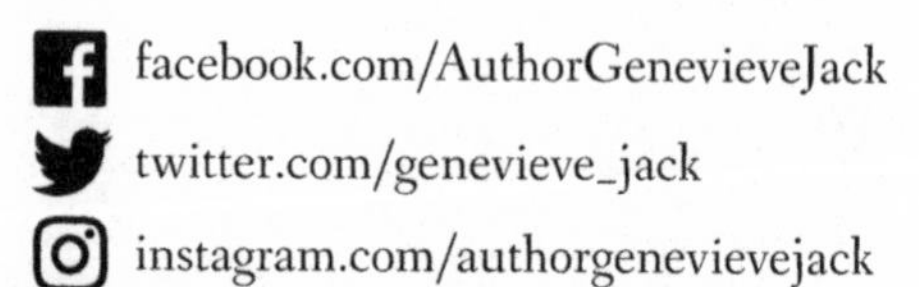
facebook.com/AuthorGenevieveJack
twitter.com/genevieve_jack
instagram.com/authorgenevievejack
bookbub.com/authors/genevieve-jack

MORE FROM GENEVIEVE JACK!

The Treasure of Paragon

The Dragon of New Orleans, Book 1

Windy City Dragon, Book 2,

Manhattan Dragon, Book 3

The Dragon of Sedona, Book 4

The Dragon of Cecil Court, Book 5

Highland Dragon, Book 6

Hidden Dragon, Book 7

The Dragons of Paragon, Book 8

The Last Dragon, Book 9

The Three Sisters

The Tanglewood Witches

Tanglewood Magic

Tanglewood Legacy

Knight Games

The Ghost and The Graveyard, Book 1

Kick the Candle, Book 2

Queen of the Hill, Book 3

Mother May I, Book 4

Fireborn Wolves

(Knight World Novels)

Logan (Prequel)

Vice, Book 1

Virtue, Book 2

Vengeance, Book 3

ACKNOWLEDGMENTS

We've come to the place in my novels where I get to extol the virtues of the team of people who make this all possible. Novel writing doesn't happen in a vacuum. If you enjoy my work, you should know it wouldn't be quite what it is today without the help of a few important individuals.

First, I want to thank Anne Victory of Victory Editing for her meticulous attention. It's thanks to Anne that my comma placement is satisfactory, my participles don't embarrassingly dangle, and all those sentences that made sense in my head but are complete gibberish on the page are made clear again. Anne has edited each of the Treasure of Paragon books so far, and I can't thank her enough for what she does for me.

Manhattan Dragon would not have been possible without the support of a few amazing and talented people. Tara was kind enough to give this manuscript an early critique and point out both areas of brilliance and where the story was a complete mess. I think we cleaned up those messes! I thank you and the dragons thank you. Sara also helped me iron out a few details. Sara, your eye for character development and ear for humor are always appreciated.

Thanks again to Deranged Doctor Designs for the cover art. Every book in this series is more beautiful than the last. Your talent is breathtaking.

And finally, to my husband, Aaron, and daughters Hannah and Madelin, thank you for understanding my occasional absence (both mental and physical) as Rowan and Nick slowly revealed their story to me. Your support keeps me going. I love you all.

Made in the USA
Monee, IL
14 June 2021